NEW YORK
ECHOES

SHORT STORIES

Warren Adler

NEW YORK ECHOES

To my Grandparents on both sides who had the good luck to emigrate to the United States more than a hundred years ago and the good sense to settle in the greatest city on the planet.

CONTENTS

INTRODUCTION

My first New York based short stories were published in anthologies sponsored by The New School, where I studied creative writing under my sainted professor, Don W. Wolfe. He had been my freshman English teacher at New York University from which I had graduated two years earlier.

Among the contributors to these anthologies were fellow students Mario Puzo and William Styron and others of equally extraordinary talent, most of whom were to suffer the indignities of obscurity and oblivion.

Not long after these anthologies were published, I left New York City for Washington, D.C., then Los Angeles, and later Jackson Hole, Wyoming, all of which served as backdrops for my 24 novels and four previous story collections.

Finally, after a half century of absence, I have returned to New York City as a permanent resident only to discover that I never really left. Being a New Yorker is not simply a geographical condition, it is a lifetime embrace, an immutable DNA marker, a soul-capturing experience, engendering a permanent state of mind in which everything is possible and all dreams an open road.

Each day New York provides new wonders to contemplate, a feast of changing images, an ever-changing kaleidoscope of experiences and endless material for the obsessively imaginative observer. For the creative writer, all that is needed is an unbaited fishhook and a drop line into this infinite human pool of New York to attract schools of story ideas dying to be caught.

This volume contains a partial result of this fishing expedition.

GOOD NEIGHBORS

"Hi, I'm Caroline Kramer," she said to the older woman in the elevator of their West Side apartment building.

"Sandra Siegel," the woman replied, nodding, somewhat taken aback by the introduction. She held a little white-haired dog in her arms. Caroline petted it and exclaimed how beautiful it was.

"Her name is Betsy," Sandra Siegel said.

"She's absolutely gorgeous," Caroline said, letting the dog lick her fingers.

As a general rule, few people in Manhattan introduced themselves in elevators. The lady with the dog was short-haired, graying, wearing slacks, sneakers, and a sweatshirt, the usual dress for a Central Park dog walk in early fall.

When the elevator reached the lobby floor, Sandra Siegel let Betsy down and snapped on its leash. Then she nodded an acknowledgement and hurried away with Betsy in tow through the lobby to the street.

Later when Jules came home from work and they were having a glass of white wine before dinner, Caroline told him what she had done.

"Brave girl," Jules snickered, helping himself to a handful of nuts and washing it down with a deep sip of the wine.

"I felt good about it," Caroline said. "I think it's awful that people don't communicate in New York apartments. Our elevator bank is a good place to display neighborliness. We live too much in isolation in these apartment buildings in New York. After all, we do live under one roof."

"I suppose you're right," Jules acknowledged. He was a dyed-in-the-wool New Yorker, having been brought up in Brooklyn, migrating to Manhattan in the early nineties. He was vice president of a media company, married to Caroline five years now, but still postponing having a family. Caroline was from Hempstead, Long Island, a freelance copywriter who worked at home. They had bought the one-bedroom co-op on the fifteenth floor of a twenty-floor pre-war building.

"Why not, Jules?" she said, as if convincing herself. "I go up and down the same elevator bank and often meet the same people. It doesn't hurt to be friendly, which is different than becoming fast friends. Why shouldn't we at the very least introduce ourselves? And she had a cute little pooch with her."

"And you fussed over her dog?"

"Her name was Betsy, and she was beautiful."

"No dogs for us, baby. Ties you down and you have to worry about kennels when you go away."

"I'm not tempted, but it was a cute dog and the lady was very proud of her."

"Cheers," he said, lifting his glass. "May she and her canine have nothing but happiness."

They clicked glasses and drank.

Caroline acknowledged that she was one of those people who were naturally friendly. She liked to engage people in conversations, make eye contact, offer smiles. On buses she talked to people and knew she had the kind of face that invited openness. She had the look of a compassionate person and with her open, white-teethed smile; round, cherubic, naturally rouged cheeks; and large, blue eyes, she made others feel comfortable.

"You're you," he said, reaching for her hand, caressing it and bringing it up to his lips. "I adore you."

"I know it's the right thing to do, to break this pattern of isolation. It startles people. They're not used to it."

"That's for sure," he said, agreeing. "I guess we New Yorkers are wary of intimacy in our apartment culture."

"I'm not talking about intimacy, just common friendliness."

"Maybe when you're surrounded by crowds everywhere you go,

people welcome privacy. Like now. You and me. Cozy, intimate and, above all, private. Delicious, quiet time." He bent over and kissed her.

"That doesn't mean people can't be neighborly when they venture out. Say hello on the elevator."

"Also," he added. "They may be too self-absorbed in their daily business. Like me. Sometimes I start thinking about the office the minute I close the door."

"You can still offer a smile and a kind word. You don't have to be bosom buddies. Just a good neighbor."

"As long as they're not nosy neighbors."

"There is a big difference between nosy neighbors and good neighbors. They don't have to be intimate friends."

"We have plenty of those," he said. "And people who are important to us on the job. And relatives, and old school chums. What I'm saying is that we have enough people on our 'known to' list."

"Still, it would be nice to know our neighbors."

"Our circle is wide enough as it is. We have barely enough time for further obligations."

"You have a point," Caroline acknowledged, wondering how the conversation had reached this strange territory. "But, you never know when you need a neighbor. After all, we do live in the same house. We share services, utilities, and doormen."

"Who can forget doormen?"

"They deserve our acknowledgement. They're always ready with a smile and a few words of greeting."

"Especially around Christmastime, and remember, we only own shares in the building. This is a co-op in case you forgot. With a board that has to approve everyone and keep the riffraff out."

"Snob," she said playfully. "As for me, I am an egalitarian and from now on, I plan to introduce myself to the neighbors on our elevator bank as a start."

"I think you are undertaking a noble venture," he said. "And I'd be flattered if a beautiful, open-faced charmer like yourself said hello to me on the elevator."

She started to introduce herself to those who came up and down with her on the elevator. Not many remembered her name, and more than once someone asked her, "What was your name again?"

She was, however, determined to remember theirs so that she could greet them by their first names whenever she met them again. There was Bob Rainey, who got on at the tenth floor, a thin-faced elderly man with a pencil thin moustache. Mary Schwartz lived on an upper floor, a youngish woman with flaming red hair. And Benjamin Agronsky, who got on at eight, a preppy-looking man in his thirties in pinstripes and button-down, white shirts and thick-soled brown shoes. Paisley McGuire, a young, Irish-looking girl with creamy skin and dark curly hair, got on at floor five. Caroline liked the idea of saying hello by name although the extent of the conversation was mostly about the weather. She did not encourage any further intimacy.

There were four apartments on each floor. One of the tenants of their four, she assumed, lived in another city and came to New York seldom. Another was a secretive bachelor named Sheldon whom she knew by sight, although he always turned away when they waited for an elevator and never even grunted an acknowledgement. The fourth apartment was occupied by a woman named Anne Myers who lived alone and apparently traveled a great deal. Anne was the only other tenant on the floor who received home delivery of the *New York Times*. Caroline had had only one brief conversation with her.

"I travel a great deal," the woman said. "It's a bother to cancel the *Times* every time I go away. Could you please not let them pile up? You know, just in case. We don't want people to know when I'm not home."

Caroline consented, since the trash bin was close to her own apartment. When two *Times* lay in front of her apartment, Caroline dutifully threw them away, always knowing when the Myers woman was home because the *Times* was not on the floor in front of her apartment.

"Why doesn't she cancel them when she goes away?" Jules asked.

"I don't mind," she countered.

Because she worked at home, she spent more time coming up and down the elevator, at times to shop, at other times when the weather was good, to take a break by walking in Central Park, sometimes watching the dancing roller skaters or observing the rowboats glide through the water or sitting on a bench by the pond and watching the hobbyists sailing their power-operated little sailboats.

One day as she worked she got a call from the woman who introduced herself as Sandra Siegel.

"Remember me?" the woman asked pleasantly. "Sandra Siegel, the woman with the little white dog."

"Betsy," Caroline said. "How could I forget?"

"I took a chance, hoping you were home."

"I work at home, freelance," Caroline responded, thinking the woman might invite her to tea.

"I hate to bother you," Sandra Siegel said. "I have a favor. You see, I twisted my ankle and can't take Betsy for her walk. And Sam, our doorman, is off on vacation. He's the only one I can trust to walk her. So I'm in a bit of a jam. The dear little girl needs to go out. It's her regular routine. I hate to ask. It would be just this once. Could you take her? I'd be so grateful. I'm sure I'll be better by tomorrow."

"You mean now?" Caroline asked.

"Say in a half hour, if you could. I really hate to ask. But you see my dilemma."

Caroline contemplated the request. She was about ready for a break, and there was no pressing time factor.

"I really hate to ask," the woman said yet again.

In the brief interval before her consent, she thought of Jules and determined not to mention it, since it would provoke his "I told you so's." She snickered to herself, deciding that to accept was still in the realm of good neighboring.

The woman lived on the twelfth floor, and she opened the door leaning on a cane and handed Caroline Betsy and the leash after first planting a big kiss on the dog's snout.

"She likes the walk that goes to the baseball field. That gives her the greatest sniffing pleasure." She handed Caroline a plastic glove. "She makes such tiny little bitsy poopies."

It was a nice day and Caroline actually enjoyed watching the little dog sniff about, and disposing of her little bitsy poops was hardly a chore. In a half hour she was back to the grateful Sandra Siegel, who expressed her heartfelt thanks.

"You are a real princess," she said. "I'm eternally grateful."

She did not include this little episode in her and Jules's review of their day, and she felt quite comfortable with her good deed, even when it repeated itself the next day, and the next.

"The doctor said I should be better in a week or so. I am so grateful."

After the first few times, it became a kind of routine, and she didn't mind it as long as the weather stayed good. Besides, it didn't take much more than a half hour out of her day. Still, she didn't tell Jules.

As part of her regular regimen, she would often take a break in the afternoon and go down to the Starbucks a half a block away and get a Frappuccino, a sort of gift she gave herself before going back to work. Usually she sat alone, thought about the work she was doing, then after draining the concoction she went back up to her apartment.

One day, a voice intruded. She was sitting at a table by herself staring into space, tranced out on her work.

"You're Carol, am I right?"

"Caroline," she corrected.

She looked up and saw Bob Rainey, whom she recognized by his pencil-thin moustache.

"You're Bob Rainey," Caroline said.

"May I join you?" Rainey said.

"Of course."

They chatted amiably as she sipped her Frappuccino. Rainey was nursing a large-sized coffee.

"Not a very good day for me," he said suddenly. She studied his face, which seemed to mirror his announcement suggesting internal pain. "I never come here, but you see, Lila is moving out as we speak. I didn't want to be there." He swallowed hard and his face seemed to grow ashen. "Eighteen years together," he shook his head. "Not a very happy day."

"Sorry to hear that."

"Problem is my wife won't give me a divorce. That means I can't marry Lila." He shook his head. "Can I blame her? She wants stability. But, you see, my wife is determined to extract her pound of flesh. No divorce, no Lila. Can you blame her?"

It seemed a question directed at Caroline.

"I suppose not," Caroline shrugged, sipping her frothy drink.

"Lila was a wonderful companion, but you see, there is no legal future for her. That's what she wants. A ring around the finger. Who can blame her?"

Inadvertently, Caroline reached for her ring and traced its smooth surface.

"I understand. I'm very happily married."

"Lucky girl," he snickered. "Lucky guy. My wife was a monster. My life was a hell until I met Lila. She was a saint, that woman, but after all, you can't live on hope alone. She wants to be Mrs. Bob Rainey, not a mistress. She's a traditional girl. I can't blame her."

He looked at his watch.

"She should be out by three. Her sister is helping her pack. We agreed, no long goodbyes. Frankly, it's a lot better not to be there, don't you think?"

"A lot better, I'm sure."

"I'm devastated," Bob Rainey said. She watched his eyes grow moist. He wiped away a tear that slid down the side of his cheek.

"Frankly, I don't know how I'm going to get through the day," he sighed. "And the night which will be worse. It will be a mighty cold bed."

Caroline wondered whether he was dishing out a seduction line, but then, seeing the man's pain, decided that it wasn't. Besides, he was elderly and too broken up to pursue such a line. Poor guy, she thought. She looked at her watch.

"Gotta go, Bob. Keep your chin up. Life goes on."

"Wonderful talking with you, Carol," he said.

"Caroline," she corrected patiently.

"Oh, yes. I'm so sorry."

She smiled and shook his proffered hand.

"Thanks. It's been very comforting talking to you."

She went back up to her apartment, dismissing Bob Rainey and his dilemma from her mind. But she remembered it later when she and Jules had their usual before-dinner aperitif and she told him about it. At times she either cooked simple meals or they ordered in or went to a neighborhood restaurant.

"Are we supposed to shed tears?" Jules said.

"I guess he needed to confide in someone," Caroline said.

"So you lent him your ears."

"Nothing wrong with giving comfort by listening."

"Save it all for me. I'm a glutton for comfort."

He smiled and patted her cheek.

"He's a real nice guy, Jules," Caroline said. "Maybe we can invite him in for dinner sometime?"

"We're not therapists. You have no obligation to comfort him."

"Just being neighborly," she sighed, on the verge of telling him about her daily walks with Betsy, but quickly retreating.

She was into the second week of walking Sandra Siegel's dog when she bumped into Mary Schwartz, who was sitting on a park bench behind which Betsy was sniffing. They had brief eye contact, and it was unavoidable for either of them to deny recognition.

"I'm Caroline Kramer from the building."

"Oh, yes, I remember. But, I don't recall a dog."

"It's Sandra Siegel's."

"Who?"

"One of the other tenants. Hurt her ankle. I'm being a good neighbor."

"I see."

She had picked up some of Betsy's poop offerings and flung them into a trash basket.

"I've been laid off," Mary said. "They're dumping all the oldies. Anyone over fifty. They deny it, of course, but it's apparent as the nose on your face. I've been sitting here figuring out ways to really hurt them, the bastards."

"I can't imagine how devastating it would be," Caroline said.

"I worked for this advertising agency for nearly twenty years. I thought I was the resident expert on media, especially the new media, you know cable, the Internet, etcetera etcetera. Sons of bitches. I trained this little rat and now she's taken over."

"I'm sure something else will turn up," Caroline said.

"They want the sweet young things, I'm afraid. I'm neither sweet nor young."

"I wish you luck," Caroline said, starting to lead Betsy away. Then she thought of something and came back.

"My husband's a vice president of a company in the media business. I'll talk to him if that's okay?"

"Why not?" Mary muttered. "You never know."

She picked up the mail and brought the dog back to Sandra Siegel, who came to the door without a cane. She picked up Betsy, kissed her on the snout and talked baby talk to her as the dog licked her face.

"I think I can hack it now, Caroline. I can't begin to thank you. You've been great."

"That's what neighbors are for."

Caroline felt good about it. After all, it didn't take much time. Betsy was an obedient dog. It generated good feelings. She supposed she could tell Jules about it now. Jules came in at his usual hour carrying a bottle of champagne with a ribbon around it and a card.

"The doorman gave it to me. It says, 'Thanks a million from Sandra Siegel,'" Jules said. "Who the hell is Sandra Siegel and why is she thanking you?"

"For walking her dog," Caroline admitted. "She's a tenant and twisted her ankle."

"Part of your good neighbor campaign?"

She held up the champagne bottle he had given her.

"Good fellowship and good cheer," she said. "And this." She handed him an invitation to a dinner party from Mr. and Mrs. Benjamin Agronsky. "The ninth floor Agronskys," Caroline said, winking. "You see what happens when you open up to them? People are hungry for companionship."

"Couple of days. Short notice," he commented, reading the invitation.

"It's the thought that counts," she said.

"I haven't really been against the idea," he said. "Only wary of involvement."

"I like the idea of involvement with people. After all, I work alone all day. It's nice to have friends to chat with."

"Like that guy with the girlfriend."

"Like him, and today I talked with another neighbor who just lost her job. I told her what you did and maybe you might see her." Caroline explained her credentials. "She says companies look askance when you're over fifty, no matter what your expertise."

In a comic mime, he looked around him as if he were checking for spies and he put a finger over his lips.

"Don't ask. Don't tell."

"It's not fair."

"Neither is life."

In the morning, when she went to get the *New York Times* outside her door, there was an envelope with Mary's resume. She gave it to Jules.

"I'll look it over," he promised. "Don't encourage her."

When she went for her afternoon Frappuccino, Ben Rainey was sitting alone at a table. He motioned her over after she got her order. It was impossible to avoid him without seeming rude, and she sat down at the table.

"I was hoping you'd come."

"Were you?"

"You were so considerate the other day. You were great."

"So, how are you doing?"

"I'm lonely as hell," he said. "I miss her like crazy. I'm barely able to function."

"Maybe there are people you can talk with," she said, hoping he might take her subtle suggestion to see a therapist.

"They can't help. They can't bring her back to me. She's gone to Europe for a long tour."

"Maybe she'll return when she comes back," she suggested. His downbeat talk was having a negative effect on her.

"No, she won't. I know her. She's made up her mind."

He then went into a long dissertation on their history together, how they had met, how they decided to live together and the things they did together, describing the most intimate details.

"I felt, don't take this amiss, rejuvenated. Every time we made love, I felt twenty years younger. We slept together like spoons."

"You'll be fine, Bob," she said, offering a big smile, suddenly wary at the reference. "You'll see. Someone will come along to recharge your batteries."

She was immediately sorry she had put it that way, not wanting to give him the wrong impression. "I'm very happily married," she said, as if to draw the curtain on any errant ideas he might be entertaining.

"I'm so grateful to you for listening, Carol."

"Caroline," she corrected again, putting out her hand to say goodbye. He took it and squeezed it in obvious gratitude.

A couple of days later, they went to the Agronsky party. Caroline counted eight guests, none of whom she recognized as coming from the building. Mrs. Agronsky, her name was Sheila, was a tall blonde in a ponytail with high cheekbones and the stringy body of a model. She was dressed in tight, shiny silk slacks and a colorful, almost sheer blouse, greeting each guest with enthusiasm.

"So glad you could come," she said. Then bending over, she addressed Caroline and Jules in a whisper. "I know it was short notice, but one couple crapped out. You guys are life savers."

Caroline looked at the carefully laid table set for ten with an elaborate flowered centerpiece.

"So, we're last minute fill-ins," Jules said.

"Be glad she thought of us."

"I'm overjoyed," he said with sarcasm surveying the group.

The guests were youngish, thirties and forties, some dressed preppy like their host and a number of the women of the type she designated to herself as "blonde goddesses." It soon became apparent that most of the male guests had known each other from college. Yalies, mostly. Not knowing anyone, she and Jules felt somewhat out of place. They had met at Queens College.

"Because you live under one roof," Jules whispered. "It doesn't mean you have things in common."

"Be a good guest," Caroline remonstrated, working the room, trying to engage people in conversation. She noted that the wine flowed copiously and dinner, which was catered, was timed so that the cocktail time would last longer.

"When are we going to eat?" Jules whispered at about nine. The guests had been cocktailing for about two hours by then, with no sign of letup.

"Ben told me you were a very interesting person," Sheila said, finally getting around to a more in-depth conversation with Caroline. By then, Jules had recognized his irrelevancy to the group, most of whom were young Wall Street hotshots. He feigned looking over the books in the bookcases.

"We met on the elevator," Caroline said.

"Did you?"

They traded the usual pleasantries. Sheila was, as she suspected, a fashion model.

"We don't know many people in the building," Sheila said. Her words were slurred. "I guess it's time we got acquainted." She was interrupted by another of the guests and moved away.

"When are we going to eat?" Jules whispered again.

"That is total bullshit," Ben shouted suddenly, directing the remark to Sheila. It was quickly apparent to Caroline that a drunken argument was ensuing.

"Look who's talking about bullshit."

"Hey, cool it guys," one of the guests said.

"Mind your own fucking business, Charley," Ben said.

"Pardon me, Benny baby," Charley said, walking away.

The obvious conflagration between host and hostess silenced the group, and Sheila finally called everyone to the dining room table. The conversation was quieter now. Caroline was seated next to a large, red-faced man who had beads of perspiration on his upper lip.

"So, what do you do?" the red-faced man, whose name was Tom something, asked. His question seemed obligatory, but she answered politely.

"Oh," he said, turning away to talk with the woman on the other side of him.

"You are a scumbag," Sheila shouted across the round table to Ben.

"Takes one to know one," Ben said.

"Are they always like this?" Caroline asked the red-faced man.

"Booze rage," he snickered, then turned back to the woman on the other side of him.

The conversation ebbed and flowed. Most of the subject matter of the conversation centered on stocks, deals, and money, sprinkled with the names of people unknown to neither she nor Jules. They used initials to describe things that she didn't understand. She exchanged glances with Jules, who was sitting between two women who were holding a conversation around him as if he didn't exist. He looked at her and shrugged.

As the evening wore on, she felt more and more irrelevant to the group and when they left, Ben, who slurred his words, walked them to the door.

"Thanks for helping us out," he said.

"Your pleasure," Jules mumbled. Ben, not getting it, smiled and closed the door.

Jules was livid when they got back to their apartment.

"Yes, we all live under the same roof, but that is not the way to pick and choose our friends and companions. We were props. They were preppy Wall Street shits. Admit it, this was purgatory."

"You can't win them all," she said, knowing he was right in this case.

"I don't think we should just accept invitations willy-nilly because we live under the same roof."

It was late and she could see an argument was coming and decided to ignore the subject and go to sleep. For the next few days she concentrated on pressing deadlines and did not go to Starbucks for Frappuccino. Then, one day, she got a call, from Sandra Siegel. By then, the weather had turned and it was raining.

"I did it again, Caroline. My ankle gave out. Could you please take Betsy out?"

"I'm in the middle of a deadline, Sandra," she protested. She looked out the window at the rain coming down in long slanting sheets.

"Please, Caroline. Betsy needs this. I tried to do it, but I could barely stand."

She heard Betsy barking in the background. "Hear that? The little girl is in pain. Please, help me, Caroline."

"And the doorman? What about him?"

"She wants you," Sandra replied.

"How do you know?"

"I can tell."

Reluctantly, Caroline complied. She put on her rain gear, took an umbrella, and picked up Betsy. Coming back soaked, she handed Betsy back to Sandra.

"Oh my God, look at the poor baby; she's soaked to the skin."

She hobbled away with Betsy in her arms without saying thank you or goodbye. Caroline went back to work, but her concentration was broken, and it was difficult to pick up where she left off. She did not tell Jules what had happened.

It was still raining the next morning and she had promised herself that she would refuse, absolutely refuse, to take Betsy for a walk. When the phone rang she picked it up, dreading that it would be Sandra and vowing that she would have to get a caller identification system for their home phone. She was relieved it wasn't Sandra, but the call offered yet another complication.

"This is Bob," the voice said, hoarse, barely audible.

"Bob?"

"Bob Rainey. I need to talk."

"Oh yes, Bob," she said cheerfully, suddenly apologetic. "I've been very busy, you see…"

Her explanation was interrupted abruptly.

"Please, Carol. I need to talk. Now."

She wanted to correct her name, but held off. The voice seemed positively desperate.

"Now? I'm in the midst…"

"Please, Carol, I beg you. I'm upstairs in my apartment. 10F. Now. I need you."

"Me?"

The phone clicked off and she debated for a few moments on what to do. She was pressed by her deadline and expected a call momentarily from a client. This was, indeed, an intrusion, but the man sounded desperate. Finally, after fifteen minutes had gone by, she went up to the man's apartment and rang the buzzer. She took her cell phone with her in case her client called.

"It's open," a hoarse cracked voice said.

Bob Rainey was sitting in his pajamas and robe in a darkened living room. The blinds were drawn, and the apartment looked in disarray.

"What is it, Bob?"

He didn't answer. He seemed disoriented and barely able to speak. She moved closer to him.

"What's wrong?"

He didn't answer, and his eyes were closing. Beside him on a table was an open pill container. She looked at the label. "Take one pill before retiring," she read. There was a warning pasted onto the container.

"Oh my God," she cried, shaking Bob, who was obviously falling into a deep sleep or coma. "What have you done?"

Having never confronted such a situation before, she was momentarily confused. Her first thought was to call Jules, but when she noticed that Bob Rainey's chin had fallen into his chest, she called 911. She had never in her life ever called 911 before, but she managed to answer the questions rationally.

"Wait there," the woman at the other end of the phone said, after taking her address and the number of her cell.

Left alone with the slumping Bob Rainey, she felt uncomfortable and irritated. The apartment was in chaos and smelled of rotting food. She shook the man again. When he didn't respond, she tried to feel his pulse and couldn't, wondering if the man was dead. Clearly, he was still breathing, his chest rising and falling. Suddenly, her cell phone screamed out a tune, startling her. It was her client.

"I can't talk now. I have a problem."

"What?" her client asked.

"I'll explain later."

"We have this deadline, Caroline. Today. I'm sorry. We have to get the copy in a couple of hours."

"I'll have it. I promise."

A half hour went by. She sat on the couch and watched Bob Rainey, concentrating on the rise and fall of his chest, wondering how long it would take the pills to do their damage. Would he die in front of her eyes? She felt suddenly panicked and called Jules, hanging up before he could answer. Why disrupt his day, she told herself, feeling increasingly panicked and upset. She wanted to cry.

Finally, she heard the doorman's buzzer ring and she answered it.

"Who is this?" the doorman asked.

"I'm Caroline Kramer from 15G. But I'm here in 10F. Is the ambulance here?"

In less than five minutes, medical people arrived with a rolling stretcher, along with two policemen. The medical people worked on Rainey and lifted him onto the stretcher while the policeman took her name and interviewed her. She explained that she knew the man casually from going up and down the elevator and had met him at Starbucks. Her explanation sounded confused and, she thought, suspicious, and she had the impression that the policeman didn't really believe her explanation although he wrote it down in a little book.

"We might need to contact you," the policeman said as they wheeled the body of Bob Rainey out of the apartment.

"He'll be okay," one of the doctors said.

"He called me. I live in the building. Just a friend," she explained.

"Potential suicides like an audience," the doctor said. "If he was serious, he would just do it."

When they had gone, she went downstairs to her own apartment. She was very shaken and poured herself a glass of wine, which she gulped down. Her hands shook and she could not concentrate on her work. Finally, she called Jules.

"You sound harassed," he said.

She wanted to explain what had happened, but could not bring herself to do it. "Later," she told herself.

"Just wanted to hear your voice, darling," she said, meaning exactly that. Hearing his voice steadied her.

"Are you okay?" he asked.

"Fine, darling. I'm fine."

Again she tried to work, but finding her concentration again was making it difficult. Then, at last, she found the words and knew she would make the deadline. The phone rang again and, without thinking, she answered it.

"This is Sandra Siegel."

"Not again," she muttered.

"My little girl needs to go out."

"Does she?" Caroline said.

"I'm so sorry to ask, but I just can't make it. Betsy is dying. She needs to go out."

"Tell you what, Sandra," Caroline said, searching for words that would make the point, finding them, pausing for a moment.

"Why don't you take that fucking dog out yourself, I'm busy."

"That's awfully rude of you," Sandra Siegel said, hanging up abruptly.

The phone rang again.

"I said I'm busy," Caroline snapped, thinking it was the Siegel woman.

"Oh, I'm so sorry. It's Mary Schwartz, remember? Remember? I dropped off my resume."

"I don't think my husband can help you," Caroline said.

"Figures, nobody wants people over fifty."

Caroline hung up without saying goodbye.

When Jules got home, she embraced him before he could sit down.

"Why the affectionate greeting?" he asked.

"I am in dire need of intimacy," she said, then poured the wine and told him about her horrendous day.

"No good deed goes unpunished," he said. "You have to pick and choose wisely."

"I suppose," she replied.

"Unfortunately, people don't wear signs saying 'I'm needy.' I guess it's a matter of luck."

Instead of dinner, they made love.

"I was very needy," she said in the aftermath. "You must have seen my sign."

"I always see your sign," he said.

"And I always see yours."

She grew cautious after her recent experiences, nodding to the various people who came up and down her elevator bank, avoiding eye contact. One morning Bob Rainey came down the elevator.

"Hello Carol," he grunted.

She smiled, nodded, and turned away.

Sometime later, she noted that Anne Myers's newspapers were piling up. Instead of throwing them in the trash, Caroline ignored them. Then she noticed that they weren't there anymore.

"You let me down," Anne Myers said one day as they both waited for the elevator.

"Did I?" Caroline said, avoiding eye contact.

"You let them pile up," she said.

Caroline shrugged. The elevator came and they both got on. She looked the other way all the way down. Pick and choose wisely, she told herself.

THE MEAN MRS. DICKSTEIN

Mrs. Dickstein, age seventy-five, sat on her favorite bench in Central Park overlooking the lake on a lavishly sunny May day reading Stendhal's *The Red and the Black*, which she had read three times over the course of her life.

A widow, she loved this exercise in delicious tranquility, and in the spring, when the weather was perfect, she would revel in this particular spot with the special view of the lake and the trees in bloom around her. Weekdays were best, for the crowds were sparse and most children were in their strollers pushed by chatting moms or nannies.

Looking up from her book, she would observe the rowboats quietly cutting through the slate-colored lake waters and people reclining on the grassy knolls, lovers embracing and oblivious, a lone man or woman, lying supine or sitting cross-legged Indian style, perhaps like her, enjoying the optimism and glory of spring.

All in all, with the exception of the loss of her beloved Henry three years ago, she could savor the best of times in her long life. She had made peace with the demise of Henry, who had been a dozen years her senior, and his departure was long expected to be before her own.

Her two grown sons lived elsewhere and were dutiful in their absent devotion, calling her at least once a week to report on their various experiences in the interim and especially on the antics of her grandchildren. Each visited a couple of times a year, and she visited them in sequence during holidays and was both happy to arrive and happy to depart.

Her children knew too that she was a habitual and inveterate New

Yorker, a native, who would never leave, although she suspected that they and their wives were happy with her chosen location. An aged parent and grandparent could be a disruption and an emotional bother, especially to a daughter-in-law. She had never ever considered a move to be near her children. Nevertheless, they did worry about her safety. They chose the next best thing to proximity. They gave her a cell phone as a Christmas gift, which she used sporadically to call friends and on occasion her sons, who insisted that she keep it charged and carry it around with her, which she did.

She had been a professional nurse in her time and since her retirement had invariably volunteered to help, as she phrased it, "the less fortunate." She assisted in serving Thanksgiving meals at homeless shelters, was active in those groups that helped orphaned children, and was one of the numerous gray-haired single ladies who volunteered at Mt. Sinai hospital, wheeling carts of books to patients or completing other chores to lighten the burden of the needy.

She believed implicitly in charity and caregiving, which had motivated her to become a nurse many years ago. Since Henry had gone, she spent most of her time with friends in her own widowed or single situation, pursued her charitable work, went to lectures at the Met and the 92nd Street Y, and generally lived what she characterized to herself as the life of the heart and the mind.

She supposed in retrospect that she had lived a good life, respecting her fellow man, avoiding all the pitfalls of mean-mindedness that seemed to afflict human endeavors, both in the past and especially now. She prided herself in not having a mean streak in her, taking the burden of affliction on herself rather than hurting other people. Not that she was self-conscious or dwelled inordinately on her goodness; she was, as she told herself, built that way.

Nor was she the type who fed squirrels and pigeons or mourned over the loss of an insect she had stepped on, but she did pride herself on her innate sense of compassion and decency. At times, when she felt wronged, she chose the path of avoiding confrontations, probably more out of fear than conviction.

Sitting here on her favorite bench, lifting her eyes to observe her favorite view, and reading a classic novel, was her version of nirvana.

There were times, of course, when her expectations had been dashed by people getting to the bench before her. When such a situation occurred she walked about the park for awhile, checked the bench again to see if there was room for her, and, if not, she would go home. Such were the limitations of habit. Thankfully, it did not happen very often.

It did not happen on this particularly glorious day, and she was able to plunge deeply into the lives of the novel's characters.

A red-haired woman sat down next to her and immediately fired up her cell phone. She chattered incessantly and, after awhile, the sound disturbed Mrs. Dickstein's concentration and tranquility. She made it a point not to decipher the specifics of the woman's conversation since that seemed an intrusion on her part on the privacy of the caller.

Of course, the woman's conduct was rude, she reasoned. On the other hand, she did not feel she had the right to intervene, since there were no legal restrictions of talking on a cell phone, and she was not one to complain about such things. Moreover, she figured that sooner or later the woman would stop and her peace would be restored.

Unfortunately, it didn't and Mrs. Dickstein, despite herself, could not avoid the substance of the woman's conversation. She was apparently making a series of calls to change the venue of a party of some kind from one restaurant to another.

To further exacerbate the situation, the woman's voice was harsh, loud, and vulgar, interspersed with strings of four-letter words. Peripherally, she noted that the woman wore large sunglasses and smeary red lipstick. She was dressed in tight jeans and wore high heels. She struck Mrs. Dickstein as snarling and hard.

Despite herself, she could not avoid hearing that the new venue was Daniel and not Cipriani's, which, for some reason, was not suitable. The party was called for tomorrow at eight, and the woman was contacting all the invitees, who apparently were considerable.

When those she called were in, a conversation ensued that went on for a long time. When those she called were out, she repeated a long explanation and asked that she be called back. Mrs. Dickstein caught her name. "Molly Harkins." Interspersed between the call-ups and the callbacks were some musical renditions that signaled that a call was coming in.

After some considerable debate with herself, Mrs. Dickstein finally reacted.

"Please excuse me, I hate to suggest it. I know these are important calls, but would you mind making them elsewhere," Mrs. Dickstein said timorously, looking around her. "There is a lot of open space around."

At first the woman merely frowned, since she was in the middle of a conversation but when she hung up she turned to Mrs. Dickstein.

"Why don't you change your seat, then?" the woman asked.

"I don't mean any offense," Mrs. Dickstein said, politely offering a smile. "I can understand one or two calls but..."

"Why don't you mind your own fucking business, lady," the woman cried, eyeing her with obvious contempt.

The rebuke seemed so hostile that Mrs. Dickstein was silent for a long time, not knowing how to react. Yes, she could go to another bench or walk around until this woman vacated and avoid any confrontation altogether. She felt frozen in place, unable to react.

The calls continued, and Mrs. Dickstein had completely lost her concentration, but still felt constrained from moving. Finally, summoning up all residue of courage, she reacted again.

"At the very least," she said. "You could talk less volubly."

"Jesus," the woman said. "Get out of my face."

At that moment, the phone trilled again and a conversation began.

"I know. I know. I do sound pissed off. Some old bag is giving me a bad time."

Mrs. Dickstein, having heard the reference, seemed to poke her nose deeper into her open book. The words swam without meaning in front of her unseeing eyes. Still, she could not rouse herself to the confrontation. Finally, the best she could offer was a shrug of the shoulders and a whispering, "How rude." But, she refused to budge from the bench.

"Why?" the woman on the cell phone said, turning a bit to avoid looking at Mrs. Dickstein. "Because they gave me a better deal at

Daniel. I was lucky as hell. Usually they're booked for months. They just had a last-minute cancellation. It will be one helluva party. And will Harry be surprised. They made a cake and the menu is to die for."

"Yada yada," Mrs. Dickstein said under her breath. At that point the best she could muster was what she decided was "a dirty look." The woman beside her paid no attention.

"I will not surrender," Mrs. Dickstein told herself, forcing her resolve to endure the harassment of the woman's voice and appearance.

Mrs. Dickstein found herself contemplating ways in which she could counter the woman. She opened her bag and took out her own cell phone and punched in the number of one son, then the other. Neither answered. In retrospect, she was relieved. Their conversation would be personal, and she had no desire to let this terrible woman into her private life.

She toyed with the idea of singing a song or making unnatural noises, but that seemed childish and unworthy and would subject her to embarrassment. She turned to face the woman and, although she held the pose for a minute or two, the woman merely looked up and offered an expression of contempt. Finally, she turned away, fearing that the woman might take it into her head to call a policeman and tell him that she was being annoyed and harassed by a crazy old lady.

Instead, she tried concentrating on the content of the book, which proved impossible. Also, the tranquil view of the lake and softly rowing boats offered no solace for her anger. She was, she decided, genuinely upset. The woman's voice went on and on, grating, vulgar, and never-ending.

It became, then, a silent endurance contest, although Mrs. Dickstein was not such a fool to believe that the battle was joined. At best, she decided to sit there, offering occasional side-glances of annoyance, which hardly made a dent on the woman or her incessant conversation.

On and on it went as the morning wore on. It must be one big party, Mrs. Dickstein thought. And expensive. Daniel, she knew, was one of the priciest restaurants in Manhattan.

One of her sons had taken her and her husband there for her seventieth birthday. It was too fancy for her tastes, and the food she found much too rich, and a brief glance at the check informed her that it was extravagant. Her husband had told her privately after the meal that the expense was in direct proportion to their son's guilt at being neglectful of their parents. She did not agree, but then she was not given to ascribing such bad motivation to people, especially her own son.

The battle to endure and not surrender went on for what seemed more than an hour. She considered herself brave and valiant to suffer through the ordeal.

Then finally it was over. The woman snapped shut her cell phone and turned an arrogant smile toward Mrs. Dickstein.

"Now you can play with yourself," the woman said, bouncing along the path in her high heels and tight pants.

Mrs. Dickstein sat for a long time, still unable to concentrate. Then an idea penetrated her mind and she giggled.

"Yes," she decided, saying aloud. "I will play with myself."

She dialed information and got the number of Daniel. The phone rang for an annoyingly long time until finally someone answered in a French accent.

"This is Mrs. Harkins," she said. She wanted to sound harsh and grating, but was unable to be less than polite. "I have reservations for tomorrow night."

"Oh, yes, I see that. Four tables. Yes, Mrs. Harkins, what can I do for you?"

"Please cancel my reservation."

"Cancel? On one day's notice?"

"I think your restaurant is overpriced, and the service is bad. Please cancel."

"But Mrs. Harkins..."

"You heard me, buster. Cancel. I wouldn't be caught dead in your shithouse."

Mrs. Dickstein hung up the phone. It took her awhile to regain her tranquility. She smiled to herself, opened her book, watched the rowers on the lake, then lowered her eyes to read.

I CAN STILL SMELL IT

They had moved three times, from their original apartment in Gramercy Park to the East Side on 72nd and finally to the big high-rise on the West Side overlooking the Hudson.

"I can still smell it," Rachel said.

"It's not possible. It's been four years."

Larry, because he loved her with the same zeal and passion as when he married her in June 2001, was patient, although, by then, he was really worried about her. September 11, 2001, had come and gone. They had considered themselves lucky, secretly celebrating their good fortune while expressing pity and compassion for those lost.

In the fullness of time, the site had been cleaned up, the building and body remains carted off to faraway garbage dumps, and some of the area was restored, although they were still arguing about the final outcome for the property.

There was no questioning the fact that it did, indeed, smell for that first year. It was a sickening odor, a mixture probably of dust, debris, and roasted flesh and bones. When the windows of that first apartment were opened even a crack, the smell seeped in and was hard to ignore. Rachel and he tolerated it like everyone else in Manhattan. It was an understandable byproduct of the horror.

That first move a year later was prompted by the idea that perhaps they were too close to the site and that their apartment might be in the path of an air current carrying the smell, which snaked its way through the high-rises in lower Manhattan and alighted with great intensity on the Gramercy Park area. That was Rachel's theory, and Larry believed it credible at the time. Her senses had always seemed more acute than his. She had a great eye for color and design, and her hearing, as judged by her musical appreciation, was exceptional. Her nose for scent was phenomenal, and she could detect perfume and sniff the quality of wine like a professional.

When she said she could still smell the pervasive odor of 9/11, he believed her, although he could no longer detect it.

"Who am I to question the quality of your nose?" he joked, often teasing her when she stuck her nose in a wine glass filled with red wine.

They tried all sorts of air cleaners, mists, plug-in devices, appliances that promised to clean the air. Apparently these things did not work for Rachel. After awhile, they began to argue about it since his own unscientific survey among his colleagues at the office and friends revealed that no one else had the same olfactory experience.

"I just don't understand it," he told her. "You must be the only one in Manhattan that still smells it. Maybe it's psychological."

"Are you suggesting I see a shrink?" she rebutted.

"What I mean," he continued, "is that it could be a memory thing. But then, when it comes to that trauma, everybody in town, the country, the world, is afflicted with that memory. Who could ever forget?"

"It's the smell, Larry. I do understand what you characterize as the memory thing. No one will ever forget that monstrous act by those terrible people. That is an indelible memory. It will be with us forever. But the smell, it's this crazy byproduct. I can't get rid of it."

With the exception of that smell, life appeared otherwise normal. She worked as a copywriter with one of the big advertising agencies, and he was an art director with another agency. Still in their twenties and earning good money, they had friends, kept in touch with parents and siblings who lived out of town, and planned a future with kids. They had had a nice garden wedding in her parents' house in Grand Rapids, Michigan, and went back each Christmas to visit with one or another set of parents. He grew up in Scranton, Pennsylvania.

If it wasn't for the smell, they were otherwise unmarked by the event, although there was no avoiding the general fear that it would happen again someday. It was always in the back of one's mind.

Of course, news of the cleanup was in the papers daily for months following the tragedy. People volunteered. Many went down to the site to assist with food service. Others carpooled. Doctors and nurses volunteered their assistance. Police, firemen, and forensic experts scoured the site for remains. Some victims were found and identified. Others were not. Everyone felt the grief of the survivors who had lost loved ones.

In the immediate aftermath the air quality, along with the smell, was annoying, but not debilitating. Some predicted that many of those who worked at the site might suffer from lung problems later in life. But, the amazing thing was how New Yorkers coped, hung in there, lived their lives to the fullest, and prevailed.

There was something intrepid about New Yorkers. Both Larry and Rachel were proud to be a part of such resilience and optimism. Three years after the event, New York was booming, bigger than ever. Cranes building big high-rises were everywhere in Manhattan. Brooklyn, too, was booming. The Bronx was resurgent.

On the other hand, except for the conflicts over what to do with the site and compensation for those who lost loved ones, people were forgetting and growing less uncomfortable about the possibility of another attack. While everybody recognized the potential threat, it was losing any sense of immediacy. The Bush administration was reviled by opponents who thought the fear factor was being used as a political weapon, and most people in New York City hated the president for invading Iraq, feeling that the invasion only exacerbated the situation. The fact was that except for security lines at the airports, the presence of police and National Guardsmen at various sensitive places like Grand Central Terminal, certain public places where people walked through metal detectors and had their pocketbooks searched, and the stories in the newspapers, the fear of an attack like the one that had destroyed the World Trade Center was dissipating.

"I wish it would go away," Rachel told him with increasing frequency, meaning the smell. "It's here in this apartment. I know it is."

"That's what you said when we lived in Gramercy Park."

"Okay, so it's a coincidence. But, it's here, Larry. I can smell it."

Larry checked with the management of the apartment house to see if anyone else complained about the smell. No one had. Larry reported to Rachel what he had learned.

"Would I complain if I didn't smell it?"

He couldn't argue with that, and he tried his best to be patient and sympathetic. In the end, when their lease was up they moved to the West Side to a brand-new apartment complex that was being built overlooking the Hudson River. The view was gorgeous, and there were wonderfully exhilarating breezes that floated over the river and reached their terrace on the thirtieth floor.

"I'm so sorry, Larry," she told him after they had lived in that apartment for a month. "I can still smell it."

"What is it like?" he asked, determined to be patient.

"Like the same as it was when I first smelled it right after 9/11."

"Be more specific."

"Like dead people, I think."

"Have you ever really smelled dead people?"

"Not really. But, it is what I imagine they might smell like."

Of course, he had asked the question before, but he was beginning to think it might be a physical thing, something that had to do with complex biological factors having to do with the sense of smell. Although he had earlier suggested that she see a shrink, he decided to offer a less threatening alternative.

An ear, nose, and throat specialist declared, after various tests, that everything appeared normal.

"I suppose that's a relief," Rachel said after they had received the test results. "Except that I can still smell it."

Finally, he was losing patience with her insistence. It was having an effect on their relationship. She was getting more restless, sleeping less, tossing at night and inhibiting his own sleep patterns. Sometimes they would discuss the problem of the smell long into the wee hours.

"I smell it now, Larry. Believe me."

"You're imagining it."

He had taken refuge in that idea, since any other possibility was unexplainable.

"Even if I was imagining it, I can still smell it."

"All the time? Is there any time when you don't smell it?"

He had asked that question repetitively, as if it might keep hope alive that she was afflicted with the odor at ever-diminishing intervals. Unfortunately, the answer was also repetitive.

"It never leaves me, Larry. But, it is most intense at home. Maybe when I am thinking of other things at the office, I can ignore it, although it doesn't go away, but when I get back to our apartment it is constant. No matter what I do here in the apartment it is always with me."

In time, it became for her a dominant obsession. It seemed to pervade everything she did, and he sensed that she was growing more and more desperate about the affliction, although she appeared fearful of mentioning it. He could tell it was on her mind by the way her eyes drifted and her nostrils twitched.

Finally, almost in desperation, she consented to a visit to a psychiatrist. She had contemplated going by herself, but she decided that since Larry was the most affected by her affliction, he was entitled to a psychological explanation, if one was available.

The psychiatrist, a pleasant and patient middle-aged man, offered an assessment that was highly technical. He referred to that section of the brain that dealt with the sense of smell, the "smell brain" he called it, and went through a series of possible physical and psychological factors that dealt with trauma and the effect it had on memory.

He had asked her many questions about her childhood. Had she experienced any childhood traumas? Did she have nightmares? What were her principal fears? Had anything happened to her in her lifetime that suggested some relationship with fear and smell? As to the phenomena of the terrorism threat, he was more than curious.

"Are you afraid that another attack is imminent?"

"No more than anyone else."

"Do you panic when you ride a bus or subway or go on an airplane?"

"Acceptance. Not panic."

"Do you have nightmares of death?"

"If you mean death caused by a terrorist attack the answer is no."

"Do news reports of terrorism attacks bother you?"

"Sure they do, but not to the point where I get too upset to function."

"Are you afraid to live in New York?"

"Of course not. I'm here, aren't I?"

His diagnosis was understandable and logical, and he did offer her some hope.

"It could be," he explained to both of them after her session when they met in his office, "that your fear of this terrorist danger is so palpable, so intense, that the odor associated with that tragedy continues to dominate your smell brain."

"But, as I told you, I don't obsess about a terrorist attack," she said. "I fear it, sure, but I don't dwell on it."

"Not consciously," the psychiatrist said. "It is an evolutionary, theory that the sense of smell was the principal defense mechanism of our ancient forebears. They could sniff danger from predators and poisons. It was their most powerful sense and is still powerful in our smell brains."

"And this explains why I can still smell debris?"

"It's a possibility."

"Have you seen other people like me?" Rachel asked him.

"Yes, I have. Fear is very disruptive to one's mental health."

"But, I don't think about it much."

"Except when the smell reminds you of it."

She shook her head, rejecting the notion.

"So, you imply that it's because the fear in my subconscious is too intense that it induces this sense of smell."

"Maybe."

"Maybe?"

"Psychiatry is not a pure science. It deals with clues, assumptions, and interpretations."

His explanation struck both her and Larry as less than helpful.

"It feeds on itself," the psychiatrist told them. "The smell induces memory, like a chain reaction. Have you ever read Proust?"

Rachel and Larry looked at each other and shrugged. Neither he nor Rachel had read him.

"The smell of madeleine cake when he was a child," the psychiatrist went on, "induced in him a lifetime of memory and served as the trigger to motivate him to write his masterpiece spanning multiple volumes, all because of the memory of that smell."

"So, what can I do about it?" Rachel asked him. "Write a book?"

He laughed politely.

"I'm going to prescribe a medicine that has worked in cases like yours. It was originally used to stop nausea in pregnant women."

"I'm not pregnant, not yet," she said, looking at Larry.

"It may not work," the psychiatrist said.

"And if it doesn't work?" Rachel asked.

"Find a way to live with it," he said. "Like titinnitis, a hearing difficulty that is rarely cured."

"That it?" Larry asked, after exchanging troubled glances with Rachel.

"One day it might simply disappear," the psychiatrist said. It was a very unsatisfactory diagnosis.

"It's already been more than four years," Larry said.

"I wish I could be more helpful," the psychiatrist said.

"So do we."

For the next few months in their new apartment, they tried to lead normal lives. Nothing changed. The pills he gave her did not work. Once again, she began to make noises about the apartment being a place where the smell became worse.

"Where can we go, then?" he challenged. Clearly, he had been patient, understanding, and cooperative, had done everything possible to help her cope with the situation.

"Maybe if we moved upstate. Somewhere in the Hudson Valley further up the river," she suggested.

"It's something inside you Rachel, not in the apartment. Will these moves go on forever?"

"I hope not."

He felt deeply sorry for her affliction. Love, he sensed, was turning to pity and compassion. They slept less and less, engaging in long, nocturnal conversations. They made love less often and when they did it seemed routine, not spontaneous as it had been at the beginning.

But, he agreed to look for a place farther up the river, vowing to himself that this would be the absolute last time they would move. Moving was an exhausting process and was financially draining as well. Nevertheless, he was determined to help Rachel.

"We'll have to commute by train more than an hour to get to work," he told her.

"I'm willing if you are."

"Maybe if we went up there and you sniffed around. You know what I mean. Trees act as filters."

"That would be wonderful."

They drove farther up the Hudson Valley, past Peekskill, but she could still detect the smell.

"Does it seem less so up here?" he asked.

"I'm not sure."

Nevertheless, they contacted a real estate broker and rented a nice house in Hudson, with a garden, surrounded by trees, and the air, to him at least, seemed fresh and clear.

It didn't help. She could still smell it.

"I'll never move again," he told her. He was beginning to see how this mad affliction was chipping away at their relationship. He tried to rationalize his situation by characterizing her as "handicapped." If she was "handicapped," he reasoned, he would stand by her no matter what. "In sickness and in health," the marriage vow decreed. Taking refuge in the idea, he felt ennobled by his sacrifice. It was a sacrifice.

She had given up her job and was working as a freelancer, doing her work at home. He couldn't, as he was needed by his colleagues in face-to-face situations. The commute was exhausting him, making him irritable and depressed. Of course, she was well aware of what was happening, but was helpless in the face of what was assailing her.

One day, he came home and she was wearing a surgical mask

obviously impregnated with heavy perfume, which smelled like lilacs.

"Does it work?" he asked.

"Only when I keep it on," she said, her speech muffled by the mask. She took it off only to eat and drink and when she talked on the telephone. She began to sleep with it. The odor of lilacs was so intense it was giving him headaches. When he complained, she changed the perfume to other flowered scents, but nothing worked as well as lilacs.

"I can't stand the smell of it," he told her often, trying valiantly to live with it, feeling guilty, finding it more and more difficult to cope with the smell.

"Now you see what I mean," she said.

"It's driving me crazy."

"For me, it's either that smell or the other. At least the smell of lilacs doesn't remind me of the other, the horror of it."

As time went on, he rarely saw her full face. Her speech behind the mask was muffled and, at times, he found it difficult to understand her words. The house was inundated with the smell of lilacs. It permeated everything, even his clothes. His co-workers would comment about it and after awhile he noticed that they preferred to keep their distance. He was too embarrassed to explain what it was all about.

Finally, his boss called him into his office.

"What is it with you, Larry? You stink of perfume, smells like lilacs. It's making some people around here nauseous. Are you wearing this scent?"

"Actually, no," he responded. "It's my wife's. It gets into my clothes."

"You'd better get rid of that stink, Larry. Really, it's upsetting people. It's too heavy. Yuk. I'd prefer if you left my office now."

As he began to leave the office, his boss called out.

"It's either my way or the highway, Larry."

At home, he tried sleeping in another room and double-washing his shirts and underwear and sending his clothes to the cleaners very frequently. Nothing helped. He explained the situation to Rachel.

"I may lose my job," he said.

"Over the smell of lilacs? That's ridiculous."

"No, it isn't," he acknowledged. "It's driving me crazy as well."

The boss kept his word and he was fired. In some ways it was a blessing because it forced him to confront his situation. She couldn't stand the smell of the World Trade Center aftermath, and the lilac scent was the only palliative that worked for her. And he couldn't stand the smell of lilacs.

He tried working from home, but it was impossible to live with the scent. By then, love had disappeared, although he did feel deep compassion for her problem and a new emotion—guilt—was beginning to take hold. As a temporary solution, he took an apartment in Manhattan and came up on weekends. Sometimes, she greeted him without the mask, but the smell of lilacs had seeped into the atmosphere of the house. He could barely wait out the weekend.

"I can still smell it," she would tell him when the mask was off and the lilac scent did not help.

Finally, he could stand it no longer.

"We're both casualties of 9/11, Rachel."

She agreed and they got a friendly divorce. It took him months to get rid of the smell of lilacs. He called her on the fifth anniversary of 9/11.

"I can still smell it," she told him.

A DAD FOREVER

Jack Spencer observed his fifty-year-old son across the table at Michael's, a celebrity haunt in Manhattan where Henry was a regular. Noting that his son's eyes swept the room with eagle-eyed intensity, nodding here and there to others in the crowded dining room, Spencer said, "You seem to know lots of people, Hank," with a touch of pride. Henry was the creative director of an important advertising agency.

"I guess," Henry shrugged, offering his father a shining, bright smile, certainly a cosmetic spruce-up. He was handsome, with big brown eyes behind high cheekbones like his late mother's. In fact, he looked so much like Dorothy that Spencer felt a pang of deep sentiment and had to squelch a sob, disguising it with a cough.

Henry had certainly enhanced his appearance since Spencer had last seen him two years ago. Apparently, there had been an eye job, which eliminated the bags that were a family affliction on Spencer's side of the family tree. Spencer had never corrected the bags under his eyes. And there was the touch-up of Henry's sideburns, once graying.

They did speak periodically on the phone. Their conversations had become, over the years, more like short news bulletins from New York than real dialogue. Spencer defined it as perfunctory, obligatory, and dutiful, but feared to protest its lack of real intimacy. He was well aware that his expectations exceeded the reality. But at seventy-five, he supposed, he was more tolerant of disappointment and more willing to accept small victories. Even lip service had its attractions.

The fact was that hearing his son's voice was comforting,

validating the existence of genetic tissue between father and son. Lately, they had communicated more by e-mail, enhancing the news bulletin definition. Like any report from a faraway place, all it lacked was a dateline and audio input.

"You look great, Hank," Spencer said with sincere admiration. His son's success was a source of pride, and he acknowledged it frequently in their telephone conversations and e-mails.

He had long ago made peace with the knowledge that his son was gay. There was, of course, only one answer to that dilemma, and he and Dorothy had confronted it when it became apparent, then finally admitted. Parental aspirations had little to do with reality. When one truly loved one's children, the only option was acceptance.

Henry's sister, Carol, had provided them with two grandchildren, which filled that void. Not that he and Dorothy had been professional grandparents. Carol lived with her husband and the kids in Los Angeles, and Spencer got to see them twice a year. Thankfully, he had had his busy practice as an internist in Chicago to keep him occupied and able to cope with the physical loss of his wife, three years ago.

He was semi-retired now, which enabled him to, as he put it, smell the roses, which was more of an excuse than a necessity. Tomorrow he would board the gargantuan Queen Mary for a trip across the pond with a group of Chicagoans to visit the literary sights of the United Kingdom. English literature had always been his hobby and private joy, especially the Victorians, and he had had a lifelong passion for Shakespeare.

"It should be fun, Dad," Henry said as they dipped into their Cobb salads. "I'm glad you're getting around more." They were silent for awhile as Spencer surreptitiously inspected his son. He felt clandestine, as if he were spying. Actually, he was remembering how it had been in their early years, the joy of his son's birth, the homecoming, the upbringing, all the things they did together as a family, how wonderful it was.

Family and work. He loved both aspects of his life then. His children were the central fact of his and Dorothy's life, and everything they did was to enhance their lives, contribute to their happiness.

Memories crowded his mind as he sat facing his firstborn, once his and Dorothy's fervent and loving occupation from sunrise to sunset and certainly in their dreams. They had marveled at the miracle of making this little boy. Surely other progenitors must have felt the same way. Family was the cornerstone of living in those days before mobility and ambition upset the balance. His and Dorothy's parents had lived in Chicago all their lives and so it had been with them. He knew, of course, when displacement had begun and, he supposed, it was partially his and Dorothy's fault.

Eschewing Northwestern and the University of Chicago, he and his wife encouraged their children to attend pricey Ivy League universities, and Henry had scored Harvard and Carol Yale, which was and still is a feather in their parents' caps. Not wanting their children to be burdened with debt, they had borrowed heavily for the tuitions and it had taken them years to pay off the debts.

They had high expectations, quickly dashed on graduation, that their children would return to their Midwest haven loaded with honors and make Chicago their permanent home. He had yearned to be the paterfamilias of a growing brood, a wise guide, steering both his children through the minefields that awaited them in adulthood. Dorothy, too, had her own ambitions to be the mother hen grandma whose long soft arms would embrace her blood progeny through the generations.

They had, of course, survived their original disappointment, learning the hard way that destiny had other things in store. Mobility had trumped their dreams, and once out of the coop, both children had fled. Memories of family joys, concerned only the first two decades of their children's lives, probably less, for soon both kids had established themselves elsewhere and condemned them forever to long distance parenting, telephonic talk, and reports from afar.

Of course, they remained connected via all those new devices and they all participated in a running documentary of their children's activities. Inquiries were made about their own lives, mostly, they suspected, with a sense more of obligation than overwhelming concern. The children seemed to accept the notion of their parents' decline, often with, what they supposed and hoped was genuine regret. Spencer assumed that their memories of childhood, those crucial two decades, continued to hold them in thrall as they did him.

They had been dutiful, even Henry, whose gaydom might have threatened the old bond, but Spencer and Dorothy felt they had navigated that choppy river with tact and understanding. Besides, there was little they could do about it.

Observing his son now, seeing the child in the man, the deeply loved firstborn, he remembered those first years, the joys of fathering, the caresses of that smooth baby flesh, the giggles and tickles as the little boy got between them in their bed to be loved and fondled, those first steps, the feel of that little hand in his, the olfactory memory of those little boy and later little girl's smells.

His pride of progeny was boundless. Drawings done by both children in first grade were still preserved forever in frames as if they were great art and continued to grace his Chicago apartment. Nothing could ever erase the angst of old illnesses, measles, mumps, croup, and all the other large and small ailments and affliction that plagued them during their childhood. Carol had scarlet fever and frightened them for days as they imagined the ultimate tragedy, the potential loss of a young child.

He and Dorothy were concerned and deeply interested parents in all phases of their children's lives. No parents were more dedicated, more devoted, more supportive of their offspring.

For years he and Dorothy had pored over the thousands of pictures they had taken of themselves and their children, during family vacations, outings, and visits to the long-gone generation of their own parents. For some unspoken reason, as the decades passed, it became too painful to look back through this tangible visibility and it felt better to resort to memory to revisit those old images.

Then, looking at his son's smooth complexion, he remembered something that he could not contain and words suddenly popped out.

"Do you remember when I gave you your first electric razor, Hank? I took you into Marshall Field's and made a big deal about it, then instructed you how to use it?"

It was hardly the most important incident in their father-son life, but it did mark the end of something and the beginning of a new chapter. Henry's thin smile and shrug indicated only the vaguest of memory.

"And the bike?" Spencer said, his memories drifting as his mind lighted on the strangest incidents. For some reason, Henry had great difficulty learning to ride a two-wheeler, and Spencer had patiently held the bike upright until Henry had finally mastered the process. It seemed like weeks until the boy was finally able to ride on his own. There were countless other incidents, but it just didn't seem the time or place to be overly sentimental.

What he kept especially hidden from revelation at that moment was the day when he called Henry aside to inform him about what was then called "the facts of life." It was summer and they were at their lakeside cottage, and he had illustrated the process by using a twig to outline in the dirt at lakeside what happens when the penis enters the vagina. Embarrassed in the telling, he used medical terms, which seemed to confuse the boy.

"Do you understand all this, Hank?" he had asked.

"I think so, Dad," the boy had answered, and that was enough to satisfy the father that he had done his duty.

The irony of the memory caused him to swallow hard and a bit of lettuce caught in his throat. So many things were left unsaid now. It had been years since they had had an intimate conversation, although he was not quite sure he knew what that would entail. In fact, except for the blood bond and the obligatory connection, Spencer felt that there had been little intimacy between them for three decades or more.

Bits and pieces of his son's adult life had emerged in passing, in the unguarded and inadvertent remark, but nothing said seemed to have the genuine feel of revelation. His son had been through therapy, had had various partners, whom he had met on occasion, but this information was merely offered as dry facts and impersonal stage asides.

Spencer often wondered if being a father meant that he had any right to any more than a cursory interior view of his son's psyche. Where, after all, were the real boundaries of fatherhood?

Spencer's relationship with his own father had been closer, but they had had the advantage of proximity and frequent face-to-face conversations. They had observed each other, and overcome reticence by familiarity. Still, he wondered if he had really known his father, the man's inner life. Or had his father known him? His memories were heartfelt and pleasant and, in truth, he now wished he knew his father better and would have welcomed some memoir that would have revealed more than he knew.

"What is it, Dad?" Henry asked suddenly.

Spencer realized he was staring at his son.

"Sorry, Hank," Spencer said. "I was just thinking about the old days when you were a kid and we were all together." Well not quite, but that was what it came down to.

"The good old days," Henry chuckled. Spencer detected a mocking tone.

"They were the best of it, Hank," Spencer said, pretending now to eat his salad with relish. He felt suddenly bereft, unbearably alone. "Do you ever think about those days?"

Henry put down his fork. His nostrils flared, and he used his napkin to pat his lips, then took a deep sip on a glass of water.

"I do, Dad," Henry said. "I do think about them." Then he added, "Not often."

Spencer could not think of a response. He tried not to show his disappointment.

"The fact is, Dad, I'm sorry to say, I really didn't like my childhood."

"You didn't?"

While the words were a shock and Spencer felt a sudden wave of nausea assail him, he valiantly tried to keep up appearances. It was a blow for which he was totally unprepared.

"I was not a happy camper, Dad."

No, the father protested, searching for soft words of refutation. It was, Spencer concluded quickly, revisionism fostered by those years in therapy.

"You could have fooled me," Spencer said hoarsely. "And your mother."

"You mustn't blame yourself, Dad. Or Mom. I know you tried. Valiantly."

"We were your parents," Spencer said, feeling a flush of anger, as he pushed his plate away, as if some gesture of impatience was needed. "We loved you and did everything in our power to give you the best of life, and, above all, to give you happiness. Are you saying that there was no joy in your childhood?"

"I assume you want me to be truthful," Henry said blandly. His attention was suddenly allayed by a greeting to someone passing their table. It seemed to Spencer a rude gesture, considering the earth-shattering importance to him of his son's remark.

"You mean your version of the truth."

"My perception is my truth, Dad."

"Are you saying that all those episodes and incidents in your childhood, our early times, what we did together as a family, all those acts of devotion and, yes, sacrifice and expense, all that loving care lavished on you by your mother and me was all for naught, bringing you nothing but unhappiness?"

"It's a lot more complicated than that, Dad. You just don't understand what it means to struggle with one's sexual identity in a potentially hostile middle-class environment."

Spencer felt his stomach tighten. He reached out for a glass of water, noting that his hand shook. It was impossible to hide his reaction.

"A hostile middle-class environment? Really, Hank. Long ago, we accepted your sexual orientation."

"It would be difficult to explain," Henry said.

Spencer was quick to recognize the dismissive nature of his remark.

"Did we live under the same roof? Or am I imagining things. Childhood begins at birth. Are you saying you never had a happy moment when you were growing up? Your mother must be turning over in her grave." And his daughter? Would she too reveal that her childhood was unhappy? Considering how this present incident had shattered him, he resolved to avoid inquiring. A double whammy would be too terrible to bear.

He felt himself wrestling with a rising rage, searching his son's face, wondering if this person who sat in front of him, was, indeed, his real son, child of his loins, recipient of his love and devotion. Or was he a stranger? At this moment, it seemed so.

"I hadn't meant to be hurtful, Dad. It doesn't mean that I don't love and respect you. Or that I didn't love Mom. Would you rather I told you that I had a happy childhood? Didn't you always teach us to tell the truth, no matter how much it hurt?"

"It cannot be the truth. No way," Spencer protested. "Why now? Why did you tell me now?" He ignored the issue of hurt since he was too wounded to confront it.

"I can't answer that question, Dad. It just came out. I guess I hadn't expected your reaction."

"It shouldn't have come as a surprise," Spencer said bitterly. "What you're telling me is that because we never really knew who or what you were, we robbed you of a happy childhood. Is that it?"

"You're overreacting, Dad. It was all so long ago. What does it matter now? Think happy thoughts. You're going on a great trip. Why dwell on the past?"

He felt trapped by disappointment. Getting his rage under control required a great force of will. He studied his son's handsome face, looked into his eyes. What was he thinking? He could feel no connection. Between them was merely empty space, a great gulf.

"So, my well-burnished image of a happy family was just delusion," Spencer muttered.

"That may be too strong an interpretation Dad," his son said with some annoyance. He hailed the waiter and ordered coffees, then turned to his father. "Let's drop the subject. It's really of no importance now."

Henry shrugged and waved to someone across the room. It was obvious that to his son, this revelation was a small thing, a passing blip on the screen of his life. It was merely confirmation of what Spencer could no longer deny to himself. To Henry, he had long ago entered the age of irrelevance. In this environment, this fancy restaurant that validated his son's success, he was a stranger, an object of condescension and charity.

His son had severed himself years ago, holding on only to the rituals of family. His periodic calls and e-mails and this little lunch were Henry's version of kindness, a painless tribute to an ancient memory, reserved mostly for obligation and, perhaps, to satisfy a tiny trill of guilt.

When the check came, his son reached for his wallet, but Spencer stayed his hand and pulled out a small wad of folded cash.

"Please, Dad, let me. New York is my town. You're my guest."

"Thanks, Hank, but I'd prefer it this way."

Henry nodded.

"I get it. Once a dad, a dad forever."

"Nothing is forever," Spencer muttered, laying out the cash to pay the check.

THE EPIPHANY

"I want a divorce," Carol Goldstein said.

Charlie, her husband, had just returned from one of his occasional foreign business trips. He was a lawyer dealing in international trade. They had been married twenty years and their daughter, Sharon, was away at college, a sophomore at Harvard.

"You can't be serious," Charlie said, trying to remain calm and summoning the mask of his lawyerly demeanor. In fact, he was stunned. It was beyond his comprehension. He and Carol had been what he believed was a sharing, compatible, and contented couple all of their married life. He had never been unfaithful and there had been numerous opportunities. She had combined a busy career with elements of traditional wifely chores.

Charlie was Jewish and Carol an Episcopalian, an issue that had been bridged without major complications years ago. To spare themselves and their parents any undue tension, they had been married in Manhattan's City Hall. Both sets of parents were secular, although they had schooled their children to respect their religious heritage. Charlie had gone to Hebrew school and been bar mitzvahed, and Carol had attended church with her parents and observed Christian holidays.

The reason for their city hall ceremony was that they did not want to confront the complications of a joint religious ceremony and the painful rituals of merging relatives of different backgrounds, forced to celebrate an event that might be uncomfortable for some of them. Nevertheless, acceptance came early, since such marriages were now commonplace in the new age of diversity. They had met at a student cafeteria at Brown University, where Charlie had been a senior and Carol a sophomore.

"He could have been a Hawaiian," Carol's mother said in an offhand moment after imbibing too much champagne at a welcoming dinner in the Greenwich, Connecticut, home of Carol's parents, Mr. and Mrs. Clark, after they had returned from their short honeymoon in the Berkshires. It was a tiny slip of the tongue and in conflict with the family's Wasp tradition of reserve. When he was in the company of Carol's parents and relatives, Charlie always felt an oddly forbidden sense of guilty pleasure in the knowledge that he, the Jew boy from the old ghetto land, had absconded with the heart and body of this "Blonde Goddess" sorority girl of legend and entitlement.

Charlie's parents, liberal and progressive to the core, wore a façade of complete acceptance. When they slipped in front of Carol, it came in the form of a joke, as in an occasional remark from Charlie's father that "shiksas made the best wives." Pure shtick, Charlie would say, laughing without any attempt at rebuke. Charlie's mother, in a typically Jewish Burns and Allen riposte, would remark that there was nothing more domestically satisfying than a nice Jewish husband for any girl, especially a shiksa.

It was a case, they both agreed, in which true love trumped tribal affiliations and outmoded irrelevant rituals. Of course, Charlie knew he was irrevocably and inescapably branded a Jew by his name and to some, his looks. He was comfortable with that. It was, after all, who he was, and he had too much pride to reject the idea that he had sprung from an ancient people who had survived centuries of persecution and pain. Just because he was not into their God fantasies didn't mean that he didn't consider himself a Jew. He could never reject such a notion, and he made no effort to hide his pedigree. Carol accepted it fully and completely and gave him no reason to think otherwise. She hadn't converted, which was okay with Charlie. There was no need to. She had equal pride in her Christian antecedents.

Nor did they feel any sense of compromise. The world had changed and they were part of it. It never occurred to him that he was watering down the faith, and she never acknowledged any hint or attitude that she had surrendered to an alien horde.

From the beginning, Carol and Charlie had asserted that they would be aggressively non-denominational and if they had children they would allow them to choose what religion they wished to identify with or none at all. Nor was it an issue between them. There was one small concession about identity that Carol had adopted early on. She called herself Carol Clark Goldstein. It was the name she used in business as an advertising executive and in her personal relationships. Completely supportive, Charlie would always introduce her to strangers with her three names.

Their social and business circles consisted of people of all persuasions, political and religious, and all skin tones and accents. The old boundaries of past generations seemed extinct in their own, although occasionally a word or gesture might hint of a mild imagined reaction in someone observing Carol when they were introduced. Goldstein? Funny, you don't look Jewish. Later, they would chuckle over the observation.

As for their daughter, with a name like Goldstein how could she deny that her father was a Jew? In fact, as she matured, she was rather proud of it, although she stayed on the edge of any formal affiliations with Jewish groups and shrugged off those areas still cordoned off by prejudice against Jews. She could not understand the bigotry, the extent of which surprised her once she got to college, but she didn't lose any sleep over it, thinking those who practiced such sentiments were bigoted fools.

Between Carol and Charlie, they made a good living and had an apartment on the Upper East Side, with appreciating art on their walls, a well-stocked library featuring leather-bound sets that Charlie had lovingly collected, and a large dining room that could seat fourteen. Carol entertained frequently, and to all appearances, they were a typical successful Manhattan couple with a wide circle of friends and an accurate image of being a loving, compatible couple with a bright, attractive, and devoted daughter. They were, indeed, and Charlie had no clue or premonition that this image was about to implode.

"You can't be serious," Charlie had replied to the sudden

pronouncement, after he had recovered his equilibrium. Carol had chosen the moment right after Charlie had refreshed himself from the long plane trip, had showered, and gotten into his pajamas and robe.

"I know this comes as a shock, Charlie. I'm sorry, really sorry."

Quite obviously, she had rehearsed this necessary confrontation over and over again in her mind. Knowing her intimately, he knew she needed to get this over with quickly, having made the decision some time ago. This was not a situation that one activates without long deliberation.

"Is there someone else?" Charlie asked, opting to cut to the chase. What other reason could there be?

"Yes, there is," Carol admitted with unflinching candor. It was as if she had predicted his responses and had studied her lines.

"May I ask who?"

"John Fletcher, a business associate. You've never met him."

"For how long?" Charlie said, finally feeling the blow, his voice constricting.

"More than a year."

Charlie felt the blood rise. He knew his face had flushed and that if he held out his arms, his hands would be shaking. He had, of course, encountered defeats and disappointment in his life, but nothing more cataclysmic than this. There was no game plan in his arsenal of reactions. He was, quite literally, emotionally crushed. Worse, he felt foolish. How could he have not known?

"The heart has its own agenda, Charlie," Carol said. She had, he decided, worked long and hard on finding that response. How else to justify such a life-changing decision? Blame it on the unknown, the profound mystery.

"No second thoughts?" he asked, taking refuge in politeness. Although he desperately wanted to show his rage, he had suddenly decided that such a reaction would imply weakness and loss of dignity, something he could not bring himself to display in front of her. He had been cuckolded. There was no other word for it. She had come to his bed after wallowing in the embrace of her lover, the remains of his sperm in her body. The image was beyond awful.

"And Sharon? Does she know?"

Carol nodded.

"You could have at least told me first," Charlie said, feeling all self-respect drained, his pride demolished. He sensed the first tiny stirrings of hatred.

"I think it needed to be a mother-daughter thing," she shrugged.

She had worked that out as well, Charlie thought, a ploy to gain sympathy and justify her betrayal of the child's father.

"We cried together. She needs to talk with you. I told her that I would be telling you tonight. She loves you, Charlie, and she needs us both."

Apparently, she had won her point.

"My God…" he began, but he couldn't go on.

It would soon be time to go to sleep, and he found himself worried about the sleeping arrangements. Perhaps as a distraction his mind began filling with the technicalities of separation and divorce, domicile arrangements, property divisions, legal details. The turmoil ahead seemed daunting.

"We have got to be civilized and sensible about this, Charlie."

Charlie shrugged. The "civilized and sensible" cliché seemed the least important item on his emotional agenda. What he really wanted to do was go into a dark room, shut the door, curl up in a fetal position and go to sleep, forever if possible, to spare himself the impending pain and agony.

Following the long-standing tradition of an amicable divorce, he moved into a hotel and, in time, into a small apartment near his office. The meeting with his daughter had been fatherly, with no bitter or hateful allusions to her mother's affair as anything more than a natural event, merely a manifestation of a midlife crisis. He resisted any temptation to characterize her mother in a way that would be emotionally disturbing to his daughter.

In his loneliness and despair as he tried to adjust to his new life, he had slowly begun to feel a growing rage, which he was finding unable to keep under control. He tried to rationalize his situation by ascribing it more to self-pity and merely a passing trauma that time would eventually heal. But, as the myriad details of separation and divorce progressed, he was growing exceedingly less understanding. They had each hired lawyers who diligently and expensively prepared documents and listed their possessions and the details of their dispossession, about which he found himself growing increasingly uncomfortable.

When they met they were polite and proper, especially if their daughter was present. As time went on they met infrequently, letting their lawyers deal with the details. Once or twice he had actually seen Carol with her new lover, John Fletcher, noting that he was definitely cut from a different cloth. Once they had met in a restaurant. Fletcher struck him as a Waspy country club frat boy, straight featured and uncircumcised, a goy down to his toenails. So, she had receded back to her roots. He was certain of this truth even as he smiled and shook the man's hand. At that moment, hatred for Carol gushed over him like a tsunami.

It was a delayed action, and his lawyer had advised him to resist recrimination, settle the matter, and go on with his life. Of course, he agreed in principal, but he knew the so-called civilized and sensible paradigm was totally shattered. He was becoming increasingly pissed off. He had been screwed, betrayed by a conniving, deceptive, lying bitch. The Blonde Goddess had morphed into the witch of the west and all points of the compass.

Living in his one-bedroom, furnished apartment while the lawyers worked out the division of property, he would often think of her living in the lap of luxury in their once prized apartment, now populated by her lover, the Wasp goy, sleeping in his bed, screwing his once worshipped Blonde Goddess, handling his cherished leather-bound books, and enjoying his appreciating art. It began to inflame him emotionally and, finally defying his lawyer's good advice, he began to throw obstacles in the way of what once was an amicable divorce procedure.

"I want all of my leather-bounds, most of the artwork, half of the furniture, and half of every fucking thing in the apartment. I want half of everything down to every spoon, knife, and fork in the silverware. I want the apartment sold immediately."

"It's your nickel," the lawyer told him, an obvious reference to his fee.

"Exactly."

His resistance was, at first, adamant. Her lawyer, at Carol's behest, tried various strategies to compromise. Of course, she had her own agenda regarding the possessions, some of which was unreasonable as far as he was concerned. It was, he supposed, a typical standoff. At one point his daughter intervened, urging both parents to make peace for the sake of their own happiness. Her plea made sense, of course, and he hated the idea of being the cause of any emotional pain to his beloved daughter. Apparently, Carol and her lover were planning to marry after their divorce was final, another item to fuel his anger.

Finally, after months of wrangling, he decided that it was self-defeating and ridiculously expensive to continue the battle, and he carefully drew up lines of compromise, although on some issues, particularly when it came to his books and some of the artwork, he was still determined to hold the line. To achieve a final settlement, the lawyers arranged a meeting in the boardroom of Carol's lawyer.

They sat at either side of the conference table, icily polite. Despite his bubbling rage, he admitted to himself that she did look quite beautiful and self-possessed. She had, after all, found a companion with whom to share her life. He had not been successful in this regard, although he had tried.

Thankfully, he had managed to compensate by working longer and harder in his practice and had increased his income, which helped with his legal bills. With discipline, he tried valiantly to effect a calm demeanor. Unfortunately, the sight of his Blonde Goddess, looking haughty and beautiful, did not stir warm nostalgic memories of the happy days of their marriage. Instead, he dwelled on the unsavory aspects of her cunning deception. How had he not known? How could she have done this to him? Worse, why had he not made peace with this affront to his dignity and self-worth? Yes, he assured himself, it was about time to shed the corrosive power of his inner rage before it destroyed him.

The lawyers calmly outlined the differences that separated them. Although it hurt, he agreed to divide the artwork, giving up some especially favorite work, and she finally consented to let him have his beloved leather-bound books. At this point, he was in a compromising mood, wanting at last to put all this behind him. He had lost and it was time, he told himself, with lawyerly logic, for dignified face-saving surrender.

She wanted to keep the apartment and through her lawyer, she made an offer. He was about to concede on this point, but he hesitated. Her lawyer said she had had an appraisal, and he handed Charlie the document citing the value.

"I'd like to have my own appraisal done," he said to her lawyer.

"Oh come on, Charlie," Carol blurted, revealing her impatience. "This is the right price."

"He is entitled to it," Charlie's lawyer said, turning to his client seeking approval.

"The fact is that I demand it," Charlie said, as if his sense of fairness felt suddenly violated.

"You people are impossible," Carol blurted.

"We people?"

"You know what I mean."

He could see the beginning of an accelerating anger.

"No, I don't," he said deliberately fueling the exchange.

"Jesus, must I say it, Charlie?"

"Yes, you must."

She drew in her breath and shook her head.

"Jews, Charlie. Jews. All you can think about. Money. Money. Money." He felt his insides curdle. "I mean face it, Charlie. There has to be a reason why Jews are persecuted and reviled for thousands of years. It took me a long time to see it. You Jews are the most impossible people on earth. You think you're smarter than the rest of us poor goyem. So fucking superior. You know everything. The fact is, as I have learned, you are a vicious, greedy people. You take. All that baloney about giving, justice, fighting for the underdog. It's all bullshit, an attempt to make you look goody-goody so people won't see the real flaws and subterfuge behind the façade." She stopped for a moment and exchanged glances with her own lawyer, who, as he knew, was not Jewish, probably deliberately chosen.

Charlie's lawyer was Jewish, but held back any reaction, looking toward Charlie with an expression of concern. He made a movement with his hands, which signaled to Charlie to restrain himself. Charlie did not need to be told. There was no defense, no possible argument to be mounted against this time-tested canard. No one, as far as he knew, especially a Jew, had ever understood the logic behind it. It was too embedded in the culture of the planet, perhaps a genetic fault in the human species, beyond explanation or rationality. He felt a sudden epiphany, the realization of an absurdity that had morphed into a universal mindset. There were, therefore, only two choices: fight or flee.

"I know I sound awful," Carol said, but without any sign of remorse. "Unfortunately, it's true, Charlie. Jews are that way. You people can't help yourself. That's the way you're programmed. You have this compulsive need to take advantage. Believe me, Charlie, I understand. It's just part of your makeup and any corrective strategy is out of your hands. And, unfortunately, out of mine."

She grew silent, as if something had ballooned inside her and some mysterious pinprick had deflated the balloon. Charlie was surprised that his own anger had abated. He thought suddenly of his daughter. In Carol's mind was she, too, poisoned by his genes? He wanted to bring up the point, but decided against it. How would such a view impact his daughter? He decided to remain silent and turned to his lawyer.

"Accept the appraisal," Charlie told him, standing up, lifting his hand and waving a tepid goodbye. Fight or flee. He had chosen the latter.

EAST SIDE WEST SIDE

"Done," Susan Charrap had said, her voice a low, hoarse whisper on the cell phone. "You're free now."

A burden removed, he had thought at first, even though it had been totally unexpected. Searching for a response, he was confused. It had been discussed, but there had been no resolution.

"You should have told me," he admonished.

"Why? I'm free now as well."

"After all, I do have some say."

"Not anymore," she said. He remembered the long silence, hearing vague background noises, horns honking, outdoor sounds. Then she said: "I don't want to see you ever again. Not ever. Do you understand? Not ever."

She had her own place on the East Side off 73rd and Lexington, a two-room apartment in an older walk-up. He lived on West 80th off Amsterdam. She spent more time at his place than her own. When he had finally accepted the ultimatum a few weeks later, he had sent her clothes and other odd possessions back to her. The fact was that he had taken it seriously for his own reasons, feeling, after long reflection, that she had it right: He was the unwilling one.

But he was twenty-five then, just starting to get a leg up with the firm. He was hardly ready for fatherhood and all its inhibiting responsibilities.

"I feel trapped," he had argued. He hated the idea.

"So do I."

"Well then."

"Well then what?"

"You know what you have to do."

It wasn't a question of money. They were both making good salaries. She was freelancing commercial art. He was established at the firm.

"People do it all the time. We don't even have to get married."

They had avoided the issue of responsibility. People in love, physically attracted, could be careless. To cite her neglect, he thought at the time, would be dishonorable. Indeed, he truly felt that this procedure was the practical solution for them in that moment. There would be plenty of time, he had told her. She seemed to have agreed and that was that. Until she called him with the news. Then it was over.

But it wasn't over, not really. Five years hadn't granted him the complete cure. Withdrawal had been difficult since he loved her, truly loved her. Not that he thought of her as often, as time went on. Other things happened. He imagined he fell in love again with Dorothy, then Barbara. At that moment, he thought Barbara was the one and now that he was thirty and had moved up in the firm, he could honestly tell himself he was nearly ready. Not quite, but nearly.

Barbara and he lived together in his larger West Side apartment and were seriously discussing the official ring ceremony and all it implied. There were pros and cons, of course. They wanted to be absolutely one hundred percent certain that they were the ones, that this was the time.

It was in the middle of that debate that he saw, of all people, Susan Charrap. He had been jogging along the main access in Central Park at 72nd on Saturday. It was late morning. He and Barbara usually slept in on Saturdays. He wasn't sure at first. Actually, it had amazed him that he had never bumped into her, not once. Admittedly, sometimes he had passed her old place, even stopped to watch, wondering what she was doing.

There were times, too, when he thought he had glimpsed the back of her head or a passing side view, but he had been mistaken, and after awhile he became less alert to the possibility.

This time he was dead certain. He was wearing sunglasses and a baseball cap pulled low against the late spring sun. If she had been alone, he imagined he might have simply stopped, identified himself, and, after a few brief pleasantries, he would jog on. But she was holding the hand of a little boy, and for some reason he did not have the courage to reveal himself.

After she had passed by, he suddenly found himself with the overwhelming urge to follow her. By then he had jogged all the way to the east side of the park. Following her at a distance, he hid, literally hid, behind a tree and watched her go into the children's playground. The little boy began to play on the nearby monkey bars with other children. She sat on a bench, opened the *New York Times,* and began to read, periodically lifting her head to observe the little boy.

So, she had probably married, he concluded after watching her for a while. Had found another life and just as he had predicted, in time she had had a child. She was still quite beautiful, he decided, acknowledging a trill of the old feeling, that pulse-quickening sensation of emotional memory. God, he had loved her.

It had taken him a long time after their breakup to make peace with his behavior. At times, especially on those sleepless, dead-of-night confrontations with the truth, he berated himself for his cowardice, his utter lack of character, his refusal to take a risk, his putting his career above his sense of honor. She, on the other hand, had seen what he was truly made of and had taken the bold step, an act of far greater courage than his, to protect her integrity.

Eventually, he forgave himself. Not quite. But, he no longer brooded over his failings. Okay, he was a lot less than heroic, but he had done the practical thing and now he had moved upward and was ready to face whatever came his way. He stopped beating himself up. He had fallen in love with a beautiful, decent, honest girl with whom he was compatible and with whom he was comfortable.

"Are you okay, Ben?" Barbara had asked when he got back to the apartment after jogging.

Of course he was okay. What had she detected in his expression or demeanor?

"Don't I look okay?"

"Maybe it's my imagination. You look, I don't know, funny."

"Don't be ridiculous."

That night he awoke in a sweat, suddenly wide awake. The little boy! He was not a good judge of children's age, but he figured that the little boy might be about five or pretty close. Could it be? He spent the next few hours running the gamut of speculation. Over and over again, he heard her words on the phone, "Done, you're free now."

"You look tired," Barbara said at breakfast.

"Couldn't sleep. Must be a cold coming on."

It was part of the protocol these days to be reasonably candid about past relationships, and he had been. Up to a point. He could not bring himself to tell her the full story. Perhaps he was too embarrassed, or a true confession would make him seem lesser in her eyes. He hadn't dwelt on it. Besides, it was over, a blip in his personal history. Or was it?

On Sunday, he went jogging again and made a beeline to the playground. There she was, sitting on the bench watching the little boy. But, this time he studied the boy. The child was tall, dark haired, freckled. Ben was tall, dark haired, and as a child had been freckled. He studied the boy's movements, the way he moved his hands on the monkey bars. Once the child looked up, and even at that distance he imagined he and the boy exchanged glances. Had they communicated some mysterious genetic attachment?

He had calculated that the boy was about five or close to it. If so, the math worked. Could it be? He hung around the playground, hidden behind the tree, watching, waiting, intuitively investigating the possibility. At about noon, Susan stirred, folded the paper, summoned the boy, took his hand, and proceeded to walk along the path toward Fifth Avenue. He followed her at a distance. Luckily, he could fade into the crowds who filled the streets, taking in the beautiful spring day.

Holding the little boy's hand, she walked for a couple of blocks and then entered a high-rise apartment building on 71st Street. She had moved up in the world. After she had disappeared into the building, he reentered the park and jogged his way to the West Side.

With effort, he tried to maintain some semblance of normality. Under the circumstances, it was extremely difficult since he was growing angrier by the minute. How dare she? In his mind, he could not mistake the coincidence of the time frame and the appearance of the child.

"Is something wrong, Ben?"

"Why?"

He supposed he was not good at hiding things, especially something as searing as this. If that little boy was his child, she had literally stolen it away from him. Clearly, it was a betrayal. If she truly wanted it, he would have honored his commitment. Despite the awkward timing, he would have found the courage to step up to the plate, to do the right thing.

All sorts of scenarios came to mind. What had she told people about the child? Was there an adoptive father? If she had married, how did she portray the child's history to his new daddy? What had she written on the boy's birth certificate? Father unknown? How could she?

He grew increasingly agitated. A few days went by. He grew listless. His mind wandered and his work suffered. Thoughts of how he had been betrayed crowded into his mind. He spent long hours in silent contemplation going over numerous possibilities about how he might react when the true situation was revealed. He had no intention of remaining silent.

Everyone around him during the next week looked at him askance, asking him what was wrong.

"Not a damned thing," he would shoot back to their queries. He wanted to say it was none of their friggin' business, but, above all, he was a practical man when it came to taking risks. In the firm, he could not look as if he were involved in anything that was not relevant to the activity of the firm. People did understand real problems like sickness or death in the family, but a person who exhibited perpetual anger and depression was not long for upward mobility.

With Barbara, he did not need to be as careful with his demeanor. She was quick to assess his moods, and when they were prolonged, she reacted with concern.

"Why are you so angry?" she would rebuke.

"You're imaging things."

"I know you, Ben. What's going on?"

"Nothing."

Of course, it wasn't "nothing." Anger was becoming rage. Susan had inveigled him, forced him into conceiving a child for her own selfish purposes. He was merely a means to an end, a way for her to realize her secret dream of motherhood without having to take him along as excess baggage. He had been taken, abused, his good nature manipulated for her own evil ends. She had stolen his seed.

Thinking back, he tried to re-imagine how he could have been so naïve. She had assured him that she was on the Pill, that she loved him. Now he was certain she had faked her pleasure in their couplings, egged him on, taken advantage of his sexual nature. He cursed his naiveté.

Three times in the week after he had first seen her with the boy, he had stolen away from the office, canceled meetings, and rushed off to the children's playground in Central Park to observe them. She was so calm, so self-assured, so certain that she had gotten away with her subterfuge.

Watching the boy, he fantasized about him. His son. Child of his loins. His conception. He viewed Susan Charrap with growing hatred, but still he did not reveal himself to her.

One thing was certain: His entire life had been turned upside down. Remembering how he had agonized over his fate, cursed his cowardice in those days after the break-up. Worse, his entire sense of self had undergone profound changes on account of what she had done. Even today, he was becoming convinced it affected him so profoundly that it had inhibited his progress at the firm. In truth, he had expected to go further. Not that he had done badly, but he could have done a lot better if the incident hadn't happened.

In fact, he looked at Barbara now in a new light. Can any woman be trusted? He was having second thoughts about the future of their relationship. After a week of this new agony, he suggested that maybe they should give themselves pause, reconsider their long-term plans.

"I don't understand any of this, Ben."

"It's my fault," he told her.

"What changed?"

"That line of questioning will get you nowhere," he told her, reducing her to tears, which, surprisingly did not move him. He remembered when Susan Charrap had been reduced to tears. Only now he knew they were crocodile tears.

It rained the following weekend, and he did not go out jogging. It was unlikely that Susan would take her son, their son, to the playground. Instead, he stayed in his apartment and stewed. It was becoming impossible to live with his rage. He decided he would have to confront her.

He toyed with the idea of calling her on the phone, but decided that such a move was cowardly. No, he decided, he would meet her face-to-face, and the most logical method would be to do this in the playground with their child just a few feet away. When he came up with that course of action, he felt slightly unburdened. As for the practical implications, the legal aspects, he would consult a lawyer. With DNA testing, he felt certain that paternity could be established without a shadow of a doubt, but he considered that a mere formality.

He wasn't certain exactly what he would ask for. Probably some form of visitation rights or, at the very least, the revelation that he was the boy's father and that such knowledge should be imparted to the boy when he was old enough to understand its implications. If there were monetary considerations, he would consider them, especially as concerned the child's education.

If she refused, he would fight her in court. In his mind, he became militant and aggressive and nothing could assuage his anger. In fact, this cause had established itself as his number-one priority. All else, his career at the firm, his relationship with Barbara, retreated against the onslaught of this personal crusade. The fact that it had happened so fast was not an issue. He was ready to cast everything else aside.

One day he did not go to the office. Instead, he waited on a park bench for any sign of Susan and the little boy. The day was bright; the trees had sprouted to full bloom prompted by the rain and the warmth that had bathed the park in cheerful sunlight.

He saw her approach from a distance, her and the little boy, his son. As before, she sat on the bench and began to read the *New York Times* while the little boy played on the monkey bars. By then, Ben's rage had solidified his resolve. He rose from the bench and moved toward the playground, his legs slightly wobbly, his breath short.

As he approached, another woman sat down beside Susan, someone obviously known to her. It put somewhat of a crimp in his strategy, but he did not falter. She looked up as he approached the bench and lifted her sunglasses, as if to make certain her eyes were not deceiving her. She folded the paper on her lap.

"Is that you, Ben?"

He nodded, but did not smile.

"I can't believe it."

She turned to the woman next to her on the bench. She was about the same age as Susan.

"This is Cynthia Raymond," Susan said, turning to the woman, introducing him. "Ben Grant."

He was about to ask whether he could speak to her alone. It was an awkward moment, since he did not expect to find another person beside her.

"Cynthia is one of my clients. I've been taking care of little Fred while she was out of town."

"I took the red-eye from California, but I couldn't wait to see Fred again."

At that moment, the little boy spied his mother and came running to her outstretched arms.

"He was wonderful," Susan said. "Not a bit of trouble, really."

She looked up at Ben and smiled.

"So how are things, Ben?" she asked pleasantly.

He cleared his throat and tried to speak, but found it difficult. They exchanged glances and he saw no fire in her eyes, no real recognition. It was as if nothing had ever occurred between them.

"Very well, Susan. I thought it was you."

He nodded repeatedly, but could not find anything else to say. The woman brought her son back to the park bench and continued to embrace him.

"Do you live on the East Side now?" Susan asked.

"Still on the West Side," Ben said, haltingly.

"Good seeing you, Ben," Susan said, turning to talk to her friend. Ben hurried away.

BIRTHDAY CELEBRATION

Al sat on a bench in Washington Square and watched the crazy lady with the pigeons. She had long made it known that this flock was hers and hers alone, and pity anyone who would interfere with her feeding ritual. Al was amused by her possessive tenacity and was particularly attentive when an errant tourist attempted to photograph the ritual and became the butt of her fury.

Al understood ritual. He had his own, although he assured himself that he had drawn the line on obsession. The feeding of the flock was, more or less, the woman's entire life, her reason for being. His own ritual was more like habit and depended on the weather.

At nine every morning, barring rain, snow, and intense heat, he would walk the five blocks from his rent-controlled apartment in the Village, *New York Times* in hand, occupy the same bench, and proceed to read every word of interest, including the stock market results, although he no longer had stocks in play. By eleven he was finished, dropping the paper in the trash bin and sitting awhile, observing the scene until noon, the time he chose to move to the Olympia coffee shop on 12th Street for the gustatory phase of his ritual, usually to eat an egg-salad sandwich on rye toast with lettuce and tomato, hold the mayo.

With Milly gone three years now and Jack in California raising his own family, he was alone, hanging on in the Big Apple, the only place he knew well enough to survive comfortably, filling up time, determined to keep his mind churning with interests and trying not to think about waiting for the other shoe to drop.

He had been a high school teacher of history at Jefferson High, where he had spent his entire thirty-year career, through all the turbulence and changes, retiring with relief. Milly had retired from her accounting job a couple of years later, and they had their joint pensions, Social Security, and rent-controlled apartment to see them through. With their one child gone off to work in California, they had tolerated their retirement quite well. Milly had done all the spadework for their social life, arranging tickets to shows, lectures, and concerts and the occasional dinner with friends. He went along happily.

With her gone, that part of his life had wound down. So-called friends had either died or drifted down to Florida, living in senior communities, which Al dubbed a fate worse than death, if that was possible. He hated the designation senior citizen, although he took full advantage of all the discounts. He was a frequent user of the New York Public Library and had continued his subscription to the 92nd Street Y lectures and often picked up discount theater tickets at the Times Square discount box office.

Occasionally, his ritual was enhanced with conversation, usually with a student from NYU, the buildings of which had completely enveloped Washington Square. Normally, he would be ignored by them. He had by then discovered a person of years was often considered irrelevant by the young. He didn't like the idea, of course, but he accepted the situation in silent protest. He wasn't exactly decrepit. Long walks had kept him limber and he looked, he believed, younger than his seventy-five years.

Today, June 16, was actually his birthday, not exactly a celebratory experience since it marked one more year on the inevitable march to oblivion. He preferred to consider it a great joke, the very idea of living three quarters of a century. It was a hoot, he told himself, regaling himself often with a laundry list of past friends and acquaintances who had checked out of the world. He was a big fan of the *Times* obituary columns, checking the ages of the well-known belated who got the big write-ups and the listings of others in the "paid for" column announcing the demise of a loved one.

At times, a student would engage him in conversation, sometimes out of politeness or seeking information or directions to this place or that. Lately, he had struck up a conversation with a young student named Marvin. He didn't know his last name. He was skinny and, it seemed, rarely shaved more than two or three times a week and wore faded jeans, black T-shirts, and scuffed sneakers, which seemed to be the uniform of choice of young people these days. He seemed pleasant enough, intense and intelligent with an open, dimpled smile. He was nineteen, majoring in computer science, and was often absorbed in banging away at his laptop.

Their conversation was sporadic. Mostly, Al asked about Marvin's brief history, his life in Great Neck, inquiring also about his parents, what they did, and about his hopes and dreams for the future. Marvin was slightly older than his grandchildren, who he saw little of these days. They were busy with their own lives in California, and Al hadn't been to California for two years.

It was a beautiful day, sunny but cool. The leaves of the well-tended trees rustled gently in the breeze, and his hearing was still good enough to hear the sounds of birdsongs despite the cacophony of the surrounding traffic. An idea had popped into his head as he shaved that morning.

If Marvin showed up, he had decided to invite him to a nice restaurant a few blocks away for what he dubbed in his mind, a birthday lunch. It would be pricey, but he felt he deserved to celebrate the event. After all, three quarters of a century was no small thing. If Milly were alive, they would have had a birthday dinner and she would have ordered a slab of chocolate cake topped with a lighted candle and he would make a wish, always the same wish for good health for Milly and himself and their son and grandchildren. It hadn't worked in Milly's case. Wish or not, she fell ill, lingered, and died in pain in six months.

The stories in the morning *Times* offered their usual gloomy testimony to a world gone mad with perpetual terrorism warnings and the continuing saga of man's inhumanity to man. He read these stories with increasing disgust although he could not resist a sense that having lived so long, he could look back to having survived the best of times in America. He had been lucky, he decided, coming through without a scratch, a combat veteran of the college of hard knocks.

He perused the movie section, unable to ignore the full-page ads hawking movies that were increasingly irrelevant to him. Kid stuff, he sighed, noting that the new movies were an index of how his age group had been excised from the popular culture.

Television, too, had written off his so-called category. Senior citizen! Demographics! He scoffed at the designations and the way people were put in these silly cubbyholes. Once he had loved the movies. Even now, he wallowed in the joy of nostalgia when an old black-and-white movie showed on television, and he prided himself on how many actors in these old movies he could name. That was when movies were movies, not the computer games that passed for stories these days.

Looking up from his paper, he watched the pigeon lady, knee deep in birds, sprinkle her feed to her flock of gray-feathered city dwellers. She was a dour, intense woman with a mean look for anyone who passed to observe her, especially those with cameras ready to focus. He kept turning away from these peculiar activities to scan the area for any sign of Marvin.

He was entitled to company on his birthday, he told himself, feeling a sense of accelerating impatience and regret that he had not made a date with Marvin in advance. He was sorry that he had invested so much hope in the idea of the birthday lunch. As he waited, growing more anxious by the minute, he realized that his presumption had only set himself up for disappointment. Then, as if it were an answered prayer, Marvin did show up.

Marvin, oblivious to the private drama that had been played out in Al's mind, plunked himself down beside him on the bench and began to open his computer.

"How ya doin', Al?" Marvin asked as he fired up his laptop.

"Fair to middlin'," Al said, enormously relieved as he watched Marvin begin to tap the keyboard.

This was always the extent of their initial greeting. Normally, Al would let Marvin work for a while before extending the conversation. But today was special. He had already gone through one crisis of waiting and had no stomach to go through the process twice.

"Got an idea, Marvin," Al said, plunging right in. "Today is your lucky day. I'm springing for a fancy lunch at Café Loup. You and me, kiddo."

Marvin looked up from his screen with a quizzical and somewhat ominous expression. It struck Al that perhaps Marvin was observing him now in a different light, perhaps as a potential sexual predator. He dismissed the idea and pressed on.

"It's my birthday," he said in explanation.

"Awesome," Marvin said. "Happy birthday."

Awesome seemed to Al a bit exaggerated, but it did appear to be a more civilized response than "cool."

"Thanks, buddy." Al said determined to appear casual. "Hence my invite. Hell, I'm entitled."

Marvin continued to tap keys glancing at the computer screen. Al could tell he was mulling over his offer.

"A bit pricey. But what the hell. It's a big one, and I'm planning to pop open a bottle of champagne."

"Big one?"

"Seven oh, pal." Al lied. "Seven gun salute, one for each decade."

"Awesome."

"Fuckin' a."

Marvin looked up and they exchanged glances. It occurred to Al that he was using his own generational expression, long in disuse.

"Why not?" Marvin said. "It's an offer I can't refuse." He hesitated a moment. "As long as I get back for my two o'clock tutorial."

"With time to spare, pal. I've reserved for noon."

He was hoping Marvin would not take his remark as presumption. Marvin looked at his wristwatch.

"Let me work this out," he mumbled tapping his keyboard.

"No sweat," Al said, going back to reading his paper, relieved now. Hell, he thought, Marvin might be good company, although they hadn't talked much to each other, their relationship, he assured himself, was more than a mere nodding acquaintance. They had, after all, exchanged dialogue but it did cross his mind that his invitation might be construed also as an act of desperation by a lonely old coot. Maybe not too far from the truth, Al chuckled, putting a humorous spin on the idea.

Aside from the bare facts, Al didn't know much about the kid, except that he was friendly, polite, and, for some reason, he had gravitated to sitting on the bench beside Al as if it were some gesture of camaraderie. After all, there were other benches and he could have chosen any one of them. Perhaps, Al contemplated, there was some unspoken, special bond between them.

They arrived at the restaurant early. It was half-filled at that hour, but the lunch rush was just beginning, mostly executives from nearby office buildings and administrative officials and some professors from NYU. They were shown to a table in what Al determined was an obscure corner. Perhaps the headwaiter had made certain assumptions about their relationship and made the selection as if they were seeking a spot for intimate conversation.

"Fancy place, Al," Marvin commented, eyeballing the restaurant. Al was pleased with his comment.

"What the hell. Not too many shopping days left."

"Seventy is not that old."

It was, of course, the expected comment. How about seventy-five, kiddo, he wanted to say, but held off. He ordered a bottle of champagne, not vintage, but okay for the occasion. Actually it had been ten years, his sixty-fifth birthday, when he had last tasted champagne. He and Milly had gone to a restaurant on the Upper East Side, long gone.

"Awesome, Al!" Marvin mumbled.

"Hell, it's a birthday," Al said.

"Cool!"

The champagne came and the waiter popped the cork with skill, poured, and placed the bottle in an ice bucket. They lifted their glasses.

"Happy birthday, Al."

"Thanks for coming," Al said.

They drank, both upending their glasses. The champagne tasted tart and cold and triggered the earlier memory of his birthday dinner with Milly. He felt a sob begin to rise in his chest and to deflect it, he pulled the bottle from the ice bucket and refilled their glasses. Then they both studied the menu.

"I read a restaurant review that praised their duck à l'orange."

"Sounds awesome," Marvin said, apparently relieved that he did not have to make a choice.

"Appetizer?" Al asked, being the good host, but hoping Marvin would reject it out of consideration for the cost.

"You?"

"I'll pass. But, you can."

"I'm okay," Marvin said. Al had ordered some chocolate cake wedges, one with a candle, for dessert. He had calculated this lunch would go for about two hundred with the champagne and tip. Hell, he hadn't spent so much money in a fancy restaurant since Milly was alive and even that was fairly rare. Milly would never have allowed the extravagance, except for very special occasions, like an important birthday. It's for you too, doll, he told himself silently, thinking of his wife, stifling another upcoming sob, masked by clearing his throat.

When the waiter came back, Al gave the order, embellishing the duck with some vegetable sides.

They drank their second glasses, and Al poured again until the bottle was emptied. He felt the sudden alcohol rush and noted that Marvin's face had flushed.

"How does it feel to hit three score and ten?" Marvin asked, his speech slightly slurred by the alcohol. It occurred to Al that he was reaching for things to say, choosing the usual cliché. After all, Al reasoned, they had little in common.

"Feel?" Al said, contemplating a response. Instead of making him feel good, the effect of the champagne was somewhat disorienting and depressive. He felt the heavy weight of loneliness. He missed Milly. A wave of self-pity washed over him. He was sorry he had chosen to celebrate his birthday with this nineteen-year-old whom he barely knew. It seemed an act of desperation.

"I'm not sure," he answered, his eyes inspecting Marvin's face. It was a child's face. He tried to imagine what the boy's eyes were seeing, his wattled, spotted skin, tufts of gray hair thinning topside, a lined forehead, and patches of wrinkles around the eyes. What was he thinking? Al wondered, watching this lonely old fart springing for a fancy lunch.

"Life's like a movie," Al blurted, remembering his earlier thoughts about reading the movie section of the *Times*. He watched the boy's expression look back at him with incomprehension.

"Yeah, a movie," Marvin said as if he understood the reference. "You mean like a dream. A dream is like a movie."

The waiter came with their duck à l'orange and sides of brussels sprouts and carrots. They ate for a while in silence.

"Good?" Al asked, signaling the waiter and ordering two glasses of white wine.

"Awesome!"

"That good," Al said, noting the touch of sarcasm that had popped into his remark. The fatuous comment was beginning to grate on him.

They ate quietly for a few moments. Al's thoughts had once again turned to movies.

"I made it, Ma. Top of the world," Al suddenly blurted aloud in a Cagney imitation. People from surrounding tables turned around, and Marvin looked at him curiously, obviously confused by the outburst. Al felt slightly embarrassed. He assumed the champagne was having an odd effect on him.

"Jimmy Cagney, from the movie *White Heat*."

"Who?"

"Cagney, Jimmy Cagney."

Marvin looked at him blankly.

"You know," Al pressed making another try at the Cagney imitation. Marvin continued to look at him with mounting confusion.

"Never heard of James Cagney?" Al asked.

"It sounds familiar," Marvin replied, although it was obvious to Al that the name was not in the boy's field of comprehension.

"How about Gary Cooper?"

Marvin shrugged.

"Who?"

"Okay, then," Al pressed, suddenly feeling irritated and combative. "Mae West?"

"Vaguely familiar."

Al knew he was faking now.

"Myrna Loy and William Powell, *The Thin Man*."

Again, Marvin offered a blank look. Al felt increasingly irritated, not only at what he determined was Marvin's ignorance, but at his own aggressive attitude.

"Is this a game?" Marvin mumbled avoiding any eye contact, keeping his head down and eating perfunctorily.

"A game?" Al said, troubled by the comment. Where was the connection with this boy? Who was the alien here? He did not answer the question. Instead he picked up his wine glass and quickly emptied the contents, as if he were trying to quench his anger.

"Fact is, Al," Marvin said. "Why should I know who these people are?"

"Because," Al said, drawing in a deep breath, his anger and frustration palpable. "Because everybody does."

"Does what?"

"Know who these people are. They are famous, goddammit. Everybody knows who James Cagney and Gary Cooper are. Everybody knows for crying out loud. Are you a fucking ostrich with your head in the sand?"

Again his voice rose and people turned at other tables. Al raised his eyebrows and shrugged in frustration. The maître d' who had shown them their table looked at them and scowled.

A high flush developed on Marvin's cheeks. He looked at Al with what seemed like total incomprehension.

"You're a college boy," Al muttered, trying unsuccessfully to mute his anger.

"I don't know what this is all about, Al," Marvin said, his voice beginning to tremble. The people dining at the nearby tables turned away.

"Knowledge," Al said.

"This kind of knowledge," Marvin began. He had put his fork down, leaving his duck à l'orange half finished. "Is it so important?"

"It's a question of awareness. It underlines your ignorance."

"My ignorance! You're wacko, man."

Al felt a rising sense of rage.

"You take my hospitality and insult me on my seventy-fifth birthday," Al fumed.

Marvin shook his head, threw his napkin on the table and stood up. "Seventy-five. You lying old asshole."

Shaking his head, he turned and walked out of the restaurant. Again, people nearby turned to look at him. Al imagined they saw him as a ridiculous old crank or worse. He wanted to make some caustic comment to the observing crowd, characterizing Marvin as a freeloading, ungrateful young jackass, but he held off and turned away, reaching for Marvin's half-filled wineglass, which he quickly upended.

He was unable to quell his feelings of loss and futility. He missed Milly, missed her presence across the table. He felt abandoned and misplaced, and the world he had known seemed to be crashing around him. He looked at his food, grown cold and unpalatable, his mind groping in a haze to make some sense out of the incident. He was deeply conscious of his own impotence and felt old and withered, a broken man confronting the abyss.

He needed to leave this place and swiveled around the restaurant to signal his waiter for the check. Suddenly, the waiter emerged from the kitchen with a wedge of chocolate cake embedded with a lighted candle. He wished he could stop the ritual, but it was obviously too late. The waiter placed the cake with the lighted candle in front of him on the table and two additional waiters joined the group and began to sing "Happy birthday to you."

Some of the people in the nearby tables joined in, eyeing the ceremony with humor and, Al suspected, ridicule. He wanted the earth to open and swallow him up, hoping that what the image portended would come soon, very soon.

He started to sob. His shoulders shook and he could not muster the strength to blow out the candle. All he could do was to look at the flame, reminding him again of that last scene in *White Heat* when Cagney's character was shot dead.

"Made it, Ma. Top of the world."

He did not say the words, but he sensed that, like Cagney's demise in the movie, the end was on its way.

THE CHERRY TREE

"There, turn left," Howard, her grandfather, said, instructing his granddaughter, who was driving, where to make the left. He was obviously remembering the names of the Brownsville streets, where he had grown up, whispering them as he viewed the signs. Saratoga, Herzl, Amboy. "Comes back."

Helen could tell that his mind was immersed in memory, and she let it happen because it apparently meant so much to him to go back to the scenes of his youth. She was unmoved, but felt the obligation to be granddaughterly since she hardly ever saw him these days.

He had been an accountant, then retired and moved to Florida in the nineties with her grandmother, who had died a few years back. He had returned periodically to New York visiting his only son, her father, who lived now in Huntington, Long Island. In her mid-twenties, Helen was working on Wall Street for a hedge fund, living in Tribeca, considering herself part of the New York scene, pretty, hip, cool, and, for her age, rich.

"Must I?" she asked her father, who had called her to do him the favor. He had a golf date.

"Why not? Go early Saturday morning while the muggers are still in bed."

"Brownsville? In Brooklyn. Supposed to be a sewer, full of gangs, drugs, and trouble. Shit."

"Just don't get out of the car."

The fact was she hardly knew her grandfather. He was not in her radar range. Even when she was younger her grandparents, although pleasant enough and, in their way, loving and interested, were sort of in the outer circle of her life. There was, of course, an obligatory affinity and respect and the necessity of exhibiting familial affection, but beyond that, there was a kind of generational distance, an unbridgeable gap.

Her grandfather, whom she called Grampa, was in his early seventies and looked a lot younger, one of those seventy types who looked fifty and acted maybe forty. He had told her father he had lots of ladies banging down his door in his widowerhood. She could not imagine going to bed with someone that old.

In the car he asked her what she characterized as grandfatherly questions. "Do you like your job? Any serious boyfriends? You like your apartment?" And the usual compliments. "We are all very proud of your success. When will you come down to Florida to visit?" And the familiar reminiscences. "You were the cutest little baby girl I ever saw." And on and on in that vein. Then there was a long silence. She was his only grandchild.

He dozed and woke up only when they reached what she supposed were the outer limits of Brownsville. In fact, he became instantly alert. Up until then he had paid no attention to the female voice on the navigational system, but when the car hit familiar streets he contradicted all her directions and became a nonstop travel guide.

"On every corner there was a candy store where you could get a charlotte russe." He explained what that was. "A piece of cake, a glob of whipped cream topped by a cherry, all in a white cardboard container shaped like a crown. And a cigarette was a penny a piece and for three cents you could get an egg cream, which had in it neither egg nor cream." He laughed and shook his head. "There were delicatessens everywhere. You could get stuffed derma for a nickel." She didn't know what that was and didn't inquire.

"A shtikl for a nickel. And hot dogs you could die for and probably did." He laughed again. "The man behind the counter would say mustard, sauerkraut, and relish as if it was a knee-jerk reaction. Like you would say, 'How are you, Jake?' and he would say, 'Mustard, sauerkraut, and relish.'" He laughed again. The best she could muster was a thin smile.

Helen was being tolerant. The drive in from Manhattan, where she had met him at Penn Station, was long and difficult. Brooklyn streets were impossible to navigate. There was no rhyme or reason to them.

"Make a right here on Saratoga, but go slow," he said, and she obeyed while he pointed out the sights that were no longer his sights.

"I was bar mitzvahed somewhere around here. One of those little houses that was converted ino a synagogue. It was a Monday, which was allowed. I did my haftorah in a place that was less than half filled with smelly old men who used snuff and spat into spittoons. Where the hell was it? Dammit, everything is changed, but then I'm going back sixty years."

"A long time," Helen said, half listening. It was too remote from her world. She was thinking about Jack, who was dating her that night. Jack worked for a mutual fund and was witty and really good looking. They'd go to one of the clubs and shake all night, then pop back to her place, hopefully still energized for sex. Getting up this early to take Grampa on his trip through memory lane would have its impact. On Saturdays she usually slept until noon.

She looked at her watch. It was barely eight, but at least it was a bright, early summer's day and the streets were pretty empty. Everybody she saw was black. She checked the door locks to make sure the buttons were down.

This was no place for white people, especially a white person driving a new car. Thankfully it was a Toyota Corolla in need of a good washing. For the moment, she was happy it wasn't a Jag, which she very nearly bought, but was talked out of by one of her boyfriends. Uncool, he had told her. Conspicuous-consumption cars are déclassé. Don't look too polished. Make believe you were born with it and didn't need to flaunt it, especially in Brownsville.

Not that she was prejudiced against black people. She had many black friends who wouldn't be caught dead in Brownsville. She was surprised that it didn't seem dangerous, not on this sun-dappled morning. What people she saw were going about their business quite peacefully. Perhaps the media had exaggerated.

"There was a little grocery store there," Grampa was saying, pointing. Her own thoughts had disrupted her attention, and she had missed some of his commentary. "My mother used to send me out daily to get groceries. Usually bagels, cream cheese, butter, and lox. The bagels were real, not like the lousy imitations you get nowadays. There were two kinds, regular and egg bagels. They sliced the cream cheese, which came out of a long wooden box, with a wire cutter, and the butter came in big tubs. The grocer totaled up the cost on the side of a brown bag with a much-used short pencil, which he wet with his tongue before making the additions. He was never wrong. In those days they taught people to add in their head." He looked at his granddaughter. "Can you add in your head?"

It was as if he was challenging her whole generation. She didn't bite.

"Suppose so," she said, although most of her additions were done by machine.

"Over there," he said, paying little attention to her answer, "were two movie houses: The Ambassador and the People's Cinema." He chuckled. "For ten cents on a Saturday you could see three movies, three comedies, a chapter, but then you don't know what a chapter is, and they would have drawings for prizes based on your ticket number. I once won a pair of roller skates."

"Did you?" she said. She didn't ask what he meant by chapter and didn't care.

Glancing at him sideways, his color had risen, and he was quite excited about what he was seeing and how it registered on his memory. Okay, she told herself, I am making my grandfather happy and that is a good thing worthy of toleration, although his nostalgic musing was far removed from her life. Like ancient history, she decided, as the car moved slowly down the street.

At the end of the street loomed the El, the subway extension that rolled out of the tunnel after Utica Avenue and followed the track outside all the way to East New York. He explained that he used to go to Rockaway, getting off at the last stop.

"Which was New Lots Avenue. Then we took the bus to Rockaway, where we went summers. My parents and I slept in one room, and Mom cooked in a community kitchen. Better than being in the city, which was hot as blazes in those days."

Still hot, she wanted to say, but she left it alone. She was certain he would tell her that winters were colder, food tasted better, movies and music were better, people were nicer. Ah, the golden glow of yesteryear.

"When I lived with my Gramma and Grampa," he said, "because my old man was always losing his job and we were dispossessed from our apartment and had to move into their little house in Brownsville, the trains would roar past on the El. Their house was a few houses down from El, you see, and the sound of the trains made it impossible to hear the radio every ten minutes or so. In those days we listened to radio, especially serials like Billy and Betty, Jack Armstrong, the All-American Boy, Omar the Tentmaker and Little Orphan Annie, which was sponsored by Ovaltine." There was no stopping him on the radio bit. "Sunday nights there was Edgar Bergen and Charlie McCarthy, Fred Allen, Jack Benny, Fibber McGee and Molly. It was a ritual to listen Sunday nights." He stopped after awhile, and there was a sudden silence as if the memories had clogged in his brain.

As they got closer to the El, a subway train that had stopped at the Saratoga station roared forward.

"Listen. See what I mean. Anyway, when I was a teenager I had odd jobs that took me into the city. We were packed in like sardines in those days." He shook his head and his voice sounded funny as if he might be wrestling with tears of nostalgia. She did not look at him, even sideways, because he might be embarrassed if she saw tears moistening his eyes.

She sensed he was looking around, searching for something outside.

"There was a fish store around here. I'm sure of it. My Gramma used to take me shopping for fish, carp I think it was. A woman stood on a high platform on which was a pool for live fish. She wore an apron stained with fish blood. Gramma would point to a live fish. The woman would net it, then lay it on a board, chop off its head and split it open, taking out the bones. Gramma used the fish to make gefilte fish, which we ate every Friday night, along with…" He went on and on with the menu. She desperately needed to change the subject.

"So where was the house you lived in, Grampa?" she asked pleasantly, hoping they would finally get to the place where she knew he was determined to go, and this was the heart of the favor her father had asked her to perform.

"Make a left here on Livonia for one block then turn left again on Strauss Street where the old house was."

As they made the turn, which was under the El, he pointed out some stores on the left, one selling secondhand clothes and the other a dry cleaner.

"See that corner store." This was the one selling secondhand clothes. "You know who hung out there? Murder Incorporated. That was where Midnight Rose Gold held court. It was a candy store where they sold cigars and had one of those walk-in humidors. Phone call would come in. Kill Benny. Kill Mendy. That was Murder Incorporated. These guys would get paid to knock off people and bury them in Canarsie. Pittsburgh Phil, Bugsy Goldstein, Lepke Buchalter. They all got the chair in 1941, I think on the same day of Pearl Harbor. Poor bastards. Couldn't even get their execution acknowledged because the Japs bombed Pearl. I remember that like yesterday."

She listened, unengaged, as if she were hearing some CD with a bad track that played over and over again.

"Next to the candy store was a pickle store. A guy and his wife filled cardboard cartons with pickles and sauerkraut right from the barrels. Winter, the guy had snot running down his nose, which he wiped frequently with the back of his hand, but still stuck them into that pickle and sauerkraut barrel. Nobody cared. Funny." He laughed again. She would care, she wanted to say, thinking of the pickle barrel and the snot on the man's hands. Yuk.

"God, whatever happened to this place," he said, as the car turned the corner on Strauss, but then she discovered that it was a one way street, which required her to carefully back out and proceed down Livonia to the next street.

"Make a left on Hopkinson, then a left on Blake, then a left on Strauss," he said. "Imagine Helen, I never forgot these street names and it's been, how long, pushing sixty years. Over. See that?" He pointed out the window. "That's Betsy Head Park, where I played ball and swam during the summers. I played outfield, although I did pitch occasionally. We had a hell of a team, and it was right across the street from the house. Occasionally a ball would be hit foul out of the park and blast into my grandparents' house, sometimes breaking a window. Pull over. Right there. Let me get oriented."

She pulled over the Toyota and parked. Again she looked at her watch. Was this going to take all day? It would be at least an hour to get back to Manhattan, then she would have to drop him off at Penn Station so that he could take the next train to Huntington. She decided that she would definitely not have lunch with him. It was bad enough to listen to his old memories without having to recycle them again during lunch.

She felt somewhat guilty thinking unkind thoughts like this, but frankly his memories bored her. Nevertheless, she forced herself to be respectful and look as if she were interested. He was, after all, her grandfather, her father's father, and it simply would not do to leave a bad impression. She remembered being bored silly when her father and mother took her to visit them in West Palm Beach at the condo complex where everybody was old. What she remembered most was going to what they called a recreation center, which was as big as a football field and filled with people playing cards.

Deliver me from that, she thought. The fact was that old people were boring, their memories boring, what they talked about was boring. Yet, she did commend herself for being respectful. Her grandfather looked out of the window.

"Unbelievable," he said. "This used to be a block of attached row houses with front porches and backyards. On nice summer days, the people sat on rockers on the porches. They also had back porches where my grandparents made a sooky during holidays."

She didn't know what a sooky was, probably something connected with one of the Jewish holidays. She let it pass. She wasn't religious although she had been bat mitzvahed.

"They had three fruit trees in the backyard: a pear tree, a cherry tree, and a plum tree. They also had vines that grew on a wooden thing and my grandfather harvested grapes from them and made his own wine. I remember that they made stewed pears from the pears and did the same with the cherries. I used to eat those cherries straight from the trees. They were sour, but I can still taste them. Made your lips pucker. But, they were good to eat right from the tree."

He looked up and down the street. Most of the row houses were gone, but there were a few still standing, unattached from their neighbors' now, although they formed the skeleton of new, undistinguished, flat facades that he did not recognize at all.

"There," he said suddenly, delighted by what appeared to be the discovery of his grandparents' house, still standing but, as he acknowledged, totally different. The houses on each side of it were demolished and had become empty lots overgrown with weeds. He unlocked the door and got out of the car and for a while seemed to be still trying to orient himself. He moved closer to the house. There were numbers over the doorway, one of them lopsided.

"2108. That's it." He looked back at Helen and waved her forward. "This is it, Helen. This was my grandparents' house. Come on."

He moved forward and perhaps out of a desire to be protective, she unlocked the door on the driver's side and got out. Remembering her father's admonition, she could not completely chase away her fear, but since the street was mostly deserted, although she could see people walking in her direction, she felt reasonably safe, although they would certainly be the only white people in view.

The house that was 2108 did not have a porch, and was small, boxlike, and undistinguished. Her grandfather stood in front of it for a long moment, then moved to one of the empty lots next door.

"There," he said. "The trees are still there. I remember them like yesterday."

He moved further into the lot. She followed reluctantly.

"Do you think it's wise, Grampa?" she said, but he paid no attention and kept on moving. At the rear of the house was a short fence badly in need of repair. There was no back porch now, but as he had exclaimed, there were three trees, one of them bearing cherries.

"Imagine that. Still bearing cherries after all those years. Do cherry trees last that long?"

He stood by the side of the fence surveying the trees for a long time. His granddaughter stood beside him while he looked. Is he watching the tree grow or eating the cherries with his eyes? It was, after all, only a cherry tree.

Then suddenly, he stepped over the fence that had fallen in one spot, and it was easy for him to pass over it.

"You shouldn't, Grampa," she said, feeling uncomfortable by his action. "This is private property."

"They shouldn't mind," he said as he moved into the little yard and placed himself under one of the low branches of the cherry tree. Reaching up, he bent the branch, picked a couple cherries, and put one in his mouth.

"Sour as ever, but just as I remember," he said, turning toward his granddaughter, who still stood behind the broken fence on the vacant lot. Then suddenly, a voice screeched with anger, and a large black woman in a housecoat rushed into the yard.

"Get the fuck out of here," the woman screamed. It took Helen a second to discover that the woman held a pistol in her hand and was pointing it straight at her grandfather.

"I was just..." her grandfather began. "I used to live..." But he couldn't go on. His complexion turned ashen.

"This is private property you sumbitch. Get your white ass out of here."

"But I..."

She could see her grandfather was too stunned to reply. Quickly, she hopped over the fence and stood between the outraged woman and her grandfather, looking down into the barrel of the pistol. She had never in her life been that close to a firearm.

"I got my rights. If I shot you both, I be within my rights. So get the fuck out of here before I blow both your heads off."

"Take it easy," Helen said, hands outstretched. "He meant no harm. You see, he lived here once."

"I don't give a shit. You have no business here. So git."

"There's no need for that gun," Helen said. The barrel of the pistol was no more than a foot from her head. "He is my grandfather."

"Who gives a fuck?"

"I do, lady. I do," she shot back. Oddly she felt no fear, only rage. "We're not here to do you any harm. All he wanted was to pick a cherry. Don't be a fool."

"Who you callin' a fool?" the woman replied, her anger unabated. "Just get the fuck off my property."

"We're going. We're going," Helen said, turning to her grandfather, who seemed on the verge of collapse, white as a sheet with fear and confusion. She put out her hand to her grandfather, who took it. It felt like grabbing the hand of a child. Then she led him to the edge of the property and across the fence to the vacant lot and led him to the car while the woman watched them depart, still holding the pistol, pointing it at them.

"She could have killed us," her grandfather said.

"Well, we're still here."

Her reaction had surprised her.

"All I wanted was to taste one of those cherries," her grandfather said, as she gunned the motor and headed under the El. As she drove, he opened his palm, which held a single cherry.

"I picked one for you," he said.

"Thanks, Grampa," she said, taking the cherry and popping it into her mouth.

"Really sour," she said, knowing then that she would never forget the taste of it.

SUBWAY LOVE AFFAIR

Just my luck to fall in love with a girl that lived way up in the Bronx. I met her that summer in Rockaway when nearly every boy in our crowd had girlfriends. I picked her up on the beach, which was the way we boys met girls. They all wanted to be part of our crowd.

Helen was sixteen, and I was eighteen and going to summer school at City College in the years when they still called it CCNY. Even so, I always made it back to Rockaway by two in the afternoon, which bought me nearly three hours with our crowd on the beach.

I loved the way Helen looked. She had a big face with big brown eyes and what they called in those days dirty blonde hair. Also she had a great big warm smile and a body that was described then as *zoftig.* I was proud as hell of Helen's looks. She thought I was good looking, too. I was tall and thin and tan, and some people said I looked like Gregory Peck.

We necked a lot in those days. It wasn't always easy finding enough dark corners to do it in, but when we were on the beach or walking on the boardwalk we always had our arms around each other. Necking was in those days a perfectly respectable way to make love. You soul kissed a lot, blew in your girl's ear, hugged and squeezed, sometimes for hours.

I really loved her. I said so lots of times and she told me she loved me, too. We were both happy being in love. I wrote her love notes, and since I was an English major I read her poems from *Sonnets from the Portuguese* and sonnets from Shakespeare. I was never certain that Helen truly understood the words of these great poets, but she never let on that she didn't and, after each reading, she would hug and squeeze me and tell me how much she truly loved me.

Of course, I believed her and I truly believed in my own undying infinite love for her.

I thought of her from the moment I awoke in the morning to the moment I shut my eyes. I'm sure I dreamed of her. My heartbeat always accelerated when I saw her for the first time each day. I could not wait to touch her, hold her in my arms, and kiss her. God, I was in love. We were in love.

Of course the necking led to what they then called petting, which meant I felt her tits and she occasionally let her hand brush against my erection. You've got to understand how it was in those days. Girls were deathly afraid of pregnancy and disgrace. They were equally afraid of getting a "reputation," which would spoil their chances of finding husbands, which was their number-one ambition and the preoccupation of their mothers and fathers.

Boys were supposed to show respect to nice girls by not being "fresh." Virginity was really a prized possession. Boys did not want to marry what they secretly felt was "soiled goods." The fact was that the whole damned value system was different. Sometimes, though, you were so much in love that you both made a deep commitment to each other, deep enough to go a bit further when you made love.

That summer I loved Helen so much and she loved me so much that she proved her love to me by letting me finally make love to her naked. It came in stages, though, and we were both pretty clumsy at it. Also we were too shy to give each other instructions. She used to jerk me off until I hurt and I was no better at masturbating her.

It was a foregone conclusion between us, a solemn pledge that one day we would finally marry. We were certain, of course, that our love would last forever and ever. Not that both of us weren't in love before. But that was considered "puppy love." This was the real thing. Boys and girls of our age truly wanted to find someone to love and to love them. That was the point of existence. Of course, boys worried about their careers and their future and making a living, but when it came down to what they truly wanted most was to be in love with a girl who loved them and would always be true and loyal and loving.

As the summer wore on and we contemplated going back to our

respective neighborhoods in the city, our lovemaking got more and more intense. You see, we had a problem. Helen lived in the Bronx and I lived in Brooklyn. To understand what that meant, one has to know something of the urban geography of New York City in the early forties. This was, remember, before everybody moved to the suburbs.

I lived in Crown Heights in Brooklyn. For me to get to Helen's parents' apartment on University Avenue in the Bronx, I had to walk ten blocks to the subway station, the one on Sterling Street or Kingston Avenue. Then I would have to change at Franklin and rattle up through Manhattan and Harlem to the elevated section of the IRT in the Bronx to Burnside Avenue. That took a good hour and ten minutes. Then I would have to walk five more blocks up Burnside to Helen's parents' apartment. Her father was a cab driver, and they lived on the top floor of a four-story walk-up.

Let's face it, it was one big schlep. Then if we were to have a date in the city, which was what downtown Manhattan was called in those days, that would be another good forty minutes to get there and another forty to get back to Helen's, after which I would have to spend another hour and a half, sometimes two, getting back to my parents' apartment in Brooklyn.

That was the reality of courtship if you happened to fall in love with a girl from the Bronx. Which was why our lovemaking got very intense as the summer drew to a close. But I tell you, I was madly in love, my heart bursting with feeling, and I was sure that Helen's heart was bursting as well.

I think it was about a week before the end of summer that we both felt compelled to seal our love irrevocably, to prove to each other that we had made a lifetime commitment to loving. My friend Harold's parents were going to the city for a funeral and planned to stay overnight, and he lent us his bedroom. We were very resourceful in those days and always managed to find places to make love. Don't forget, few, if any of us had cars in those days. But, there were porches and occasional empty bedrooms and blankets on the beach.

We finally did it in Harold's bed. It was a real emotional scene with both of us sobbing like babies as we finally went all the way, which was the way it was described then. Physically, it was a lousy experience for both of us. I did the deed, but it hurt us both like hell.

But, to tell the truth, that really was not the important part. The sexual thing was not as connected as one might think. Maybe it was because of the way we were brought up and thought about the opposite sex. I wasn't doing it for pure pleasure. It was for love, for bonding. Even in our own minds, we did not call it fucking. There was something holy about it nor was it something that I was going to brag to the boys about. This was really private stuff, intimate. It had to do with love.

We only did it once that night and, of course, I wore a rubber and we clung together for the longest time. Helen got hell from her parents for coming home late. The very next day, I remember, I bought her an ankle bracelet, which we called "a slave chain." We loved each other deeply. We had been with each other every day and night for almost three months. We had been inseparable, like Siamese twins.

I'm sure that others in our crowd that summer were having the same experience, although I don't think many of them went all the way like we did. Strange to say, we boys never discussed that part of it, not about the girls we loved. Of course we liked to brag, but never about the girls we loved. Never that.

That last night, our crowd spent the night on blankets around a bonfire on the beach. We weren't much for drinking then. After we toasted wieners and ate our spuds, we paired off on blankets and made love while the fire burned low. Most of us were under the blankets as well and, of course, Helen and I had our pants off and were kissing and hugging and crying as we made love.

I'm sure we both pledged undying faithful love to each other. I know we both meant it. I'm sure I did. God, I loved that girl.

When we got back to town, I called Helen every day and saw her every Friday and Saturday night. I got into the swing of things at CCNY, which was a long schlep from Brooklyn in itself, all the way up the West Side. But, every chance I got I either called Helen or went up to see her. Her folks never invited me to stay over and I always went home, usually getting there when the sun was coming up, but not before Helen and I had made love on the living room couch. Ironically, her folks never got out of bed to catch us at it.

I think they trusted Helen. But I was never sure they liked me. Thinking back, maybe they thought Helen was too young to make a long lasting commitment. She was still a senior in high school. Also, I could never be sure, but I don't think girls confided as much in their parents as they do today.

But the facts of distance did not mean our love diminished. In fact, I think it got stronger. When we met we were like hungry lions and couldn't get enough of each other. Even the sex part became better. It was really awkward and very frightening to make love on the living room couch while Helen's parents were sleeping in the next room. We never got totally naked, and since there was only one bathroom and you had to go past her parents' bedroom to get to it, I used to have to wrap all my used rubbers in Kleenex and put them in my pocket. I wouldn't throw them away until I got to the trashcans at the Burnside Avenue station.

Once I had a real scare. When we made love for the last time on a certain night, I heard her father get out of bed and go to the bathroom. I pulled up my pants, hastily zipped and belted, and said good night. It was probably three or four in the morning by then. Anyway, I left the house before her father got out of the bathroom and walked down the four flights and started up the hill to the Burnside Avenue station.

When I got to the station, I discovered that somewhere between Helen's parents' couch and the Burnside station, the rubber had slipped off. I was petrified with fear. Suppose it dropped off inside of Helen's parents' apartment, right in the center of the living room. Or in the hallway. Or just outside the front door. I don't think Helen's parents would have understood.

It was still dark out and, panicked, I retraced my steps back up toward Helen's apartment, my eyes peeled to the ground, looking for that used rubber. Christ, my heart was pounding, and I'm sure I was calling for help from every celestial being known to man. I got back to Helen's apartment house without finding it. I even retraced my steps up the stairs. Still no sign of it.

I got to Helen's door and searched the area in the hall, but couldn't find it. But, I didn't have the guts to ring the bell again and scare the shit out of everyone. I can tell you I didn't sleep that night. I couldn't wait until I called Helen the next morning. Her mother answered. She wasn't home, but she seemed very polite on the phone, which relieved me somewhat. Later when Helen called back, she laughed when I told her my story. I never did find out what happened to that rubber.

I wrote Helen love notes every chance I got. I managed to study and get passing marks, but my mind was never once free of thoughts about Helen. Sometimes I would talk to her for an hour on the phone. It was hell being away from her.

Sometimes when I got off really early from school, I would pop up to her place in the middle of the week, but I would always go home earlier because usually I had classes the next day. At times, because I couldn't get her on the phone, I sometimes surprised her, which was quite exciting for both of us. Not once did I question the mutuality of our love. Not once.

Sometime in February, when the nights were very long and the weather very cold, we happened to get off from classes early. I think one of the professors was sick. There wasn't any homework to speak of and, besides, that's the way I passed the time on those long subway trips, reading mostly. I read all the novels in my European history class going from Brooklyn to CCNY.

I tried to get Helen on the phone. Nobody answered. I got to Burnside Avenue just as it was getting dark and started to walk swiftly up the hill to Helen's apartment filled, as always, with expectation and love. I remember there was a candy story a block before University where a crowd of boys and girls about my own age used to hang out. In those days hanging out around the candy store was a way to pass the time.

But what I saw startled me. It was Helen standing against a brick wall next to the glass front of the store. She was kissing a guy, actually kissing a guy, right there in the street. Nobody was paying much attention to them. People did that in those days.

I stopped dead in my tracks. My heart banged against my chest.

It wasn't just a question of disbelief, I was physically hurting. My breath came in short gasps. I had to actually lean against a street light for support. It was awful and the sense of pain beyond any that I had ever experienced.

But it wasn't only a sense of overpowering betrayal and defeat that I was feeling. I was embarrassed, ashamed, and it only exacerbated my emotions to feel that and make me more ashamed of my shame. After all, it wasn't me who should feel that. I wasn't the one being disloyal and untrue. I vowed not to look at them, but, as in all vows like that, I could not keep my eyes away.

By then, they had separated and were merely holding hands, which, in that context, was equally as bad since it implied a relationship. I had had no warning. I had been with Helen just three days before, had not the vaguest hint of something like this. I hung back in the shadows, watching them, further humiliated by the act of spying. Was that really Helen, my Helen, my true love? Thankfully, they moved away, still holding hands, heading up the hill.

I watched them until they faded from sight, trying to hold down a feeling of nausea. I really wanted to vomit. I gagged, but held it down. I had no idea what to do, where to go, how to cope with this monumental disaster in my young life.

I could never remember how I got home. I felt dazed, punchy, like a person who had been emptied of all life and hope. I know I didn't sleep. In the mirror the next morning, I saw a pale, bearded face with circles under my eyes. I felt feverish, sick at heart. My Helen. I still longed for her, wanted to hold her in my arms. I must have run through a gamut of emotions, all new.

And yet, when Helen called me next day, the sound of her voice momentarily chased the pain. I told her I was sick.

"I'll come over if you want," she said. Not a hint. Not an iota of guilt did I detect. I couldn't understand it.

"No. I'll be fine," I said.

"Do you love me?" she asked.

"Of course I do."

I knew I was saying it by rote, although I also knew I loved her still. But, a totally new feeling had crept over me, a kind of aura of self-protection. It even over-rode the sensation of jealousy that was now growing inside my gut. What could be bigger than jealousy? Betrayal. I was sure of that. I could not stand the idea of being betrayed, and I was determined to exorcise it from my system. I have since learned that nothing, but nothing, beats being betrayed as an act of inhumanity.

I didn't let on to Helen what I had seen. Deep down I tried to tell myself that it was all a mistake. Perhaps the guy she was kissing was an old childhood friend, maybe a cousin? It was all harmless kidding around, I speculated, searching for the bright side, if there was one. After all, I still loved her deeply. But, I sure had doubts about its reciprocity.

It must be understood that, in those days, a great premium was put on faithfulness. Divorce was more a rarity than the norm. People made pacts with other people and kept them. Or so it seemed. Certainly, it was supposed to be that way with Helen and me. We had made a pact, an irrevocable one. We had vowed to love each other forever and ever. I had not the slightest doubt that, from my end, my commitment was iron bound.

But, I was not a fool. Before I was going to do something I might regret for the rest of my life, I had to be sure. To be absolutely sure I had to commit myself to be a shadow. Put her under surveillance. That meant neglecting everything and dedicating my energies to the service of that one purpose. That wasn't, of course, very practical. In those days we had to be practical. There wasn't much room to maneuver. We hadn't any money and to get ahead you had to keep up. And applying yourself to college was one of the ways you got ahead. So, I wasn't going to jeopardize that under any circumstances.

Sick at heart, doing my best to mask my feelings, I did not waver from my pattern of calling Helen every day. We talked, and I tried to keep my voice from cracking and my conversation light enough.

"Are you okay?" she asked.

"Still a little down," I told her.

"Friday I'll make you a very happy young man," she told me. "I love you so much." At those words, I thought my heart would break.

On Friday I appeared as usual at her apartment.

"Good news," she said grabbing me around the neck and giving me a deep kiss. "Mom and Dad won't be back until very late. They've gone to a party on Long Island."

That meant that we could spend the whole evening together in her bedroom. Ordinarily that would have been a wonderful event. Not tonight. That night I was planning to be clever, manipulative. I was going to force the truth, one way or another. However the chips fell.

We hopped into bed and got naked and made love. It is possible to separate your mind from your body. I hoped she was not noticing any difference in the way I performed. I even whispered to her, as I always did, telling her how much I loved her, how much she meant to me, how I would love her forever and ever and ever. I'm sure she said the same things to me as we lay there locked in each other's arms. All the time, on another level, I was thinking about what I was going to say and when I was going to start. I waited until I cooled down.

I held her in the crook of my arm, and we both lay there looking at the ceiling.

"Helen, sweetheart, I often wonder what you do when I'm not around." It was, I thought, blandly put as a matter of idle conversation, typical afterplay talk, I supposed.

"I go to school, do my homework, talk to my girl friends, listen to records. The usual."

"And you miss me?"

"That especially," she said.

"You don't hang out with a crowd?"

She stiffened slightly, although that could have been my imagination.

"Not really," she said.

"Does that mean yes or no?"

I was deliberately not threatening, just coming on the subject easy, not wanting to scare her.

"Sometimes I go down to Murray's with my girl friends and kid around."

"The candy store."

"Down the street," she mumbled.

"Every night?"

"Not every night."

"Every other night?"

"Maybe."

Still, I didn't look at her. But I was sure she knew something was up.

"Lots of boys there?"

"A whole crowd."

I could tell that she was getting just a wee bit defensive. I was afraid of that. I was still hoping to get her off guard.

"I can't blame you, I suppose," I said, changing my tactic slightly. I wanted to keep lulling her, afraid of going too far too soon. "I'm all the way down there in Brooklyn. You've got to have some fun when I'm not around."

"It's just hanging around with people I've know for years," she said. I could tell she was slightly relieved.

"I don't mind," I said.

"I don't see why you should," she said, with just a bit too much innocence showing. I held my breath. It was, I was sure, time to strike.

"I don't even mind your going out with that guy," I said blandly.

She stiffened now, lifted her head, and looked me in the face. I made sure I was smiling.

"What guy?" she asked, but a frown had already wrinkled her forehead.

"You know how it is," I said, as if it didn't really matter, as if I wasn't bleeding inside. "You hear things. People talk."

She wasn't sure what to make of it, but I could see that she was getting really scared now.

"They're all busybodies. Bernie doesn't mean a thing to me."

It was a dagger in my heart. Bernie? God, I hated Bernie.

"That's not what I hear, Helen," I said.

"They're all liars," she said with some vehemence, sitting up in the bed. It was getting tougher and tougher for me to keep up the game. I could feel rage and jealousy mounting inside of me.

"They say he's more than just a friend," I pressed.

"People are such bastards," she said, her own anger mounting.

"They say you go out with him," I said, my voice no longer gentle.

"You can't believe them."

"I know you went out with him," I said, taking the shot in the dark. I really felt like a prosecutor and it pained me, especially the answers I was getting.

"Just once or twice," she admitted cautiously. I could tell by then that she was lying through her teeth.

"Or more?"

"Maybe more," she said. I was not giving her enough time to think, to be evasive.

"A lot more," I said.

"No. That's not true."

"He did it with you, too. That I know for sure."

"I didn't," she snapped, on the verge of hysteria.

"Listen. I know the truth. Why are you lying to me? Everybody knows."

Tears rolled over her eyes, down her cheeks.

"I didn't," she repeated through her sobs.

"Bernie told everybody, Helen. Everybody knows."

Her sobs became louder. Her shoulders shook.

"I only did it once. I swear it. He made me," she cried. "Only once."

"Lots more than once Helen," I said as if I knew.

She really started to bawl then, crying like a baby. Clutching me around the waist. I felt her warm tears on my naked chest.

"I didn't mean it, Kenny. I swear I didn't mean it. He made me. He pushed me. It's you I love, Kenny. Please, please, Kenny, forgive me. I'll never do it again. I swear it. I swear on my mother. I swear."

It became a litany, all this swearing never to over and over again. I felt sick to my stomach and soon the dykes broke and the tears ran down my cheeks and onto her hair. I was still holding her, you see, still hugging her, still loving her. But I was also grieving, grieving for this lost pure love. I had, I truly believed, given her my essence, my soul, and she had betrayed me. It had dealt me an awesome, monumental, painful blow.

I don't know how long we lay there, but I do know that for me it was the end of the world, the absolute end of the world. I've been through lots of defeats since, lots of betrayals of one sort or another, but nothing ever had the force and power of this betrayal.

I knew it was over then, although we did go through the motions of making love. I'll never understand that. I knew it was over, that I would never, could never see her again, and yet I made love to her. I even whispered in her ear how much I loved her and heard her whisper that to me.

I think that kind of farewell eased the parting for both of us. I never saw her again after that night, and I don't think I ever loved anyone as much.

SPORTY MORTY

Every time Max Ruben passed Bloomingdale's, he thought of Sporty Morty Millstein. Even now in his late seventies, Max found that Sporty Morty was the dominant character of his long-term memory.

From their earliest days together hanging out in front of the candy store on Saratoga Avenue in Brownsville, Brooklyn, Sporty Morty was the acknowledged leader of their pack. With his nifty double-breasted, blue serge suits, jaunty gray fedora, ties that screamed out their authority with large Windsor knots on gleaming white-on-white spread collar shirts, pointy-toed, mirror-shined shoes, Sporty spun stories of female conquests that boggled the mind of his deprived sycophants who were relegated to the dubious delights of Madame Palm and her Five Sisters.

No one really knew how Sporty could afford his lifestyle, although he broadly hinted that he was involved in various enterprises that smelled like number running or bookmaking, far more romantic undertakings than his supposed front carried out behind the counter of his father's delicatessen on Pitkin Avenue.

The candy store was renowned for once being the headquarters of Murder Inc., the Jewish mob that was hired out to dispatch enemies of the mob bosses in the twenties and thirties, a number of whom wound up in the electric chair. When Max, Sporty, and the other boys got there, that era had ended, although the romance of the mob's exploits remained to fire their imaginations.

Most of the gang, like Max, were good boys who got decent marks in high school and dreamed of the prosperous life in the professions. Becoming a doctor, of course, was still the highest rung of the success ladder in that first-generation Brooklyn Jewish neighborhood and many became such, while others became lawyers and accountants, and the more idealistic of the crew became academics, writers, and artists.

Sporty Morty would have none of that. He was a high school dropout, and his life seemed obsessively devoted to his Casanova exploits. At times, he showed off his conquests to the candy store crowd, good-looking girls who wore their big boobs like flashing headlights and strutted and posed and swarmed over Sporty like ants over honey.

There was nothing mean-minded about Sporty Morty. He was generous, gregarious, and loved the spotlight, performing mostly for the benefit of his envious crew. They coveted his lifestyle, especially his remarkable success with girls, a fact that he publicized at great length and with vivid images.

"Keep this up and it will fall off," was the mantra of his jealous buddies who yearned to drink the magic elixir of his success. As Max remembered, this was long before the sexual revolution, and getting girls to go all the way, for most of the crew, was a task akin to climbing Mount Everest barefoot. Not so for Sporty Morty.

"I make them feel like Queen of the May," he instructed them. "The name of the game is focus."

"But how?" his buddies asked.

"I guess I was born with the knack."

At times, he would regale the crew with the results of a triple header, meaning having serial sessions with three different ladies in a single day, moving from bed to bed with the zeal of a grasshopper. The crew supposed, from the samples Sporty Morty brought around to exhibit, that they were all gorgeous with tits that would grow an erection on a dead Indian.

Sometimes, goaded by their envy, he would illustrate the point of his prowess by visiting Bloomingdale's and picking up the salesgirls. Apparently, this was his prime hunting ground. Max and his friends would watch out of the corner of their eyes as he pretended to buy something, and before they knew it he had stashed the girls' telephone numbers in his little black book. He did have a little black book and sometimes showed them its jottings with numbers denoting not just a box score, but the quality of the girl's sexual performance.

The Bloomingdale's spiel went something like this:

"Hey, doll, I couldn't help noticing your striking resemblance to that movie star."

"Which one?" the girl countered, wary, but strangely engaged.

"The name escapes me, maybe Myrna Loy or Veronica Lake. Someone like that. I see the same aura."

"You're kidding me," the girl replied, skeptical for form's sake, but visibly moved.

"No, really. There's something about you." He peered soulfully into the girl's eyes. "I can't put my finger on it." He smiled and showed his dimple. "These things happen. Suddenly you're there. I can't explain it."

"Come on," the girl said, blushing, but obviously enjoying the repartee.

"Honest to God, I wish I could buy something, just to keep your attention. But by not making a purchase it will give me an excuse to see you again. That is, if you'd like me to?"

"I can't say I would mind," the girl said.

"Nor would I. In fact, if you could grant me your telephone number, I will show you my sincerity."

Invariably that first step was granted and thus the prelude was achieved. What was most remarkable was the yearning look the girls offered as Sporty Morty moved away. To the onlooking crew, her response was both baffling and miraculous.

When Max or one or another of his friends tried to ape Sporty Morty's technique, they were rejected so resoundingly that it left them socially stunted for weeks on end. Sporty Morty's talent was a given, like that of an artist. Was it in the smile, the look, the dimple, the walk, the clothes, the gleam? The words were, after all, so simple, silly transparent meaningless clichés full of false flattery that anyone with half a brain could decipher.

Long debates would ensue on the mysterious subject of Sport Morty's magnetism. All of the boys were certainly presentable, and a number of them were movie-star handsome, far more handsome than Sporty Morty, although one had to admit that Sporty had great teeth, a cleft chin, and dimples. His complexion, though, was often ashen, which the boys attributed to his overworked libido and a massive loss of semen.

Looking back, Max calculated that Sporty Morty worship probably lasted no more than three or four years. Most of the boys went off to college and became the professionals their parents wished for them to be. Max Ruben became a certified public accountant, raised a family in Huntington, Long Island, had two sons, both of whom migrated to the west coast. When his wife died, Max moved to Manhattan to a one- bedroom apartment on the east side, ironically a couple of blocks from Bloomingdale's.

The old candy store gang drifted apart, and when Max would meet one or another of them casually invariably the conversation would get around to Sporty Morty.

"Whatever happened to Sporty Morty?" became the refrain of all these chance meetings. One or another heard he had moved to Manhattan where he became a full time bookmaker, a salesman for Vegas casinos or a pornographic film producer. No one knew for sure. Somehow Sporty had to be connected, at least in the mind of his old friends, as someone involved in illicit trade like gambling, jewel thievery, or some other romantically roguish activity.

Sporty Morty was always the central point of these chance meetings. For long periods of time, as life became crowded with other experiences, Max did not think about Sporty Morty. It was only when he became older, widowed, and lonely that memories of Sporty Morty surfaced like a long-latent storm that had been gathering for years.

How did he do it? What was his secret? It became somewhat of an obsession for Max, especially now that he was alone. He wanted, needed, longed for the fleshly pleasures of ladies, preferably young ladies. His fantasies became lewd and, experimenting with the benefits of the new erection drugs, he discovered that he could maintain a respectable performance instrument despite his age.

In his married life, sexual events had become gradually tepid and in the end ceased altogether. Desire had disappeared and although he had a wonderfully affectionate and loving relationship with his wife of more than fifty years, that part of the equation had lost its luster. Alone now, retired, with more time for reflection, he rediscovered erotic longing and began having exciting fantasies, stimulated by the numerous websites he had found on the Internet that could feed his newfound lust and bring him to a solitary climax. Naturally, he would much rather have reached consummation with a live partner.

For some reason, he was not attracted to women of his own age. Their sagging flesh and aged bodies could not move him sexually. There were some forays in that direction, but in the end, they became brief and unsatisfying. What he found was that he longed for young flesh, pretty girls, the kind of girls that Sporty Morty brought around to the candy store in those halcyon days of his youth.

As an accountant, he had a trained analytic mind, and a daily assessment in the mirror told him that he was hardly a magnet for any woman, no less a woman under thirty. Or even forty. In fact, with his graying, sparse hair, his yellowing teeth, baggy eyes, and growing jowls, he was hardly a sight to stir any woman, except those desperate enough to have somebody, anybody, a live male body, to shepherd them around.

Somehow he managed to buy into the idea that age was merely a matter of attitude and that today's eighty, a milestone he was fast approaching, was yesterday's forty. He became determined to remake himself into the youthful image of himself that had grown in his mind. He prevailed, over the objections of a reputable plastic surgeon, to tighten his face, remove his jowls, lift his chin, and eliminate the bags under his eyes. With liposuction, he removed the fat on his belly and the love handles that had grown above his hips. He had his rotted yellow teeth replaced with white porcelain.

He hired a trainer to help tone up what was left of his muscles, dyed his hair, tweezed his eyebrows, and, satisfied that he had done what he could for his body, bought a new wardrobe at Bergdorf's, favoring Italian designers. His sons, who passed through New York on their various business meetings, thought he had lost his mind or regressed into a severe form of senility. One of them suggested he see a psychiatrist. Privately, they both thought his makeover hideous.

In his own mind, he felt that he had armored himself for the battle of the sexes, determined to pick up ladies by following the path of Sporty Morty Millstein. With the new erection pills, the cunning wisdom that came with age, and a pocketbook bulging with excess bucks, he felt he was ready to embark on a twilight career of seduction.

Carrying the mind baggage of total recall of Sporty Morty's chatting technique, he charged the Bloomingdale's floor looking for a likely target. It wasn't easy. The sales staff at Bloomingdale's had changed radically since the days when Sporty Morty prowled its precincts. He remembered that Sporty Morty found his best prospects in the jewelry department and after careful study, he found a likely mark, a well-stacked blonde with a boyish haircut and a big-toothed, welcoming smile.

"Hey, doll," he said, offering a flash of his implanted teeth and winking his bagless eyes. "I couldn't help noticing your resemblance to that movie star."

"Really?" the girl said. "Like who?"

"Marilyn Monroe comes to mind."

"My God, she's been dead forever."

"I mean in her heyday," he corrected, changing course. "I'm not kidding," he said, forgetting his lines.

"Can I show you some jewelry?" the girl said. "We work on straight commission."

"Honest to God," he said, flashing his implants again, "but if I bought something now I wouldn't have an excuse to see you again."

"Yes, you would. I would sell you something else."

"We should really discuss these things over dinner."

"You're kidding."

"Dead serious," he winked.

"What, are you nuts, old man? I'm selling jewelry here. Why don't you take your great grandchild to the carousel in Central Park and get out of my face."

Max felt words congeal in his throat. "Old man? Hell, this new me cost nearly fifty thousand dollars," he wanted to say, but he held back. Sporty Morty would have known how to handle this situation.

He felt himself flush and hurriedly left the store.

Of course, he was mightily discouraged, although he did try the technique at Lord & Taylor and one time at Bergdorf's, experiences that left him depressed and feeling ancient despite the cosmetic rearrangement of his face and the attempt to sculpt his body. He toyed with the advice one of his sons had given him about seeing a psychiatrist, but finally rejected it. He would not be able to bear the shame of revealing his inner life to a stranger.

The repetitive rejections seemed to accelerate the aging process. He lost interest in living alone in his one-bedroom apartment. He stopped cooking for himself and took fewer and fewer pains with his grooming. Life slipped by without incident. He no longer experimented with erection drugs, no longer frequented the porn sites on the Internet, slept most of time, lost all interest in watching television, and generally drifted in a haze of nothingness.

Finally his sons, seeing the condition of his apartment and his declining physical state, put him into a nursing home on East 71st Street. It was a compromise since at that point he refused to leave Manhattan. There, he languished, reluctantly joining the various programs devised to keep the inmates, as he called them, from dying of boredom.

One day, sitting in the main room, dozing, his attention was arrested by a well-dressed elderly gentlemen sitting on a couch surrounded by three or four ladies of uncertain age, one of whom was in a wheelchair.

The women were apparently mesmerized by the story he was telling and, despite their age, giggling coquettishly and hanging on his every word. The man was vaguely familiar, someone from long ago, etched now by age and infirmity, but nevertheless displaying a familiar swagger that had crossed his path many years ago. Incongruously, he apparently had taken great care with his clothes and grooming. His shoes were spit-shined and he wore a suit, very rare in this environment and, more incongruously, a white-on-white shirt with a colorful tie done in a Windsor knot.

It didn't occur to Max until he was alone in his room and in his memories that evening. Of course. The epiphany exploded in Max's mind and memory. It was none other than Sporty Morty. My God, Sporty Morty, Max exclaimed, suddenly revitalized, as if he had shed ten years in an instant.

At breakfast in the dining room, he inspected the man and was even more certain. At the table were four giggling ladies listening intently to every word. Occasionally, a wizened hand would pat a lady's arm or stroke her cheek, setting off titters of pleasure. And there it was, the smile, the cleft, the dimples, untrammeled by time. Sporty Morty, with the luster and magnetism as intact as ever.

After breakfast, the group shuffled into the main room, and Sporty Morty took his place in the center of the female group, smiling, patting, winking while the aged ladies fought for his attention.

"Sporty Morty," Max said. "Remember me? Max Ruben from the candy store."

He felt Sporty Morty's inspection as he struggled for recall with dim eyes. Then came a flash of vague recognition.

"Yeah, Max. From the candy store."

"The same, a little older, but not much wiser," Max cracked, hoping for the dimpled smile and nod.

"Yeah," Sporty Morty said tentatively. "I think I remember. Was it Max?"

"Max from the candy store."

The nod was slow, but accelerated as Sporty observed him. He turned to the women surrounding him.

"Meet my old friend, Max, from the candy store," Sporty Morty said, introducing him to all the ladies by name. Max acknowledged them politely, but it seemed impossible for any of them to tear their attention away from Sporty Morty.

Max wasn't sure he had been remembered, but he did look for Sporty Morty after lunch, which was nap time at the home. He had found Sporty's room number and knocked timorously, hoping he could renew old acquaintance.

"The door's open," Sporty Morty said.

There he was, unashamed, smiling his dimpled smile as he lay sandwiched between two of the ladies Max had seen with him earlier. All three were under the covers, crammed together on the bed, the women resting their heads against Sporty Morty's shoulders, enjoying his tender, patting embrace.

"It's okay," Sporty Morty said. "We're cuddling. It's therapy. Right, girls?"

Embarrassed, mumbling excuses, Max hurried away. Up to his old tricks, he thought, then giggled. Good old Sporty Morty.

At dinner that night, he followed Max into the men's room and both men stood side to side in the urinals, relieving themselves in slow motion.

"Max is it?" Sporty asked.

"From the candy store," Max reminded.

"Yeah, the candy store. Long time."

In the long interim, Max Ruben pondered the nagging question.

"How do you do it, Sporty Morty? What is the secret?"

"Focus, Max, focus," Sporty Morty said, nodding after some cogitation. Then looking downward briefly he said: "Good job, fella. You've been a loyal and faithful friend."

"Me?" Max asked, confused.

"Not you, Max." He pointed downward, this time with his chin. "It," Sporty Morty said, showing his dimpled smile. He zipped up, rinsed his hands, patted his hair, turned to Max, winked, and went out the door.

THE DIVIDING LINE

Lavine was sitting in his East Side apartment reading the *New York Times*. From time to time he lifted his eyes to peer out the window, where across the street a glass-walled, spanking-new condominium was taking shape. His wife, Betsy, was sitting opposite reading the arts section of the *Times*. Occasionally she would glance upward and look at her husband.

"We'll just have to get used it," she said.

She was, he knew, a pragmatic woman. She knew how to cope, make do, steer around controversy and, mostly, how to keep him content. He was, now that he was seventy-five, eager to find tranquility, a tough chore in today's global environment. The news from everywhere was awful, a bill of fare of suicide killings, mass murders, car bombs, ethnic slaughtering, and terrorism fears.

They had been married twelve years now, and she was twenty years his junior. She was his former secretary when he was in full-time law practice, having worked for him for nearly fifteen years. The firm had a mandatory retirement age of sixty-two.

As his secretary, Betsy was exemplary, efficient, competent, and understanding. Their relationship was friendly and beyond reproach, even in his widowhood. Neither would have dared to violate the stringent new politically correct rules regarding office behavior.

With that stricture gone with his retirement, she swallowed her pride and approached him with both trepidation and courage.

"If you ever marry again, consider me as your perfect choice of wife," she told him when he considered his future on the cusp of retirement. "I know all your faults and virtues. I know your business. I have spent more time with you than anyone you know. And…" She winked at him. "I have always loved you."

Oddly, he was not shocked by the boldness of her assertion. He had always felt her special interest in him, and he harbored a vague attraction for her, even in his married days. She was, after all, quite attractive, with the kind of full figure he had always admired, and she came to work perfectly groomed and attired in ways that set off her strong physical points. At times she had even entered his fantasy world, but he was too ethical, hidebound, and cowardly to open that window of action.

He did mull over her offer. With retirement came the loss of his work routine, which enhanced the loneliness of his widowhood. His two children were grown and lived on the West Coast, and although he was still fit and not without sexual urges, he could no longer compensate with the ingrained habits and long hours of a fervent legal career. Nor was he in love with Betsy. Attracted, yes, but not, as he defined it, in love.

After retirement, they continued to see each other. She became available to sort his papers and continue to serve him in a business way. Without the conduct restrictions mandated by the firm, and the legal barriers imposed, they now socialized in dating mode, and with the boundaries broadened, they developed a relationship, meaning they became sexually involved. To him, it was a revelation. She was remarkably giving, uninhibited, adventurous, and exciting as a sex partner, and it served its purpose as a profound bonding mechanism. Besides, they were already bonded in the practical ways of domestic cooperation.

At one point in their new relationship, Betsy suggested in her practical way, that he live with her for a trial period and see if it worked out. It did and they married. She smoothly transferred her secretarial skills to their domestic life and organized and comforted him and, as vanilla ice cream goes with apple pie, she completely revived his interest in sex. These days that pursuit was achieved with some pharmaceutical assistance. She interpreted her own healthy sexual appetite as making up for lost time. He was delighted, and the process went a long way to further bond with her and, by the miracle of chemistry and attraction, he fell in love with her.

Their life in Manhattan was filled with theater going, concerts, opera, lectures, and dinner in restaurants or with friends. He served on a number of not-for-profit boards, and she had her opera club and circle of female friends.

"It's not that bad," she told him, referring to the glass-walled condominiums. "Better than that heap of old brick."

"That heap of old brick was built in the early thirties," he said. "Like me. I hated to see it go."

"The new condo is an improvement to the neighborhood," she said in her gently persuasive way.

He started to concentrate on the *Times* again, then looked up at the emerging building.

"What is the dividing line?" he asked.

"The dividing line?"

"Between the old and the new. Relevance and irrelevance."

"I don't get it."

"That's because you're transitional."

Her forehead creased and her eyes narrowed, which was the way she often expressed skepticism.

"You're fifty-five, a baby boomer. I preceded you by twenty years. You have a dividing line as well, but you're not conscious of it."

He knew he sounded like he was playing the wise man, a bit pompous and all-knowing, but he felt the need to illustrate what had started in his mind as a vague concept and was fast coming into full bloom as an important and essential truth. In an odd way he felt that the two of them were transported into a *New Yorker* cartoon waiting for someone to write a caption.

"I was sitting in my doctor's office last week. Picked up *People* magazine and I didn't know a single one of the featured people, nor did I care. I can't even name them."

"Some of them are foreign to me as well. I do know some, the older ones."

"At some point the editors will phase them out. Like for example Eddie Cantor."

"Who is that?"

"Who is Eddie Cantor? You're kidding."

"No. I'm not."

"He was the biggest movie star and comedian in the early thirties. He had a wife named Ida and five daughters...I think it was five daughters. He was also on radio every Sunday night along with Jack Benny, Charlie McCarthy, and Fibber Magee and Molly."

"Sorry. I don't remember. I wasn't born until 1949. Who was Fibber Magee?"

He sighed and shook his head, showing an amused smile.

"My point about the dividing line. When do memories become irrelevant?"

"You mean when do they fade out from the collective memory?"

She seemed serious, but he had the impression she was humoring him.

"There has to be a dividing line, a point where living memory becomes merely history, where things have become obliterated and lost except to those whose memory is still alive. A point where what used to exist, buildings, neighborhoods, once famous actors and politicians, fade from memory and become merely history. Like my reference to Eddie Cantor and that old pile of bricks that has disappeared." He pointed with his chin to the new condominium rising outside. "People fade away and die out and with them goes their memory."

"I will always remember that pile of bricks that has disappeared," he muttered. "Not for its aesthetic value, but for its being there."

He knew he was groping for some clear way to express what he was suggesting and searched his mind for other examples. "Take theaters. The Loews Paramount, the Capital, the Roxy. All gone. And 52nd Street, Swing Street in my time. Leon and Eddie's, the Downbeat Club. And 42nd Street. Grant's, where you could get the best hot dogs, and all those movie theaters where you could go for a quarter and get a double feature." He felt himself on a roll. "And Lindy's, the real Lindy's, and Shrafft's, and the Third Avenue El, and the Fifth Avenue double-decker buses and trolley cars. The subway was a nickel. Take politics." He mulled the thought for a moment.

"Who was Harry Truman's vice president? And Fiorello

LaGuardia. He was once a person, yet most people will remember his name merely as a New York airport."

"Lots of airports, high schools, streets, towns, and colleges are named after people that no one remembers. I don't know where you're going with this."

"I'm searching for the dividing line," he said, somewhat testily. "Like when was the moment when the curtain went down on the memory of Eddie Cantor and the Roxy and the Paramount and double-decker buses."

"And Harry Truman's vice president. I know that one. It was Alben Barkley. I read McCullough."

"Not fair. That was history. He was, by the way, referred to as 'The Veep.'"

"So, how many people now retain this bit of information as living history?"

"Life goes on, darling. People who knew Shakespeare and called him Willy or Will or Bill are long gone. Think of all the things that have disappeared, never mind people. My mother wore a corset and hung her clothes on the line. My father wore a fedora and chain-smoked cigarettes. What man wears hats, and only young idiots or fools smoke cigarettes. And the sun. No one told us you could get cancer from the sun."

He nodded, went back to reading the *Times,* but he couldn't concentrate, and looked up again at the building going up. But the ideas they were discussing continued to hold his attention.

"I guess that's why I love black-and-white movies of the thirties and forties. My time. I love to look at the details, the backgrounds. The clothes my mother wore, the décor and furniture, the telephones, the old appliances, the old cars, the slang. Words like scram and mug and sucker. Laurel and Hardy, the Marx Brothers, the Ritz Brothers. Jean Harlow. Do you know she died when she was twenty-seven years old? Imagine." He felt a lump grow in his throat and unaccountably a sob began deep inside of him and, for a moment, his eyes teared. I am a sentimental old fool, he told himself.

He hadn't realized that she was watching him.

"Remember, darling. I watched those with you, mostly for the stories. I love those old stories."

"And I point out who those actors are?"

"Yes you do."

"I do appreciate your trying to enter my past. I love you for that."

"Now I know why you called me transitional. You have twenty years of living memory on me. Some day my dividing line will come. My range of celebrities and memories will fade away from the public consciousness just like yours."

"It's all changed too damned fast," he muttered. "You don't even get much of a chance to savor it. And you don't know how good it was until it's gone."

"Now you're getting maudlin," she admonished.

He ignored her criticism, knowing she was right.

"I can't keep up," he sighed. "Once I thought I was actually computer literate. I could do e-mail, use Word for my writings and briefs. I could read an Excel sheet. Now, just a handful of years later, all I know is fast becoming obsolete, old hat. I am falling behind. I feel overwhelmed by change. I find my greatest comfort in looking backwards."

They exchanged glances. Her gaze seemed alarmed. She sees my fear, he told himself.

"Did it ever occur to you, darling, that things are better than they were. That you're living longer, that we've grown smarter in some ways, what with all the technological advances. Did you ever see a computer in those old movies?"

"Maybe I'm just bitching about the changes that are happening so damned fast, and as you grow older you become more and more irrelevant, locked in some place and mindset that doesn't exist any more." He rustled his paper and went back to reading the *Times*. "Look at this. Horror upon horror. Then again, we did have our horrors and bloodbaths. Of course, we didn't have instant reporting back then and the reach of communications."

He sensed he was heading for something more cerebral than emotional now, forcing himself into a lawyerly mode to justify his premise.

"You're just looking at the surface of things, darling," she said after a long silence. In her pragmatic way, she had been mulling over her own thoughts. "The more things change the more they remain the same."

"Tell it to my mirror," he chuckled.

"I mean human nature. The way we are. Our inner core. That never changes. No matter if that pile of bricks is demolished. External change happens, but through it all we remain the same. As humans we are constant in our emotions and our behavior. Like Shakespeare, who I just mentioned. You know why he survived for five hundred years? He knew the everlasting, unchanging immutability of human nature."

"My, my," he said chuckling. "You are so profound and eloquent today, my love."

Suddenly she rose, left the room, and was back in a moment. She stood before him and opened her palm in which was a little blue pill, which he recognized, of course.

"Take this," she whispered, bending over and kissing him on the lips. "Finish your paper and contemplate your lost world over there for the next hour. Then I'll illustrate how human nature hasn't changed very much at all."

He took the pill from her and swallowed it.

It might not be a complete answer, he thought happily, but she did have a point.

"By the way," he said as she started to leave the room again. "Let me tell you who Fibber Magee was."

She turned, looked at him, and, putting her hands on her hips, she straightened her posture in a mocking, haughty, and indignant manner.

"Frankly, Scarlett," she said. "I don't give a damn."

Then she pranced out of the room.

THAT HORRID THING

"No politics please," Irma said.

"I don't talk politics. Only common sense," Bob replied.

"Okay, then. No common sense. I mean it. I'll never forgive you."

He was helping her fold the linen napkins in a special way to make them look like birds in flight. There would be six guests, she had told him, agonizing over the placement of each person in the dining room of their East Side apartment. They were her people, meaning people from her law office, partners mostly and their spouses. He was a salesman for a firm making ladies' underwear, which might as well have been an occupation on another planet.

After five years of marriage, Irma placed a great deal of importance on these little dinner parties for building consequential relationships outside the office with spouses or significant others in attendance. This one, he knew, was particularly special, and he was being duly warned to control his behavior. Occasionally, he admitted, he had become a bit too confrontational, especially when the subject veered toward what others might misinterpret as political. He did not see it in those terms.

"Above all, don't show that horrid thing."

"Whatever you say," he promised.

He had been sitting in his office on the twenty-second floor of an adjacent building working on a big order for a Midwest chain on September 11, 2001, when he first saw that horrid thing. He had stopped by the video store on the way to work to pick up his video camera that had been in for repairs and was lying on a leather chair in his office when he heard the strange noise.

His office window was directly in the line of sight of the Twin Towers, and when someone in the office screamed, he turned and saw where the first plane had sliced into the north tower. It was such a bizarre occurrence that, at first, he thought it might have been an accidental collision. Then, in swift succession, another plane smacked into the other tower.

By no means was he a video buff. He had taken occasional pictures at outings and other events, but did not have that special visual curiosity of the dedicated photographer. Nevertheless the proximity of the video camera and the circumstances at hand were motivation enough, and he found himself standing by the window pointing the camera at what was quickly becoming a major catastrophe.

It took him a minute or two to get the damned thing focused and working, but when it was finally buzzing he saw through the lens finder the incredible spectacle of people jumping out of the windows like little puppets whose strings had been cut. There was little time for reflection nor did the horror of it register as reality. It was as if he were watching a special-effect-laden movie.

At some point, the truth of the incident set in and the collapse of the buildings set them all running from their offices. By then, he had filmed at least twenty minutes of the episode.

Although his office building was unscathed, the evacuation was orderly and he, along with others in the building, marched like robots down the twenty-two floors to street level and hurried from the chaos as fast as they could.

What he had captured on that video was, even now, something so horrendous, so weird, so horrifying, that it became over the years one of those visual atrocities that challenged the very idea of authenticity. You saw it, but it was difficult to believe it had happened before your eyes. You saw it over and over again to assure yourself that it was an exact representation of something that had occurred to real people in real time in his city and not simply a slick camera trick.

To see human beings falling like stones from high windows, surrounded by other items floating in the air beside them, like shoes, papers, and miscellaneous debris, as they jumped to certain death and smashed and exploded like ripe melons against the cement of the street below, was not exactly family fare.

Nevertheless, in those early days, he had shown it on demand. Other times he watched it by himself. As time went on, he mostly watched it in secret, as if he needed to validate its authenticity again and again to prove to himself that the memory must be preserved before it disappeared completely from the public consciousness.

In the early days, showing the video was the centerpiece of any social gathering, especially in their apartment, but as time went on it became, as Irma characterized it, sort of like pornography. After numerous showings, the effect wore off. She began to call it "that horrid thing."

"I will not watch it again," Irma had protested finally. They were still considered newlyweds then and while she indulged his insistence that it be viewed by them and shown to their friends and acquaintances, she began to find it repulsive, disruptive, irritating and, ultimately, boring.

The media drumbeat about the falling towers and the loss of thousands of people continued for months. By then, the area had become a shrine. The gates of the nearby church and armory were enshrouded by photos and artifacts. People continued to mill about in hopeless pursuit of their lost relatives. Clean-up crews worked day and night to clean up the mess. It was, of course, the most awful thing that had happened in New York in his lifetime.

A few months ago he had bought a giant flat-screen television that took up one whole wall of the den. He told Irma he had bought it to watch sports events, but he knew the reason that he had bought it was to watch the footage he had shot of the people jumping out of windows.

"Can't you stop watching that horrid thing?" she would ask him often.

"I need it to remind me."

"I'd rather you'd try to forget it. It's so unnerving."

"It must never be forgotten," he would counter. In his daily life he had observed that people were talking about it less and less, shutting it out of their memory.

"We all know it's a historical fact. Constantly dwelling on it is sick."

"The danger seems to be increasing," he told her. "Look what's happening throughout the world, suicide bombings, Muslims protesting everywhere. Look at the signs they wave: 'Death to America,' 'Kill Christians and Jews,' 'Behead the Infidels,' 'Bush is a murderer, a terrorist,' 'Jews are Nazis.' What does that tell us?"

"So, the world is a mess. Some Muslims hate us. What else is new?"

"They want us dead, all of us. As we speak, it would be naïve to believe that we are safe. Our future is in doubt. The people who are not afraid to die will win."

"What will watching people jumping out of windows do to solve the situation?"

"It will remind us," he insisted.

"You're going to drive yourself nuts, Bob."

After awhile, he found himself watching the tape surreptitiously when Irma was out of the apartment or had gone to bed. It was as if he was viewing some masturbatory fantasy, performing some dirty little secret act.

There were many reminders of that terrible day, but nothing, nothing equaled the tape in intensity. The surviving relatives were determined never to let people forget what had happened to their loved ones. As with everything that happened in the city of New York, competing interests inflamed emotions, and the battle over what would take the place of the Twin Towers continued over the years.

The images that he had captured and had viewed hundreds of times left him increasingly haunted by the idea that a similar and more horrendous event would indeed happen again, and he became vocal on the subject to the point of obsession. When people would accuse the government and the president of scare tactics it was like throwing a match on dry tinder.

After repeated rants and eruptions, he was well aware that people avoided any remark that would set him off. "There goes Bob again," he imagined people were telling themselves. He didn't care. He knew he was right, a one-man early warning system.

In their circles, his views on the subject were becoming increasingly isolated, since most people they associated with were adamant about their political choices and believed that scare tactics were being used for political gain by the president and his party. The Iraq war and its difficulties only exacerbated the situation. There were moments when, as Irma told him, he became downright offensive and rude.

He knew, too, that he had become a one-issue broken record. He was not a committed Republican or Democrat, although most of his circle could be characterized as liberal Democrats. Because he defended the war on terrorism, people thought he was a Republican. He tried to explain that fact, but to no avail. Most of those in their circle were highly educated, articulate, insistent, passionate. Although they professed to be reasonable and open to challenge, their core view of the world was incapable of change. As time went on, their views hardened into hatred of the president himself, and when he challenged this one aspect of their viewpoint, the terrorist threat, they would overwhelm him with invective that eventually became personal.

"The other shoe will drop," he would insist. It became his opening cliché. "Those people want to kill us. They don't care if they die, as long we die."

"You're being hysterical," someone in their group would say. Their arguments were predictable and, to him, infuriating. The president lied. They are attacking the wrong people. Saddam was not involved in terrorism. It's all about oil and big business. Our soldiers are dying needlessly. This mad president must be impeached. Al Qaeda is a fringe group. Muslims as a whole are reasonable people. On and on.

Why didn't they remember? He was able to stoke his memory by replaying the video. Irma would get increasingly furious when she caught him at it. At times, she would attempt to reason with him, pointing out the dangers that might come of such an obsession.

"Your addiction will consume you," she said. There were

moments when he agreed with the logic of her reasoning. She had a point. Sometimes a big noise in the middle of the night, or a plane flying too low, or even walking through Grand Central Terminal, or riding a bus or a subway would send a brief shiver of fear through him. It was unavoidable. He wondered if such sensations passed through the minds of other people.

Perhaps Irma was right about his obsessing too much. She was, after all, his wife. She had his best interests at heart. He decided to wean himself away from watching the tape and withdraw from the information highway, since everything that he read and saw underlined his belief that a terrorist event was in the planning stages, its execution inevitable.

Sometimes, by sheer will, he could summon the self-discipline and stay away from the news media. He would avoid all information on the Internet and on television that dealt with current events. He stopped reading the news section of the *New York Times*. When he was within earshot of people who expressed themselves on the subject, he would force himself not to listen, although that was very difficult. He tried not to respond to their comments.

Still, he could not stay away from watching the video. The longer he stayed away from absorbing information about the prevalence of terror, the more it rushed back at him when he became open to it again. It was like a sore that could not heal.

Lately, he had been more vociferous than usual, and he suspected that Irma warned people in advance to stay off the subject. She used the umbrella phrase "politics" to telescope the meaning. For the dinner party in preparation she was adamant, repeating her warning again and again to be sure it slipped into his consciousness.

He felt himself fully committed to cooperating. This was too important a gathering to create a scene, especially since he knew that Irma was up for a partnership and the spouse of such a candidate was scrutinized for any signs that might be disruptive to a potential partner. He knew how important it was to her. He and Irma were very supportive of each other. After five years of marriage, they were still affectionate and considerate to each other. He believed they were still in love. He had no reason to think otherwise.

The dinner was prepared by an expensive caterer who supplied two waiters to help. Bob was the designated bartender. Three of the guests were partners in the law firm, two males and one female. They were all sophisticated, well-dressed, and participatory. They knew how to be good guests, and he was determined to be a good and responsive host.

Except for his marriage to Irma, their occupational worlds did not intersect. They were mostly involved in Wall Street matters, security work, corporate affairs, while his business involved women's undergarments, a matter of little interest to any of them. While he was certain he could match any of them in income, he was well aware of the divide between them.

Most of them and their spouses, his included, were the product of Ivy League schools: Harvard, Yale or Princeton. They encompassed that triumvirate of upward mobility. Irma was Harvard, then Yale Law School. He was used to their airs, their superior sense of their own assertions, their talk of old school ties, roommates, and reunions. He knew they did not think of themselves as snobs, although they still were. It did not faze him; he was not in the least jealous. Sometimes their antics were laughable.

He was a graduate of the School of Commerce at New York University and proud of his own earning power. In the end, he had learned, salesmanship was the key to success. But there was no denying that in this little group of corporate Ivy League lawyers, he was an outsider. He got a kick seeing Irma maneuver herself in this world. She was sure to make partner, and he was her greatest cheerleader.

As they sipped their drinks, mainly white wine or vodka on the rocks, the conversation was mostly focused on law firm gossip, economic themes, and the state of the market. One of the senior partners, Harry Lillienthal, was the obvious "eminence gris" of the group. A man in his sixties, he had met Bob on other occasions. He wore a polka dot bowtie on a striped blue shirt and a dark striped suit with a vest from which hung a Phi Beta Kappa key. His wife was mousy, mostly silent, and morose. With a self-important person like

Lillienthal for a spouse, Bob could understand her persona.

The lady partner was Sharon Folker, carefully groomed in a black dress and a string of clearly authentic white pearls. Irma had described her as a committed activist. Her spouse was a psychiatrist with a disconcerting nervous blinking twitch, whose lips seemed fixed in a perpetual Cheshire cat smile, as if he could read the assembled guests' thoughts and was amused by them.

The third partner was colorless with a pale narrow face. His name was David Arnold and his wife was a social worker for the City of New York, with tight gray hair and large glasses that magnified her intense eyes, and the general demeanor of one who, to Bob, seemed the quintessential stereotype of a do-gooder, the kind that had no doubts at all about the righteousness of her cause whatever that may be.

After drinks and hors d'oeuvres with the initial socialization rituals of the group, they moved on to the dining room. The table was festive with a large floral centerpiece and the proper glasses and plates sparkling from the reflection of the crystal chandelier that hung over the table.

Inevitably, despite all of Irma's precautions, the talk turned to the present state of world turmoil. Irma shot a cautionary glance at Bob, to which Bob nodded his understanding. No politics, no matter what.

"This president is ruining our country," Harry said, responding to a remark by the do-gooder spouse who, as he had predicted in his mind, was fixated on civil rights. "We are losing our freedoms."

"They are certainly whittling down our rights," the social worker said. "The Patriot Act is a travesty. This is merely the opening gun of a campaign by these Right Wing fanatics to make us slaves to their self-righteous notions, most of them fostered by the evangelicals."

"No question that our rights are being eroded," the lady partner agreed, seconded by the activist who nodded her approval. "This is the worst administration in memory."

"He should be impeached," the psychiatrist said.

"Of course, the war will settle his mess," Lillienthal said. "It was a stupid blunder and has robbed us of young people and treasure. It will end in disaster."

"It was a stupid move," the lady partner said, her lips curled in contempt.

"Think of all the billions we are wasting that could be used to help the our growing underclass," the social worker said.

"The uneducated morons are taking over," the lady partner said. "And the president is the chief moron."

The conversation proceeded along those lines, with Irma glancing at Bob and trying all sort of ploys to deflect the conversation to another area. Bob listened as the vitriol grew more and more intense. The president, Rumsfeld, Rice, everyone connected to the present administration was subjected to withering criticism, roundly agreed to by everyone. There was, of course, no dissent, as each person eloquently articulated the prevailing opinion of the group as if, in their business and social travels, they had never heard one word of opposition. Bob, determined to keep his promise to Irma, kept his silence, although he answered their criticisms in his mind.

Even Irma, being the good hostess, offered her opinion of the general catastrophe by agreeing with their views. It struck Bob as somewhat ingenuous since she managed to avoid expressing such thoughts with such adamant conviction when they were together. She exchanged glances with Bob, as if to say that she was merely being diplomatic. It struck him suddenly that she was, indeed, on the same wavelength of these people, not just sucking up.

Her attitude seemed to give him permission to finally join the conversation, as if she had violated some unwritten rule. There seemed no point in remaining silent, although he promised himself to be cautious and circumspect.

"What about terrorism?" Bob said gently, watching all eyes turn toward him. He caught Irma shooting a glance at the ceiling. "We haven't been attacked in more than four years."

"We've been lucky," Harry Lillienthal said.

"Thank the Lord," the lady partner said.

"Maybe the threat is overblown," the psychiatrist said. "Generating fear is good politics for the crazies who run our government."

"It got the son-of-a-bitch elected," the lady partner said.

"Surely something the administration is doing is protecting us," Bob said without sarcasm.

"They'd like us to believe that," the social worker said. "Gives them a good excuse to bring us closer to dictatorship."

"Isn't that a bit harsh?" Bob said.

"The handwriting is on the wall," the lady partner said. "It's all a ploy."

"The president has brought us to a potential disaster. We are paying the piper for his stupidity," Lillienthal said, his cheeks coloring. "The man is a disaster, an ignorant fool."

"A graduate of Yale and Harvard," Bob said, unable to contain himself, breaking his promise, although he delivered the comment as a kind of joke.

"He wouldn't be the first fool to have graduated from those schools," Lillienthal said, going along with the joke.

"He should never have gone into Iraq," the psychiatrist said, his eyes blinking uncontrollably. "That was not where the terrorists came from."

"They were all involved," Bob said. "All the Arabs."

"Are you saying there are no good Arabs?" the social worker asked. "Isn't that a rather intolerant assessment?"

"Not all Arabs are terrorists," Bob said, "but all terrorists are Arabs."

"Timothy McVeigh was not an Arab," the lady partner shot back.

"Point well taken," Bob said, retreating. "We have our own homegrown fascists. I can't deny that."

"Yes, we do," the lady partner said. "Right Wing fanatics."

Bob was silent for a long moment as each of the guests in turn expressed themselves with what he termed in his mind, the usual clichés of their political persuasion. A quick glance at Irma told him what was going through her mind. He knew he was totally isolated, probably dismissed, irrelevant and powerless, a mere underwear salesman.

"Don't any of you remember what happened on September 11?"

"Of course they remember," Irma said, her voice on the edge of panic.

"An awful experience," Harry Lillienthal said. "Who can forget?"

"We were attacked by people that want to kill us," Bob said. "They still want to kill us. The threat has grown, not abated. I'm surprised none of you realize that."

"We do realize it," the lady partner said. "We are not stupid. It's just the way this president is going about meeting the threat is counterproductive."

"The president is using fear tactics to limit our civil rights, make us subservient to his will," the social worker said.

"Aren't we getting too political?" Irma intervened in obvious desperation.

"I think you all forgot what happened," Bob said.

"That's ridiculous," the lady partner said. "How can anyone forget?"

"I beg to differ," Bob said, trying to retain an air of politeness. After all, he was the host.

"You mean you agree with that man," Harry Lillienthal said, a clearly lawyerly challenge.

"Are you saying that you don't believe we are fighting a war for survival, fighting a foe that has no respect for life? Who wants us in the West to buy into his corrupted view, his Islamic fascist fantasy? He wants to kill us if we don't conform. He has no mercy, no human compassion."

"I guess we have a different view of things," the psychiatrist said.

"I feel sorry for you," the lady partner said. "You just don't see the conspiracy they are hatching."

"And you are all suffering from memory lapse."

There it was, he knew. He had crossed the line. It was too late now.

"I'd like to show you something," Bob said.

"Not that, Bob. Please," Irma begged.

"What do you want us to see?" the lady partner asked.

"I wouldn't, Bob."

"But I would," Bob said. He got up, went into his bedroom, got the tape from a bottom drawer, and brought it out. He could tell that they had been talking about him.

"I wish you wouldn't," Irma said, her voice cracking. "Not that horrid thing."

"What is it you want to show us?" the psychiatrist asked.

"It isn't necessary, Bob," Irma pleaded.

"Yes, it is. Come on. This is important."

They followed him into the den.

"What is it we'll be watching?" Harry Lillienthal asked.

"You'll see."

"I wish you wouldn't, Bob," Irma begged.

"These people need a refresher course," Bob said. "They are looking through the wrong end of the telescope."

"He just won't give it up," Irma cried in frustration.

"Maybe we should listen to her," the psychiatrist said.

Bob popped the tape into the machine, and the images appeared on the big screen.

"I took these myself," Bob said. "You probably have never seen this."

"I can't watch it. Not again," Irma sighed.

The tape unreeled in all its portrayed horror. The guests were glued to the images, watching people jumping out of windows, shoes flying. They were mesmerized.

"You shot this yourself?" the lady partner asked.

"Pure coincidence," Bob said, not explaining the circumstances.

From the corner of his eye, he saw Irma start to leave the room.

"How absolutely awful," the lady partner said. "Why did they have to jump?"

It seemed too self-evident to deserve an answer.

Suddenly a sharp crack in the screen distorted the images, which continued to run. Irma had thrown a piece of sculpture at the television, producing a lightning like fissure.

"I can't stand it anymore," she cried, rushing out of the room.

"I see what she means," Lillienthal said. "This is horrendous."

"I never saw this," the social worker said. "It's beyond belief."

The images continued to move on the cracked screen.

"Good God," the lady partner said. "Desperation makes people act without logic."

"What would you have done?" Bob asked.

The group continued to watch, unable to tear their eyes away from the screen, despite the crack on the screen.

"I guess you've played this many times before," the social worker said. "It is hard to watch."

"Yes, it is," the wife of Lillienthal agreed, breaking her silence. She turned her eyes away.

"I can see why Irma is so stressed," the psychiatrist said. "You should have spared her."

"I had to remind you, didn't I?"

"Do you think we needed a reminder?" the lady partner asked.

"Desperately so," Bob said. "You people are a menace. You are looking through the wrong end of the telescope. I think…"

"I think we had better leave," Harry Lillienthal interrupted as he looked at Bob.

"You just don't get it," Bob sighed. "Your minds are closed."

"I feel sorry for you," the lady partner said.

"Don't you believe the evidence of your eyes?" Bob asked.

"I think you better go and comfort your wife," the psychiatrist said. "We had better go now."

They started to file out of the apartment, awkward and embarrassed. The plates with the main dish had been taken away and replaced with dessert plates. Bob could tell that even the catering people were embarrassed.

"It's okay," he said when the guests were gone. "Just clean up and I'll write you a check." He shrugged. "Shit happens."

In the bedroom, Irma lay supine on the bed, head down. She had been sobbing, but when he came into the room, she lifted her head.

"You've ruined everything," she said hoarsely.

"They needed to be reminded," he said. He felt no remorse.

"You've ruined everything," she repeated.

She was right, of course.

He knew then that it was over between them. Another score for the terrorists, he thought. They were winning.

ACTORS

"My name is Bruce, and I'm your server," Bruce said, yet again. He prided himself on memorizing the specials. He was, after all, an actor and he had been a server for nearly two decades now, working in upscale restaurants in Manhattan and Los Angeles while pursuing what he considered his true vocation, acting.

He lived with Marilyn, his girlfriend of three years. She too considered herself an actress, having done a number of commercials and small parts in off- and off-off-Broadway shows. When she wasn't working at her craft, which was most of the time, she also waited tables in various restaurants in their neighborhood in the East Village.

They shared the rent in a tiny one-bedroom apartment and earned enough to live on the fringes of a gentrified New York lifestyle, largely because they were able to defy the Internal Revenue Service by not declaring all of their tips. They attended acting classes, usually in the early morning hours or between the lunch and dinner hours and could afford workouts at a sports club a few blocks from their apartment. Above all, actors had to keep in shape and, of course, continue to hone their acting skills, a lifetime career requirement.

Bruce was always on the lookout for someone in the business who could make hiring decisions. He was not bashful about supplying someone with a picture and resume; a long shot, he knew, but cheerfully offered. One never knew when lightning would strike. It had once when he got to play the part of the gravedigger in *Hamlet* at the Dorothy Chandler Pavilion in L.A. by playing pickup basketball in the schoolyard of Beverly Hills High School.

"It's all about contacts and connections," he lectured to his various girlfriends or anyone who would listen. It was, of course, the prevailing opinion in the business. "It has nothing to do with talent. We know we have talent, but in our business, you need a platform to truly display it."

The gravedigger part lasted approximately six weeks, and so far it had been the highlight of his so-called career. He was not loath to mention it repeatedly to the various agents with whom he was briefly attached and with whom he periodically parted company when they didn't or couldn't deliver. After ten years in Los Angeles, he went back to New York, where he concluded people were more genuine. Besides, as he told himself, he preferred live stage to film. Not that he was averse to taking film roles or commercials if offered, and he did have some film walk-ons or one-liners through the years, but his real love, as he trumpeted often, was live theater.

Although he was generally considered reasonably handsome with a rugged, sculpted face, a cleft chin, and good, well-whitened teeth, and a full head of hair now graying at the edges, he saw himself now as a character actor and, as he aged, felt that his casting opportunities might increase as others dropped out of the business. One of his girlfriends told him that his main attraction was that he was handsome, with a body still defined by musculature, and above all, not gay.

His father had been an insurance salesman in Portland, Maine. He was in a nursing home now on the public dole and could not recognize his only son. He had not encouraged his son's setting off on an acting career.

"The world belongs to the salesman," his father had preached.

"Yeah, like Willy Loman," Bruce had countered.

"Who?"

His mother, who had grown up in a tiny town in western Maine, hadn't a clue of her son's passion and died still befuddled.

Some of Bruce's breakups, especially with women not in the business, seemed to have the same root cause, his commitment to his career, more so than settling down and pursuing family life. He framed his excuse in economic terms, pointing out that until he made it, he wouldn't be able to support all the obligations of marriage and the possibility of children. As for the women he lived with who were in the business, it was a given that they were as obsessed as he was in making it in their chosen profession.

One of them had been cast as a regular in a sitcom lasting two seasons, a career spike that was always a prime breakup reason for couples in the business. She now worked as a receptionist in a dental office in the Valley. Considering all the angst, competitiveness, and rejection in the business, he considered waiting on tables as a reasonable enabler, until his acting ship came in. He had steeled himself against the possibility it wouldn't, learning long ago that any negativity and its implications would be counterproductive to his aspirations.

Besides, he had reached an age where other career possibilities had narrowed and he knew in his gut that he would never surrender his dream, no matter what. Marilyn had told him during the first week of their affair that what she admired most about him was his optimism and hopefulness about his career.

"It will happen," he assured her. "You can't get wet unless you're out in the rain."

"That's really inspiring, Bruce," she told him.

Lately though, Marilyn was beginning to sing another tune. She was thirty-six and considered by people of the business as hard to cast, no longer an ingénue and not old enough for real character parts. She continued her acting and voice lessons and had once been an understudy in a long-forgotten off-Broadway musical. A Midwestern girl, she had been helped along early on by her family, her cheerleaders ever since she got the lead parts in her high school plays. They felt certain, along with her neighbors, cousins, and classmates that she was headed to stardom.

By the time she met Bruce, her parents had died, still convinced that she was a star or, at the very least, headed for stardom. She rarely went back to her hometown, fearful of facing those who were once convinced that she would end up on the silver screen or as the toast of Broadway. She had been married for two years to an aspiring artist she met while waiting tables in the meatpacking district in

Manhattan. Frustration and lack of traction as an artist in New York had driven him off to the west somewhere, and she was still searching for him in an effort to finalize a divorce.

With Bruce's never-say-die attitude and optimism, she felt comforted and continued the pursuit of acting jobs. When she was younger, she had studied dance and voice and had been to numerous unsuccessful auditions for the big musicals that left her depressed and disgusted with the process. Once, she had taken a course in how to audition, but it didn't help.

Somehow she soldiered on, bouncing around with various boyfriends until she moved in with Bruce, who seemed the perfect antidote for her galloping sense of failure. Lately, his cheerleading was having less and less effect.

After yet another unsuccessful audition, unable to face the rest of the day, she called in sick for her table-waiting job, went back to the apartment she shared with Bruce, and contemplated her future. It was time, she thought. Time to let go. Although she had come to that point before, Bruce had put her back on track and gave her the push to keep going. Until that moment.

He found her curled up in a fetal position on their battered couch. She had finished a half bottle of wine, which had given her, instead of a high, a massive low.

"Not even a callback," she said. Such tiny bursts of hope were fast disappearing.

"Tomorrow is another day," Bruce said. "Put your head down and move forward."

"Isn't it time you desisted from that bullshit, Bruce?"

"Now, now. You're letting negativity take over. Didn't we agree? No more negativity. We stay in pursuit, always in pursuit."

"Get real, Bruce," she muttered.

"I am real. Stay the course. We're the lucky ones. We know what we want and are willing to follow our dream wherever it takes us."

"Over the bridge that goes nowhere," she sighed, uncurling from her fetal position and pouring herself another glass of wine. She took a deep sip and looked at him with glazed eyes. "Look at me, Bruce. My looks are in decline. I'm thirty-six years old, and I haven't had an acting job or anything close to it in three years."

"Negativity, negativity. Don't you realize how debilitating it is to think like that? That kind of attitude is counterproductive. You've got to look in the mirror and say: I can do it. I can do it. Do you really think that by giving up your dream you'll be better off?"

"Maybe," she shrugged. "There are other things in life."

"Not for people like us, Marilyn. We need the dream. It makes us run. In the end, we'll prevail. You'll see."

"Computers," she said suddenly. "That seems to be the thing. Computers. Or maybe even becoming a personal trainer. What's wrong with switching careers? You've got to be flexible."

"You're an actor, Marilyn, a performer. That's what you are. One day…"

She stood up, paced the floor over the threadbare Oriental rug that they bought at a sale a couple of years ago. Then she looked around at the mismatched furniture, mostly castoffs that they purchased at the Salvation Army store.

"This place sucks," she said. "A dump." She sighed. "The American dream."

"Marilyn, cut it out, you're filling the place with bad Karma."

"And you're filling the place with bullshit."

Bruce laughed or wanted it to be seen as a laugh. He could see it coming. He had seen it all before. Why are these breakups such clichés, he wondered? He would have said so, but he had no desire to hurt her.

"Maybe in the morning," he muttered, singing a few bars of the *Annie* song. "The sun'll come out tomorrow…"

For a long time, she continued to pace. He watched her as she moved with ever-increasing speed up and back, moving her lips as if she were talking to herself. Finally, she turned.

"Do you really believe you're an actor, Bruce?"

Here it comes, he thought.

"In my gut, Marilyn. In my gut."

She paced again, shook her head, and turned to face him.

"You're not an actor, Bruce. You're just lying to yourself. You're a goddamned waiter, that's what you are, a fucking waiter. And I'm a waitress. That is what defines us. That is our occupation. We are not in show business. We are in the food industry, hustling tips to get by, barely." She grew silent for a moment, paced, then began again. "Look at this dump. Where are we going, Bruce? Yeah, we're actors, but in the play in our head, a fucking fantasy. Look down the road, Bruce. Where are we going? I'll tell you where. From table to table, telling people about the specials. Something something on a bed of something something."

Suddenly she screamed, then collapsed on the couch.

"Enough is enough," she muttered.

Bruce had listened with patient resolve. He had heard it all before. She was jumping ship. It was useless to convince her otherwise. Sometimes he had seen it happen by degrees. Sometimes, as with Marilyn, it would happen suddenly, like an epiphany. Out of her own frustration, she had lashed out at him.

"Nobody, but nobody," he told her gently, "will ever take away my dream. Not ever. If you were a real actor, a committed actor, you would understand. I am an actor. I will always be an actor until the day I die."

That said, he went into the bedroom, brushed his teeth, rubbed on night cream, put on his pajamas, and got into bed. He had to get up early. He had an acting class in the morning.

GONE

It was her choice, a McDonald's in the East Village, and he stood for awhile, out of view, looking through the window. Of course he was afraid, anxious, uncertain. He hadn't seen his daughter in three years, since she was sixteen and had disappeared. "Leave that alone," he begged himself.

When you turn something over in your own mind for three years, it becomes a lingering, chronic pain. Everything changes. The anger solidifies into icy rage. He needed to squelch that now. It was bad strategy.

From this distance, he could only see her in profile, vaguely familiar, under a profusion of harsh red hair that used to be silky blonde, golden in his memory. She wore dark sunglasses, a strange accessory in this sunless environment. Apparently, the place had just opened and the customers were a tired, scruffy lot of all ages and genders. The November weather was cloudy, chilled, and cast a pall of drabness over everything, which he noted, was drab to begin with, despite the attempt of the restaurant to contrive joy, a commodity that just wasn't there.

Her complexion was ashen, unhealthy, the once-round, naturally rouged cheeks flattened, and fiery red lipstick was heavily laid on. She was wearing a long-sleeved, beige, tight turtleneck that emphasized how thin she had gotten. Worse, she looked ten years older, maybe more. Oddly, he hoped that he was mistaken and this was not his daughter. Her entire demeanor seemed to fit in with the gloomy atmosphere.

He waited, watching, trying desperately to control himself. A sob shook his chest and he sucked in some hard, deep breaths to steady himself. Finally, he walked in, forcing a smile, feeling his face cracking.

"Peggy," he said.

She nodded, and he knew her thin smile was as forced as his own. "Daddy."

He feared bending to offer her a kiss, and she made no move to stand. In front of her was a cup of coffee. For a moment, he stood watching her, but since he could not see her eyes, he was unsure about any contact.

"What shall I get you?" he asked, stupidly. After all, they were there for breakfast. There had been a go-between from back home in Boise, Charlotte Gordon, an old classmate who was attending NYU in Manhattan. She had seen and reported Peggy's whereabouts. By then, he lived in Los Angeles, the family splintered, the blame for which sat in front of him, the missing daughter.

Since neither he nor his wife could understand a reason for her disappearance they had blamed each other, and her sibling blamed them both. There was no secret between them where the blame really lay; it simply could not be abided. There was no cure for it but separation.

What he had wanted to know for three years was why. She seemed perfectly happy, the picture of a loving daughter, integrated into their world. There had been no hint, no clue, no issue, no abuse, nothing apparent, however they had searched themselves and the environment that surrounded her. There were just no answers, only questions.

"I am going away. I hate it here." The words were scrawled on a little paste-up square, now wrinkled from the perpetual folding and unfolding. Why? He and his wife had gone the usual route: police, missing persons, private detectives, and long, introspective self-analysis and confrontations with each other. What had they done? It was increasingly impossible to live without answers.

She had disappeared with nothing but her clothes. Her room had remained exactly as she left it. His wife left it untouched as a kind of shrine, and after awhile, going into that room for him had become unbearable. Inexplicably, his wife spent much of her time there. The blame had become insidious, like acid, eating away at them.

How could they not have suspected? No matter how hard they tried they could find no secret life, no evidence of adolescent unrequited love, no gender confusion, no drugs, no cult seduction, no argument, no visible anger. She lived in a loving, supportive family environment. All of her friends and classmates were as baffled as they were. Such bafflement and confusion became a way of life, a creeping emotional upheaval that exploded, finally, into a kind of silent chaos, and there seemed no solution but for him to leave. There were no tears on his wife's part, as if such a move was ordained, necessary, a logical outcome brought about by the missing daughter.

Perhaps it was his obsession to find her. He left no stone unturned. No expense was too much. Then, out of the blue, a classmate, Charlotte Gordon, had seen her and got in touch with him. Charlotte had explained that she had been sworn to secrecy, but that if he came to New York, she might call him at his hotel and maybe, just maybe, she might see him. And she had, hence this meeting.

Their conversation had been short, practically nonexistent. She simply informed him of where they were to meet.

"So what would you like?" he asked.

"Big Mac and fries, large Coke," she said, her voice harsher than he remembered. He wanted to say: "For breakfast?" but desisted. Standing in line, he got her the Big Mac and ordered a chicken sandwich and a coffee for himself. He had no appetite and looked at the mushy mess in its paper wrapping, hoping he would not gag.

"I'm glad you could see me," he said, watching her pick up the Big Mac. Her nails were painted fire-engine red, and they shook as she lifted the sandwich and bit deep into it, not dainty as he remembered her. His daughter. How could this have happened? No, he forced himself, leave that alone.

"Charlotte meeting you, quite a coincidence."

She nodded between chewing. He studied her face, but the dark glasses continued to hide any clue to contact. She poured ketchup into a cardboard plate and dipped a salted fry into it.

"So, what is your life like?" he asked cautiously.

She shrugged and smiled thinly.

"Cool," she said.

"Meaning?"

"Not bad."

"What are you doing?"

"Things."

"Just curious." He grew silent for a moment, speculating. Was she a prostitute? A drug addict? Her exterior seemed hard, her aspect vulgar. How did she survive?

"I'm sure you know that we've been looking for you a long time."

He felt this overwhelming need to know. She continued to eat, as if she had not heard his words.

"I am your father, Peggy."

Her use of the old term "daddy" had probably encouraged him. But then, that was the only word she had used for him from the moment she had learned to talk. He was daddy. Daddy. Perhaps he should have put it differently: I am your daddy.

"I'm Betty now," she said.

"Not Peggy?"

"Peggy no more."

"Do you use your last name?" he asked. Obviously not, since she was untraceable under the family name.

She shook her head.

"What is it now?"

"It's not important," she said.

"Are you married?"

Instinctively, he looked at her left hand. There was no wedding ring.

"No way," she said.

He watched her in silence as she ate her sandwich, occasionally washing it down with a sip of Coke. Frustration was beginning to gnaw at him. He wanted to tear away her sunglasses. Why are you hiding? He wanted to scream out the questions. Finally, he said:

"Is there anything I can do? I mean to help."

She shrugged.

"I don't know."

"Look Peggy...I mean Betty. I'm not asking for an explanation. It's too late for that. You know that the family has split. Charlotte must have told you. Someday..." He felt himself losing control, took a deep breath, then began again. "I have an idea." He had been thinking about this ever since he learned where she was. "At the very least, call your mother and brother. Even to just say hello, even to say 'I'm alright.' Just that even."

She appeared to be listening, but made no comment.

"Better yet, you might hop a plane. I'll give you money for the ticket. Just drop by, even if it's just to chat, or give us a telephone number. Having contact, even at a distance, wouldn't hurt anybody."

He had rehearsed a thousand speeches in his mind and this was coming out badly. His emotions were charging and recharging, running the gamut, eroding his discipline. She remained silent. Beyond the dark glasses, he couldn't even tell if she was listening, although he seemed to sense that she was watching him. There were so many things he wanted to say, especially the one statement meant to spur guilt: Your disappearance broke up the family. How could you?

He held back, of course, fearing her anger. Because she was nineteen, he had no legal hold on her. Before he had met her, he had taken out five hundred dollars from an ATM. He hadn't very much more in the account. If she needed anything, anything, he would have found a way to provide it. He was her daddy, for crying out loud. She was his child, he thought. Why was she doing this?

"Tell you what," he said, forcing a broad smile. He wanted to reach out and embrace her, forgive her, end this baffling alienation. "As I said before, no explanation needed. I just want you to know that we are there for you, always and evermore. You are our daughter. Nothing can ever break that bond. Do you understand that, Peggy?"

"Betty," she said, finishing the Big Mac. She wiped her lips, and he noted that the napkin was smeared with lipstick.

"Betty," he repeated, continuing his smile. His eyes hurt from trying to see beyond the dark lenses. He removed the cash from his pocket. It was folded, mostly fifties. "I want you to take this. No conditions. If you want to see your mother, you could buy a ticket. I live in L.A., and if you want to join me there, you are more than welcome. Do you understand what I'm saying? Whatever has happened is water under the bridge. Maybe someday…" He stopped short. Going there seemed pointless at that moment.

He reached out and touched her palm. It was cold. But the touch of her flesh triggered memories. Suddenly, he saw her for the first time from behind the glass of the maternity ward, a tiny bundle of flesh, her features contorted with crying. Was it the cry of joy or pain? Had she been sorry to be born?

He pushed the bills into her hand and closed her fingers over it.

"Remember, if you ever need anything."

She nodded and her lips seemed to offer a smile, but he wasn't sure. Then she stood up and looked around.

"Be back. Off to the ladies' room," she said pleasantly. He watched her go.

"I'll wait," he said, but as soon as she was gone, he went into the men's room. It was empty, and he leaned against the sink, broke down, and sobbed like a child. He could not stop. As a man came in, he dipped his head into the sink and tried to stop sobbing by sloshing cold water on his face. Finally, he succeeded and wiped his face and eyes on a paper towel, looking briefly at himself in the mirror.

"Why?" he asked his image, striking out with his hand against the glass. It did not break the mirror, although he did feel the pain in his knuckles. Taking a deep breath, he did the best he could to appear calm and went back into the dining room and sat at the same table where his chicken sandwich lay, cold and soggy. He lifted his coffee container and sipped, but the coffee was cold as well.

He waited for her return, watching the door of the ladies' room. He continued to wait. A heavyset, young Hispanic woman was cleaning dirty tables, and he gave her five dollars to check on his daughter in the ladies' room. She came back quickly.

"Gone," she said.

He sat for a few moments more, got up, went outside, and looked in either direction. There was no sign of her.

THE OBITUARY READER

"It's the first thing I read," Barry Fine said, referring to the obituaries.

"That's ridiculous," Mildred, his wife, said. "It's like a kind of death watch."

They sat over breakfast every day in their Manhattan apartment reading the *New York Times*. He looked at the table of contents and always insisted on reading the obituaries before other parts of the paper.

He had just turned seventy and although he had always read the obituaries casually, he spent more time at it these days, reading the small paid-for obits as well as the headlined deaths. It was not uncommon for him to find familiar names among the paid-for obits since he had grown up in New York City and had gone to elementary, high school, and college in New York and had worked there all of his life.

Of course, it was mostly males he had known who periodically showed up in the paid-for obits, which were inserted by relatives of the deceased or organizations that they had joined. Not everyone inserted these paid announcements. Still, it was the only way he could possibly be informed about the death of anyone he had known in his lifetime. It was less likely that he would find females he had known because the chances were that most of those from his generation used their married names.

Barry was still healthy at his age and busy with his accounting practice, but he had already attended a number of funerals of people in his age bracket, both relatives and friends, and the idea of diminishing time was beginning to occupy his thoughts.

"Today's seventy is like yesterday's fifty," his wife told him, irritated that he was dwelling too heavily on the subject of life's end. She was sixty-five, and they had been married forty-one years. Their two children were grown, had their own families, and lived in other parts of the country. It was one of their regrets that the kids hadn't stayed in New York, but, as they both acknowledged, the world had changed and mobility in pursuit of career advancement and economic self-interest was the operative word these days.

With regret, both husband and wife discussed this often, since they were what were called empty nesters and, although they saw their children and grandchildren a number of times each year at holiday occasions, it wasn't the same as growing up within easy reach of grandparents, aunts, uncles, and cousins who all lived in the New York area. Both of them had been brought up within close proximity of extended family circles, which was less the norm these days.

Barry admitted that he read the obituaries from right to left, meaning that he read the ages first, comparing them to his own. When he saw reports of people dying in their late eighties and nineties, he felt encouraged about his own future, and when he saw people who had died younger than himself, he counted himself among the lucky survivors with, admittedly, some secret satisfaction. Mildred insisted that he was being ghoulish and obsessed with dying, although, to be sure, she too read the more publicized obituaries of the various celebrities whose deaths were sensationalized.

He would often mutter the same comments each time he read the obituaries, much to his wife's amusement; like "Everybody dies" or "Our world is disappearing," especially when a movie star, politician, sports figure, or popular singer's death was announced. They were, after all, part of the culture of his time and their dying was certainly a benchmark event, a chapter ended, one more nail in the coffin of their generational experience.

At times, he would discover that when he mentioned people popular in his youth to a much younger person their eyes would glaze over with non-recognition. The older he got, he noticed that whole categories of younger men and women had no knowledge of the people who were significant to his generation. At first, he had attributed this lack of knowledge to ignorance, until it became apparent that the names, like products that had disappeared, were no longer applicable or relevant and had disappeared from any mention in the media.

Although he tried to keep up with the popular culture, he could no longer identify the names of people about whom he read in the gossip columns or in the magazines he skimmed through while waiting for his doctor or dental appointments. When he spent any time with his grandchildren, he would see how truly far the gap between the generations had widened.

Another thing, aside from optimism or luck, that he gleaned from the obituaries was a kind of stimulant to long-term memory when he read the obituary of someone he had gone to school with or who touched his life in some significant way.

One day, he read in the paid-for obituaries the death of Aaron Schyler. He hadn't thought seriously about Aaron for many, many years, although the incident that hung forever in his mind had occurred more than fifty-five years ago. Not that he had been in denial, but it was, certainly at the time and in the immediate aftermath, a memorable event in his experience. Not long after that event Aaron had disappeared from his life, and he had never heard from him or about him. Until that moment.

As teenagers, perhaps during a two-year period, say ages thirteen to fifteen, they were inseparable, true buddies. They played together, studied together, were always in each other's houses, which adjoined one another in the Brooklyn neighborhood where they both lived. They went to the movies together every Saturday, were on the same baseball team, had puppy-love affairs with girls who were also fast friends, did their homework together, and supported each other in all of their endeavors.

They joined the Boy Scouts the same day and went to Boy Scout camp together in Narrowsburg, New York. Not a day went by when they didn't see each other. Seeing Aaron's obituary brought back the old memory of that time in Boy Scout camp that could never be

WARREN ADLER

completely erased or dismissed.

While at camp, they often took overnights with their camp mates
and invariably shared a pup tent. What had happened between them,
in retrospect, was merely a minor incident and one that was common
among teenage boys in that era and probably more common today.

It was, he remembered, a particularly cold night, and they shared
a sleeping bag and found themselves sleeping like spoons. What had
happened was that during the night Barry had awakened with an
erection and induced himself to orgasm by putting his penis in the
crack of Aaron's rump. The activity had awakened Aaron and instead
of objecting, he had said, "Now me." And Barry had reversed
himself.

Being teenagers, they were seduced by the pleasure of their
orgasms and spent the entire night masturbating each other.
Although rarely discussed at the time, it was quite common for
teenage boys to display their erections and engage in what was then
known as circle jerks, where the trick was to see who squirted first.
The laughable assertion in the Boy Scout handbook of that time that
masturbation led to insanity was a source of amusement and ridicule
at that moment of raging hormones and the discovery of the
mechanics of penis erectus.

It was, after all, ages before sex education in the schools, and
teenage boys usually gleaned their knowledge about the mystery of
sex from other teenage boys. Neither Barry nor Aaron's parents ever
discussed sex with their sons. It was considered one of those hidden
dirty subjects, never to be mentioned, and it was certainly not
considered a parental responsibility to enlighten them about it. Barry
acknowledged that this might not have been a universal experience,
but it certainly was his and Aaron's. It was an era long before
pornography in magazines, film, and video were readily available.
Indeed, teenage boys would rifle through issues of *National
Geographic* looking for topless African women for a furtive glimpse
of the naked female breast to induce sexual fantasies.

Teenage girls, Barry remembered, were even less educated on
that subject, and some mothers actually taught their daughters that
kissing led to pregnancy. In fact, fear of pregnancy was the

146

absolutely primary hysterical fear of all teenage girls at that time. Such fears not withstanding, the girls were not averse to what was then called necking, and "feeling up" was what petting meant.

As for homosexuality, it was barely on their radar. In that era and in those old Brooklyn neighborhoods, people with such propensities were effeminate and fey and known as queers or homos and always seemed to be elsewhere or anonymous, at least in Barry's circles. None of the sexual acts engaged in by teenage boys seemed outside the range of normal conduct. Barry could honestly not recall anyone he had known in those days as queer. Such memories, Barry knew, were private and unexpressed in those terms in these enlightened contemporary times and would be considered politically incorrect or misinterpreted or even homophobic by today's standards. The world certainly had changed, Barry reflected, and he knew at least in that respect he had changed as well.

Such thoughts rose in his memory after reading the obituary of Aaron Schyler, largely triggered by that long-ago experience. It had baffled Barry for years why after he and Aaron came home from Boy Scout camp that summer, things had changed between them. It wasn't exactly an abrupt cleavage, but something was decidedly different between them. They drifted apart slowly. Aaron developed new friendships and Barry kept his hurt to himself, never confronting Aaron for reasons for this slow alienation.

Sometime later, the Schyler family moved out of the neighborhood and Aaron and Barry's friendship became a faded memory, although on occasion, triggered by an errant thought, Barry would ponder the puzzle of their strange drift. Was it because of that night in the pup tent? Or something else? Something inadvertently said? Some innocent slight?

It had often baffled him that although he had grown up in New York and had known hundreds of people during his childhood, youth, and business career, he rarely met anyone from elementary or high school and only on rare occasions someone from college. Perhaps, he decided, it was a New York thing. In the frenetic mixing bowl of a huge big city, people dispersed, moved to other places, other suburbs, other neighborhoods, and formed other friendships and alliances connected to their careers.

Occasionally, he did observe on the street what seemed like a familiar face, but often age had done its work, and it was difficult to identify for certain someone he had known long ago and he usually passed them by. He had never seen Aaron Schyler again after he had moved out of the old neighborhood, had never even seen anyone who remotely resembled Aaron in all the years that had passed.

At the breakfast table that morning, such questions came to the surface and once again stimulated the old mystery of their alienation. In the obituary he noted that services would be held in the Riverside Chapel at eleven that morning and, without any clear reason or intent, Barry decided he would attend.

Barry took a place in the rear of the chapel, noting that the auditorium was respectably filled. The coffin lay in front of the chapel, and a man in a dark suit spoke first. It was not a religious service, and the man who spoke offered heartfelt words of praise for Aaron Schyler, who had apparently touched many lives.

It wasn't until a second man spoke that Barry got the obvious message. Aaron Schyler was gay, and most of the people in the chapel were males, although there were a number of women.

"I lived with this giving person most of my life," the second man said. "He was a good loving person and made my life meaningful and important." As the man spoke, tears inexplicably moistened Barry's eyes and rolled down his cheeks. He did not comprehend any more of what the man was saying, but his sense of loss and grieving was beyond his understanding. Still, the mystery of their alienation persisted. Was the night in the pup tent some epiphany for Aaron? Was there a lot more to it for Aaron than teenagers having a little sexual fun?

Was their intense friendship more than met the eye? Barry knew his grief was real. Had he loved Aaron in a different way? Had Aaron loved him and felt uncomfortable by the feeling or the thought of it? Or was Barry indulging himself in something that he could never understand, since he had never had any urge to make love to a man and considered himself throughout his life unalterably heterosexual?

Finally, the service was over, and the group waited as others filed out behind the coffin, then the audience began to leave and he with them. For some reason, perhaps it was because of the preponderance of men, or something else, he felt oddly different, as if he did not belong there.

In the street, he walked toward the subway, still filled with this overwhelming, inexplicable, and profound sense of loss.

THE DOG STORY

"How am I supposed to work?" Milton complained. "The mutt whines all day long."

Milton wrote mysteries and worked at a computer on his desk most of the day. His room was on the other side of the wall from Mrs. Martinez's apartment. It had actually been a second bedroom, but he and his wife, Barbara, had converted it to his writing room. The room had built-in bookshelves and a studio couch where Milton stretched out to nap, usually in the afternoons, when he completed his self-imposed writing allotment for the day.

Mrs. Martinez, a widow, shared a landing on their fifteenth-floor co-op on Madison and 81st Street. There were only two apartments on their floor, but the configuration was such that the wall of Milton's writing room was the same wall where the Martinez's dog was ensconced all day long.

Invariably, the dog, which was of some small white fluffy breed with coal black eyes, began to whine just about the time that Milton sat down at his desk to write, which apparently was the same time that Mrs. Martinez went off to work at some job in Wall Street. It was an eerie sound, like a low human whimper of pain, but the fact that it was on the other side of his wall, probably no more than a couple of feet from his computer, gave it special significance, at least to Milton.

It wasn't that way when the Frazers lived there. They spent six months in Florida and even when they lived in the apartment, the bedroom that was on the other side of the wall, was rarely, if ever, used.

Ever since Milton had complained to Mrs. Martinez about the

dog's whine, her attitude was frosty. Not that she had ever been friendly, but she did offer a smile and a pleasant greeting, although it was clear that she had no intention of socializing with her neighbors. Neighborliness had a different connotation in Manhattan than it did in the rest of the country. Proximity did not equate with intimacy.

Mrs. Martinez, an imperious type with ramrod posture, was always immaculately dressed and coiffed, her jet black hair parted in the middle over a high forehead and a decidedly feral and suspicious look in her eyes, which grew more hostile after Milton's complaint.

"As you know, the building allows pets," Mrs. Martinez replied indignantly without apology. Milton's explanation, he quickly discovered, was futile and immediately dismissed.

"The fact is," Milton explained to Barbara, "this dog and I are the only two residents on this floor during the day."

He was able to ascertain by deduction, since he was a mystery writer, that the little dog was paper trained and rarely taken out for walks except on weekends when he noted through the door peephole that Mrs. Martinez carried the dog into the elevator and Harry the doorman confirmed that she took the dog for a walk, probably in Central Park, which was a half a block away from their apartment.

At first, Milton was reluctant to bring up the matter with the co-op board. A disciplined writer, he was very selfish in the use of his time and was not inclined to set off a protracted struggle with the detail-oriented, overzealous board, most of whose members were lawyers.

"It's such a cute little pooch," Barbara said.

"You don't have to live with his whining all day long."

"Buy yourself some earplugs," she suggested.

"I did. They're uncomfortable and I can't hear the downstairs buzzer."

She was more amused than sympathetic. The fact was that she was very partial to dogs and spoke lovingly of Bitsy, the standard poodle she had owned growing up in New Hampshire, and often expressed regret that they didn't own a dog.

He had rejected the idea. He didn't want the hassle and

convinced her that it would be unfair and too confining to have a dog in a New York apartment.

For similar reasons, they had postponed having children. Besides, they were fixated on their careers. He was into his third book of his mystery series, which had given him a modicum of notoriety, and she was a rising executive in academic administration. Both were on the cusp of forty and they had grown too used to their lifestyle and unwilling to take on further responsibilities.

The whining little dog next door had become, at least for him, a disruption. For her, it was barely a blip on her environmental radar.

"I never hear it," Barbara told him.

"Of course not. You're at the office. It stops when the lady gets home from work."

Barbara was out of the house during the day at her job as an assistant dean at Hunter College, not far from their apartment. On weekends, she rarely went into his writing room and the fact was that apparently, he had deduced, Mrs. Martinez gave the dog the run of the house during those days. It seemed obvious, too, that the little mutt's whining sounds were probably signs of loneliness.

Milton's work began to suffer. He became irritable and distracted. He was not meeting his five-page-a-day allotment and, worse, he couldn't even take his daily nap.

"I must say, Mrs. Martinez," he told her, catching her on the landing as she left for work in the morning. "I'm trying to be neighborly but your dog's whining during the day is really interfering with my work. In fact, it's driving me crazy. Perhaps if he wasn't cooped up in that room all day long. You see, we share a wall…"

He could see that Mrs. Martinez was becoming indignant, her eyes narrowing, a flush rising on the high cheekbones of her dark complexion.

"Don't tell me how to live my life," she sneered. "Besides my Vickie is not a he. She is sweet and gentle and quite content in her room during the day."

Her room, Milton thought startled. She has a whole room for herself.

"Hell," he complained to Barbara. "Imagine that. Think of the cost. The woman is crazy. Her second bedroom is for her dog."

"She loves her dog. People become very possessive about their pets. I can understand that."

"If she's so attached to the pooch, she should take it to work with her."

"Why not suggest it?" Barbara said, chuckling.

"I value my life."

"Then find a way to cope. Write in the kitchen."

"The creative life requires ambience. I love my room."

He could tell that Barbara was not as sympathetic as he would have liked. At one point he persuaded her to postpone her leaving for her job and listen to this doggie serenade that was making his life an agony.

"I can see where it can be somewhat of annoyance, but I'm sure you can find a way to cope. I mean it's not real loud, not vicious watchdog barking. Why not try music? You like music. Use your iPod. Beethoven's Fourth would do nicely."

"Not while I write. My muse doesn't like music when I'm creating."

Milton had the impression Barbara was not completely on his side. Finally, he decided to bring the matter up with the co-op board, who agreed that they would hold a meeting to discuss the matter and he was welcome to state his case.

Mrs. Martinez, as a member in good standing of the co-op, was also invited to rebut his complaint. She brought Vickie to the meeting and some members of the board petted and fussed over her. Vickie was remarkably silent, very friendly. She delicately licked fingers and was downright charming.

He rehearsed his plea with great care and thought he had made an impassioned case for his rights as a creative artist to work in peace within his own boundaries. At the tail end of his argument, he delved into the psychological.

"I'm telling you she makes these whining sounds as soon as Mrs. Martinez leaves, as if she were crying out of loneliness. It is, in my opinion, not a healthy situation for anyone who loves animals. The dog is a prisoner in the woman's apartment."

"You sound like a dog psychologist, Mr. Preston," one of the board members commented as he stroked Vickie's head.

"She is a member of my family. I love her as my own child," Mrs. Martinez said with passion. "People who love animals will understand. This man hates animals."

"She has her own room," Milton interjected. "Can you imagine? One of the rooms in this co-op is reserved for a dog."

"I have every right to use my apartment as I see fit." Her eyes roamed the faces of the dour board members like spotlights. "This is a free country, and property rights are its foundation."

"I have the right to my privacy," Milton opined. He could tell that he was losing the battle, and the next day he was proven correct.

"We've canvassed all of the co-op members," the Board Chairman told him in a telephone call. "No one has heard anything that would constitute grounds for any action."

"I live on the other side of that wall. It annoys the shit out of me and interferes with my livelihood. I demand action."

"You always have the option to sell your share in the building, Mr. Preston," one of the board members said with obvious irritation.

Milton was furious.

"Apparently an animal in this building has more rights than a human," he muttered as he left the meeting.

"A dog gets more respect than a creative artist," he complained to Barbara.

"I will not move," Barbara said when he reported on the meeting. "Under no circumstances."

It became increasingly difficult for Milton to work. The rhythm of his life had been totally disrupted.

"I'd like to strangle that little bitch," Milton cried. "I want her dead."

He sensed that he was entering the tunnel of a deep depression. As his work diminished, then stopped altogether, he grew despondent and began to fantasize about ways to eliminate his nemesis. He was, after all, a mystery writer and pretty nimble when it came to creating murder scenarios.

On the Internet, he researched various poisoning methods,

finally concluding that he would, under the circumstances, be the logical culprit and a lawsuit or worse was sure to ensue in the wake of the assassination.

Disposing of Vickie soon turned into an obsession, and he spent what was normally his writing time figuring out ways to eliminate his tormentor in a way that would not come back to haunt him. His first step would have to be breaking into Mrs. Martinez's apartment, no small feat, since every apartment door was equipped with excellent locks.

Harry the doorman and his night replacement Barney kept duplicate keys in a small cupboard near the service elevator. Both were trusted employees of the coop and when an apartment owner forgot a key, they would produce the proper key and open the apartment door. Security procedures were very strict and no one was able to enter the apartment without being announced and the doormen controlled the self-service elevator.

There had never been a break-in or burglary in the apartment building in anyone's memory, and the tenants felt secure in the care of their ever watchful doormen and the other employees of the building including the superintendent, the porter and the managing agent. It was an older building built in the early thirties of the last century with twenty floors.

Most of the apartment owners, including Milton and Barbara and the Martinez woman, allowed the doorman to enter their apartments with the duplicate keys when a delivery was special and would be safer inside the apartment and such action was arranged in advance by the owner.

Such details were crucial to Milton's plans as he plotted during every waking hour how he was going to eliminate his nemesis and promulgate the perfect crime, avoiding any proof that he was the perpetrator. As for the process of elimination, he determined that he would somehow get the dog out of the apartment, find a way to get it out of the lobby without arousing the suspicion of the doorman and drive it outside the city for disposal.

The disposal issue became a test of his nature, which was decidedly non-violent, and it became apparent after much soul searching that he could not be a murderer even if the victim was a dog. Instead, he determined that he would remove the dog's registration medallion and deposit her anonymously at an animal shelter. The rest would be up to the compassionate shelter people and those who might wish to adopt the dog, who was obviously expensive, pedigreed, and cute enough to attract a new owner.

After due deliberation, he realized that the first place Mrs. Martinez would look would be an animal shelter in the city. He rejected that idea in favor of finding an animal shelter outside the city limits, perhaps Westchester County.

He felt more and more exhilarated by his plotting effort. Perhaps someday it might find its way into a book.

As for the effect of his action on Mrs. Martinez, he could generate little pity. Collateral damage, he assured himself. Of course, he would have to survive her scrutiny and accusations, but he felt fully prepared for such an onslaught. This was a core issue in his life and it had to be resolved.

"You seem in fine fettle these days, Milton," Barbara told him. "You no longer are fixated on Mrs. Martinez's dog."

"I'm coping," he replied with a snicker.

There were steps to be taken. He had to establish a pattern, one that would pass muster in any investigation. Under the pretense that he was researching a new book, he would roll a small suitcase through the lobby, offering Harry, the doorman on day duty, the comment that he was transporting books back and forth from the library for research.

"Not so simple being a writer. Lots of reading required," he would tell Harry as he entered and exited the apartment lobby. After a few weeks of establishing the pattern, he pretended to have lost his key, which gave him an opportunity to follow Harry to the place where he kept the keys, which were neatly hung by apartment number on hooks in the key cupboard behind the elevators.

By establishing Harry's work patterns, he was able to determine when Harry popped out briefly to order a sandwich for lunch, a matter of a few short minutes, but just enough time for him to filch the key to the Martinez apartment, open it, then bring the key back to its proper place in the cupboard. Of course, everything had to work like clockwork. He had to get his car out of the nearby garage, find a parking spot away from where it could be seen from the building, execute the key theft, remove the dog, and achieve his getaway.

This required numerous dry runs. Of course there were still risks. Above all, Vickie had to be quiet when he passed through the lobby with his small rolling suitcase in which she would be sequestered. He had to take other precautions as well like wearing rubber gloves to prevent any fingerprints on the door or interior of the Martinez apartment.

He was, he knew, breaking and entering, perpetrating a burglary and kidnapping a dog, or dog-napping as he referred to the action in his own mind. He was, he knew, committing an illegal act and, if caught, would require prosecution. Weighing all the risk factors, he decided that it was a question of his sanity and his career. To him, this was the most serious crisis in his life. He felt that he had no choice.

When he was certain that he had laid the groundwork, he picked the date for his action. He had done his research well, finding an animal shelter in Westchester County and "casing" it carefully. To further disguise his identity, he bought a wig, glasses, and false moustache from a magic shop in Greenwich Village. His plan was to get to the animal shelter, drop the unidentified dog off at the shelter, and quickly disappear.

It turned out that the numerous fictional plots he had concocted as a mystery writer was remarkably prescient. On the chosen day, at exactly noon, he took the elevator to the lobby. Harry had ducked out to get sandwiches. Quickly, he found the key on the hook labeled by the number of the Martinez apartment. He dashed back to the elevator, which he had switched to stop, went up to the fifteenth floor, opened the door to the Martinez apartment which he kept open by a wooden stopper he had prepared, then went down again and quickly replaced the key. He had also taken the precaution of wearing rubber gloves to hide any fingerprints.

In the Martinez apartment, he found little Vickie in her own room, paper spread on the floor on which she had peed and defecated her tiny leavings. He was able, in a split second's observation, to see how beautifully Mrs. Martinez had decorated the room, all in pink with a pink little bed, a pink food-and-water bowl, and low pink upholstered furniture for Vickie to lounge on. The pink bed was located exactly on the opposite side of his wall, no more than, at the most, a foot away.

Seeing him enter her room, she stopped whining immediately, wagged her tail excitedly, and stared at him with her large coal black eyes. She was surprisingly light and cuddled caressingly against his arm as he carried her out of the apartment. Then he carefully locked the door to the Martinez apartment, placed Vickie in his rolling small suitcase in which he had wrapped the wig, moustache, and sunglasses in a plastic case, and proceeded down the elevator.

Moving quickly, he waved to Harry who was eating his sandwich and rolled his suitcase into the pleasant sunny spring day elated with the brilliance of his well-prepared exercise in dog-napping. Once in the car, he took Vickie out of the suitcase and sat her beside him. As he drove toward the West Side Highway, she cuddled close and, despite the hatred he had harbored for her all those months, he found himself caressing the soft fur of her shoulder.

Do not waver, he urged himself. Show no sentiment. If you want your career back keep going. By then, he convinced himself that Vickie was sure to find a new owner who would lovingly care for her. After all, she was an expensive breed, beautifully groomed and, at the very least, paper trained, and would make an excellent pet for anyone who appreciated beautiful animals. He was tempted to attach a note to her that might read: *Do not leave alone.*

He parked his car a few blocks from the animal shelter, then donning his disguise, he waited for just the right moment to drop the dog off at the shelter. He felt certain he had not been observed, and this method of dog disposal without comment was probably a common occurrence, given the guilt and shame that might be associated with such abandonment.

Two hours later, relieved and exultant, he was back at his computer, luxuriating in the retrieved silence as he attempted to pick up the threads of his mystery novel. Expecting the impending storm when Mrs. Martinez returned from work to find Vickie missing, he had trouble finding his creative muse as he lingered over the scenario of what to expect and his own rehearsed reaction.

The hysterics arrived on cue, and the activity on the landing picked up steam just as Barbara returned to work.

"What's going on?" Barbara asked as she entered the apartment. "There're two policemen on the landing and Harry the doorman as well. I caught a glimpse of Mrs. Martinez. She is totally deranged."

"What could it be?" Milton asked innocently.

Not long after her arrival, Barbara opened the door to the policemen, who demanded to see Milton. But before she could invite them in, Mrs. Martinez, hair askew, clothes in total disarray, her expression belching fire, pushed her way into the apartment.

At that moment, Milton, hearing the racket and steeling himself for what he knew was coming, came out of his now quiet writer's room wearing a contrived expression of confusion and surprise.

"There he is, that bastard," Mrs. Martinez screamed. "What have you done with her? I'm sure he did it. He is the one. I want him arrested and jailed. I'm sure he murdered her. He hated her. You filthy murdering swine. You rat…" She continued in this vein until she tried to push past the two burly policemen and physically attack Milton. One of the policemen grabbed her and dragged her out of the apartment, although her screams did not abate.

"Her dog is missing," the remaining policeman shrugged. "She thinks you had something to do with it."

"That is ridiculous," Milton said, exchanging glances with his wife, who looked somewhat skeptical. She invited the policeman into the kitchen where, seated around the kitchen table, the policeman, a thin Hispanic looking man, took notes.

Milton calmly explained what had transpired over the last few months, how he had complained about the whining dog because it had interfered with his work. He was careful not to leave out a single detail of his campaign.

"I lost the battle," he said finally. "I had to live with the annoyance and find ways to cope."

To his credit, the policeman probed deeply, taking notes. He was thorough and properly suspicious, and Milton answered all his questions with, he thought, believable deniability. He doubted, however, that he would have the skill to beat a lie detector.

Finally the policeman slapped shut his notebook, shrugged, and left the apartment.

"All this for a dog," Milton sighed.

"To Mrs. Martinez she was family, her child," Barbara said.

"She probably couldn't stand being left alone and beat it."

"How could she possibly do that?" Barbara said.

"Stranger things have happened."

Milton knew that the investigation was far from over although he feigned disinterest, although Barbara, he suspected, looked at him with suspicion. From Harry she learned that the disappearance was indeed a mystery and that Mrs. Martinez had apparently lapsed into a deep depression, which apparently required hospitalization.

"Are you sure you had nothing to do with this Milton?"

"Such a question is demeaning," was his response.

Nevertheless, as he had expected, the investigation continued. He was interviewed by a plainclothes detective the next day and had to confront questioning from the board at a hastily convened meeting two days later.

"I am the logical suspect," he told them patiently fielding their questions. "I understand your concerns."

Racking his brain to see if he had overlooked something, he did experience a trill of panic when he realized that the rolling suitcase might have revealed some clue, like the scent of a dog and some white doggy fur. He attended to that as soon as it occurred to him, discovering that it would indeed have nailed him as the culprit.

Nevertheless, despite all his planning, all the emotional fences he had erected, he was discovering that he could not quite avoid a pang of conscience, not for Mrs. Martinez, despite her unfortunate reaction, but for Vickie. Hell, he had only been exposed to her clever dog wiles for an hour or so, the time it took him to drive to the animal shelter. Her fate began to trouble him. He grew anxious and, once again, his work suffered. He could not concentrate.

He was certain that one glance at Vickie and a potential pet seeker would adopt her immediately. Mrs. Martinez did not engage his compassion. She deserved her fate. She had, he decided, cruelly abused Vickie, leaving her alone, cooped up in a room, forced to perform her ablutions on paper. No wonder she whined. It was heartless. He wished he could justify his action to Barbara, who normally would have provided him with emotional sustenance. Unfortunately, it was impossible to confide in her.

Worse, he was discovering that it was getting increasingly difficult to justify his actions to himself.

Vickie's fate began to gnaw at him. He could not work, could not sleep. His appetite suffered.

"What is wrong, Milton?" Barbara asked. "You look like hell."

"A cold coming on," he replied, growing more and more morose.

Finally, summoning up his courage, and disguising his voice, he called the animal shelter in Westchester. Their response shocked him.

"We have not received such a dog."

"A little fluffy white female, well cared for. Answers to the name of Vickie."

"You knew this dog?"

"Not really."

"Typical," the voice harrumphed. "Abandoner's remorse."

He could not find the words to respond.

"Shame on you," the voice said. "But the fact is that we have no record of such a dog. People like you..."

Milton hung up, stung by the rebuke. He could barely catch his breath. His heartbeat pounded. He broke into a cold sweat.

"Am I dreaming this?" he asked himself. He recalled the events of that day. He had come to the shelter, brought the dog inside, then quickly exited. Perhaps someone had stolen the dog. He was baffled. Worse, he felt sickened, nauseous, the initial elation at his cleverness dissipated.

Mrs. Martinez returned from the hospital. Through the peephole in his door, he saw her, a mere shadow of her former self. She had lost weight. Her dark complexion looked like gray clay and she seemed zombie-like, lifeless.

"Poor woman," Harry told him. "She really loved that dog."

"People do get attached to their pets," he said.

The people on the board whom he met on the elevator avoided his eyes. He was, he knew, persona non grata in the building. Milton was certain that everyone in the building suspected him of foul play concerning the missing dog. They had it right, of course.

As the days passed, he grew more and more remorseful. The absence of the dog did nothing to help his work. In fact, he had gone dry, confronted with a mammoth writer's block. He lost his appetite, paid little attention to his grooming, stopping shaving, and could not bear to look at himself in the mirror.

"I'm finished," he complained to Barbara.

"I'm really worried about you, Milton. Maybe you should see a shrink."

"Not a bad idea," he groaned, although he couldn't even consider such a possibility since he would have to reveal what he had done.

Soon he could not bear to walk into his writing room. There were too many reminders of what he had done. The worst of it was the uncertainty, the inexplicable disappearance of this innocent abused creature. He spent most of his days sitting on a park bench in Central Park like some homeless person waiting out his time.

One day, about a month after he had perpetrated his perfect crime, he heard something that made him feel certain he was hallucinating. For some reason he had felt compelled to pay a visit to his writing room as if drawn by some mysterious emotional magnet. What he heard froze all movement.

There it was, the familiar whine. He was certain it was an illusion, an imagined oasis. I am losing my mind, he told himself.

Nevertheless, the whine continued. He put his ear to the wall. He was not imagining the sound. There was a dog on the other side of the wall, the sound unmistakable. The first thought that came to mind was that Mrs. Martinez had bought another dog, a not uncommon cure for replacement of a loved pet. But the sound was so true to its original owner that he could not believe that this was another dog. No question about it. This was Vickie's whine.

For a moment, he was tempted to employ the same subterfuge that he had used to gain access to the spare key from the lobby. But it was long past noon. Instead he went down to the lobby and confronted Harry, who was shaking his head the moment he saw him.

"Damnedest thing, Mr. Preston. Damnedest thing. Bout two in the morning Barney tells me, this little dog, a bit scraggly and dirty, starts scratching on the lobby door. Barney said he looked more like a rat than a dog. But there was no mistaking it."

"Vickie?"

"Like a miracle. I swear. Barney calls upstairs and the Martinez woman rushes down. You'd think it was her long lost daughter. Hell, I guess it was. A goddamned miracle, that's what it was. Wherever the hell he was for a month, he sure knew the way home."

Milton felt something shift inside of himself, a sense of resurrection, perhaps. Born again. He could not contain his joy. He went upstairs to his writing room, lay on the couch and listened with pleasure to Vickie's undulating whine.

"She's back," he told Barbara when she came home from work.

"Who?"

"Vickie." When she didn't react he told her again. "The dog. Mrs. Martinez's dog."

"Good for her. Now you have a better excuse for not writing."

He didn't answer her fearing that he would give away his elation. He tried writing again, and again the dog's whine was inhibiting. He felt enormous pity for the creature, cooped up alone all day in its room. He discovered that when he tapped on his side of the wall, the whining stopped.

It was then that he had his eureka moment. He placed his iPod against the wall and programmed it for hours of classical music, putting it on its lowest volume. The whining stopped.

Apparently his muse understood. He began to write again. A story about a lonely dog.

PREGNANT

"I think I'm pregnant," Sheila said.

Her assertion was casual. He could see her in profile, looking up at the ceiling of the motel room, in the Holiday Inn tucked neatly in the shadow of the West Side Highway across from the Hudson River. The docks still berthed some of the cruise lines and the fleet. For them, both East Siders, it was well off the beaten track and a reasonably safe place to carry out a clandestine affair.

Suddenly Harold wished he had a cigarette. He had given up the habit ten years before, but there was still a memory imprint when he became anxious.

"Are you sure?" was about all he could muster.

"I've been through it once before, Hal," Sheila said. "Believe me, I know the signs."

Her little girl was five now. Sandra, little Sandy, played with his Liz, and they attended the same nursery school, which was where Sheila and Harold had met and where this conflagration had begun. They had been drawn together like magnets, catching them both off guard. Fearing discovery, they had adapted to this weird, twice-a-week routine that had been going on for seven months. It was a first time for both of them.

Their relationship transcended guilt or conscience, and their only real fear was exposure, since neither of them intended to sink their marriages. For both of them, the sheer ecstasy of this erotic explosion was worth the candle and the risk. *Don't overanalyze* was their mantra.

Because he was a manufacturer's rep and could make his own hours and she was a stay-at-home mom who had gaps in her day when Sandy was in nursery school, they had figured out together that they could meet at this out-of-the-way Manhattan motel and conduct their business in delicious isolation and without fear of discovery by the prying eyes of their normal social circle.

For two hours, raging lust ensued and left them both gorgeously drained and tranquilized by the effort.

"I think about you all the time," Harold had admitted, after she told him about how she grew moist at the thought of him.

"It's crazy," she told him often.

It began always with a wild frenzy, clothes strewn everywhere, erotic imagination in high gear as they tried everything they knew to try or had ever heard about. Oddly, their intimacy had its borders. They rarely talked about life at home with their spouses, as if that occurred on some other planet. As far as anyone knew, they were well-matched in marriage, good parents, respected, well-off. They knew each other socially and were often together as couples. Her husband, Bob, was his regular squash opponent at the University Club.

Both were from good stable families with undivorced parents. Were they in love? Hard to say, they admitted to each other. Call it overwhelming need, he told her. *Erotic overflow* was a phrase they bandied about with giggles.

They were both thirty-five, both Sagittarians. They were certain that this place on the zodiac had something to do with the fury of their suddenly discovered libidos.

Neither of them had ever stepped out of line. In fact, Sheila admitted, she had been one of those rarities, a virgin when she married. Her wedding night was a painful ordeal, and it took her a week for her husband to make his official entry. This was about the most intimate detail about her marriage that she had ever confided. He told her nothing about his marital experiences, nor did she ask.

Often, in the aftermath, cooling down in a temporary recess, they talked of their kids, never tiring of describing their antics.

Harold was surprised at his own ingenuity, the logistics and planning required to enjoy their few hours of sexual bliss. He had figured it all out time-wise, and it had worked exceedingly well, without a hitch. He was dead-certain that neither his wife nor her husband had the slightest suspicion.

He let the revelation of her pregnancy sink in, the shock of it taking some steam out of the routine. Up to then, the possibility of pregnancy posed the least risk of all.

"How could that happen?" he asked. "You said you were on the Pill."

"I am."

"It's supposed to be foolproof."

"I might have forgotten or something."

His mind was racing with possibilities.

"Are you dead-certain?" he asked, turning to her, leaning on one elbow, his hand tracing her profile, then tickling her down to her nipple, which was instantly erect. Her hand moved to caress him. As always, he rose to the occasion and they did it again, more slowly this time, ending it more quietly than at the beginning. They had gotten each meeting down to a triple-header.

But while his body reacted in its usual fashion, his thoughts were busy with deciphering the impact of her news.

"What do you intend to do?" he asked when they had finished. He looked at his watch. There was still time. She didn't answer him, but got up to use the shower. She was always first, leaving ahead of him. He sat on the edge of the bed, mulling the consequences of their complicated future. Finally, he got up and went into the bathroom while she toweled herself dry. He repeated the question.

"Do?" she replied. "I'm not sure."

"Abortion?"

She shook her head and made a face.

"Why? Isn't that procedure for unwanted children?"

Dismayed, he got into the shower and adjusted the taps to make it hotter than normal, as if it were a form of punishment. In his mind, he characterized the revelation as a disaster. She was putting on her makeup when he returned to the bedroom and began to dress. Finally, he asked the central question that had been bugging him.

"Whose is it?"

She shrugged.

"I haven't got a clue," she said turning to him, smiling. "I couldn't begin to calculate."

"There is a scientific way to find out. A paternity test."

"There's that. I thought of that."

"It will prove who the father is."

"Probably."

"Isn't that important? Wouldn't you like to know?"

She put a brush through her hair and didn't answer.

"Did you hear me, Sheila? Wouldn't you like to know?"

Their eyes met in the mirror.

"Would you, Harold?"

Coming up with an answer stumped him. If he was the designated father, then what? Neither of them was going to give up their spouses, and it was certain that neither of them was willing to go through the trauma of confession or anything that would endanger the stability of their normal lives, especially the lives of their children.

"Aren't you upset?" he asked.

"More surprised than upset," she confessed.

"Does Bob know?" Odd, how fucking Bob's wife had changed nothing in Harold's relationship with her husband. It was as if, in this manly arena, wives didn't exist. What surprised Harold as well was that he had no pangs of conscience as far as his own wife, Alice, was concerned. He supposed it was the same way in the relationship Sheila had with his wife. He had not observed the slightest bit of tension between them in those social situations that brought them together as couples.

"I haven't told him yet."

"Why did you tell me?"

"Because we share a secret. And you could be the father. And…"

"And what?"

"You supply a lot more little sperms to my eggs."

"It's not a matter of quantity, Sheila. It has to do with timing."

"I don't keep track. With Bob, I do my wifely duty on a regular basis. I'm not the instigator." She smiled. "We're hardly as active in that department as you and I."

"Are you saying that because of our greater frequency, I am the likely father?"

She sighed and shrugged.

"I wish I knew."

He looked at his watch. It was getting late. Somehow the dilemma had taken on greater urgency.

"Then how will we ever know?" he asked.

"What will it matter? I'm married. Whoever is the father, the child will have a good home. If it's a boy, Bob will be happy. He always wanted a boy and, eventually, we were planning to have one more child."

"Frankly, I don't understand your attitude, Sheila," he said, irritated by her apparent indifference. Throughout their intimate relationship, they had never had an argument. If there was tension, it was always the underlying thought that their affair would be discovered.

"I've thought about this, Harold. I've made peace with the idea."

"I don't get it," he said, feeling his anxiety accelerate.

"Okay then, suppose it is your child. Are we prepared to make this admission? Are you prepared to tell your wife that you have fathered a child with another woman? I certainly am not prepared to tell my husband. Why rock the boat? Who needs the aggravation and anxiety?"

"I say abort it and get rid of the problem."

"I thought about that. Tell you the truth, I hate the idea. Besides, suppose there are complications. Then what? What do I tell Bob? That I secretly aborted his child?"

"Or mine."

"Never that."

"I always thought you were pro-choice."

"What has that got to do with it? Yes, I am militantly pro-choice. And my choice is to have this child." She turned to him and patted his cheek. "Hey baby, during my first pregnancy, I felt real sexy. Nothing will change for us. You'll see; it won't be long before things get back to normal."

"Normal? This is normal?"

"Look, Harold. It's not like I'm single. That would be a whole other matter. I'm married to a good, solid man. We are quite comfortable, as you know. The child will be well cared for, just look at our girls. Stop being a worrywart. Having a child should be a celebration."

"But whose child?"

"Mine."

"And mine." He paused. "Maybe."

"There is no downside here, Harold."

"Yes, there is. If it's mine, Bob will be raising another man's child, paying the bills, being Daddy, a deceived man."

"So," Sheila replied. "He won't know he's been deceived. He'll love this child like he loves Sandy. And if it is yours, you can be content in the knowledge that he is being well cared for."

He began to pace the motel room, looking nervously at his watch.

"But he might look like me. Be easily distinguishable. If it's a boy, he'll grow bald early. Bob has a full head of hair. He's shorter than me. His eyes are a different color. Look at my nose, my chin. If he's a male, he won't look anything like Bob. It could be obvious to anyone who observes closely. And if it's a girl, she could look like my daughter. Her ears are exactly like mine. Not to mention the differences in our DNA."

"You're overanalyzing, Harold. We agreed. None of that."

"This is not in that category, Sheila. This is serious stuff. We're talking about a human being and that human being has a right to know who his or her father is."

"Okay then, let's make a determination."

Then what, he asked himself. It all came down to the aftermath.

"You should have been more careful, Sheila," he said.

"Well, I wasn't, or the Pill didn't work. In that case would you like me to sue the manufacturer?" She laughed suddenly and touched his crotch. "Did it ever occur to you that this is the culprit?"

"Or Bob's."

She patted her hair and slung her pocketbook over her shoulder, then kissed him on the cheek.

"Gotta go."

"There is only one obvious solution," he said.

"Not to me."

"How can you expect me to live my life without knowing for sure?"

"Don't be so dramatic, Harold. Nobody's life will be disrupted. I'm okay with it. Why shouldn't you be? Nothing will change for you. I'll bet there are millions of women in the world who have led their spouses to believe that their children have been fathered by them, even if they weren't. Don't sweat it. If he's not the father, Bob will never know." She looked into his eyes. "Unless you tell him. I certainly won't."

"You talk as if we men are just around to supply the crucial ingredient."

"But you've got to admit that you guys certainly enjoy the process."

"I haven't heard any complaints from you."

"Who's complaining?"

They exchanged glances and he knew in that moment that this clandestine physical affair was over, but that their attachment would linger for a lifetime in other more mysterious ways.

"You know what I think, Sheila?"

"What?"

She was going out the door, pausing to look back at him.

"You women don't understand the profound significance of fatherhood."

"You're right, Harold. We don't."

She closed the door behind her, leaving him alone with his uncertainty.

BETTER THAN DONNA REED

"I'm so excited I could scream," Peggy said as she and Charlie moved out of the Port Authority bus station on 42nd Street into the light-spangled city of New York on a mild autumn day just as the sky darkened. Culture shock could barely describe their disorientation.

Charlie rolled their suitcase through the solid wall of people, trying to get his bearings. Confused by the signs, they had already made a number of wrong turns and had to ask people directions just to get to the exits. In the street they stopped other people, whom they found, contrary to expectations, surprisingly polite, although not informed. Two people had accents neither Peggy nor Charlie could understand.

Finally they made it into the lobby of the Metropole Hotel, which, as had been advertised, was two blocks from the Port Authority terminal in midtown Manhattan.

"Like being inside a zoo," Charlie remarked as they finally arrived, but she could tell he was as excited as she was.

"Like in the movies," Peggy said in contradiction, remembering New York scenes.

The movies were her point of reference and her obsession. It was at the very heart of the dream she had for her daughter. Above all else, she yearned to be the mother of a movie star and here at last, she knew in her soul, that Aggie had embarked on the first rung of the ladder that was going to take her straight to stardom. She was absolutely certain that this was going to happen. God's will, she told herself.

"One day, you'll see," she told Charlie. His response was invariably a hopeful shrug. Of course, she knew, he wanted it to

WARREN ADLER

happen but it was obviously too remote from his expectations. But then, he had never had big dreams. Peggy was convinced that, at last, this was to be the beginning of her validation, the ultimate "I told you so."

For months now she had noted that friends, relatives, and co-workers at Wal-Mart had, she was certain, exhibited a kind of smirking expression of sarcastic disbelief in the notion that her daughter Aggie was on the road to celebrity and movie stardom. She admitted to herself that she had been a bit outspoken when Aggie left three years ago for New York to pursue the route to stardom from actress in plays, to discovery, to roles in motion pictures, a path mapped out by her mother from the moment Peggy realized Aggie's potential.

"My daughter is destined to be a star, just like Donna Reed," she told everybody within hailing distance in Denison, Iowa, where they lived. It was the same town where Donna Reed had come from and was now a kind of shrine to that late actress who had won an Oscar for *From Here to Eternity*. "Actually Aggie is more talented and better looking than Donna," she would whisper as an aside to close friends, although to others she would acknowledge that Donna was Aggie's role model.

In addition to talent, which everybody agreed she had in spades, Aggie was quite beautiful with cerulean blue eyes, a perfect nose, natural shiny blonde hair that she wore long, and a perfect figure that was the envy of every young woman in town. A miracle, Peggy had decided, considering that both she and Charlie weren't exactly Brad and Angelina, even when they were younger.

Aggie turned eyes everywhere and was the acknowledged celebrity of Denison for her starring roles in the high school plays. She was an absolutely knockout Annie when she was twelve years old and was a wonder as Juliet, not to mention as good as Betty Hutton in *Annie Get Your Gun*.

"Another Donna." Everybody said so.

"Better," Peggy would say with what she hoped was a haughty pose and a knowing wink.

In the last year, she deliberately hid her enthusiasm,

acknowledging that Aggie was out there in the Big Apple honing her skills and waiting for her big chance, which was sure to come. She did note, however, that people were asking her less and less about what was happening with Aggie's career. At times she got downright edgy about it.

Once when she was sitting together with her co-workers in the coffee-break room for employees at Wal-Mart, Daisy Parker, whom she never liked, made some sarcastic inquiry about Aggie's career, referring to her as a "Donna Reed wannabe," and Peggy exploded.

"What does a fat ass ignoramus like you know about such things, Daisy? Your kids are ignorant dropout scumbags with the ambition of petrified turds and an intelligence that registers lower than a snake's asshole."

"Listen to that overbearing, bragging cunt," Daisy countered, flinging a stream of lukewarm coffee at Peggy that stained the front of her red Wal-Mart smock. "Thinks she's hot shit because her little girl is in fuckin' Noo Yawk waving her pussy around and sucking cock to make it in the big time. Hell, did any of you ever see her in one single flick? Maybe in the pornos."

That was too much for Peggy to bear and she lost it and swung a fist right into Daisy's face, knocking out two front teeth. The incident brought her to the attention of the manager, who mandated that she take a month's therapy in anger management or lose her job. She complied, of course. The company, thankfully, paid for Daisy's dental work. Unfortunately, the incident was broadcast all over town and greatly diminished any further temptation for Peggy to offer any news about Aggie's progress in New York.

The anger management course seemed to help, although Charlie told her that he would often hear her mumbling nasty curse words in her sleep. Apparently while she was learning to inhibit any overt anger, agitated emotion was seeping into her dreams.

The undeniable facts, as Peggy interpreted them, were that Aggie was destined by fate and the miracle of talent and beauty to be everything that her mother dreamed she would be. In school, she starred in every play from the fifth grade on. Peggy had made certain that she was taught all the skills required by a budding performer.

She could sing and tap dance, and she had taken acting lessons from Mrs. Meyers, who had appeared in two movies and one Broadway show in her career.

"Just like Donna," Mrs. Meyers acknowledged about Aggie, although she had come to town long after Donna had gone.

"You're gonna be a movie star, baby," Peggy enthused. The line became a mantra, and it was apparent as Aggie matured that she had absorbed its message of unbridled hope as certainty.

Watching her daughter perform on stage was the absolute zenith of Peggy's early motherhood experience. She would attend every single performance, and invariably when she saw her daughter onstage, her eyes would fill with tears of pride and it was all she could do to restrain her sobbing. It was, she acknowledged to herself, a profound spiritual experience.

Peggy had drummed it into her daughter that, under no circumstances, was she to go steady with one boy, that God had singled her out to be a movie star celebrity and nothing, but nothing, must interfere with that goal. She had dates, of course, and it was perfectly natural for her to go out with the stars of the athletic teams, which she did. What she feared most was that Aggie would get pregnant like many of her friends and find herself in a situation where she would be waylaid from her career goals.

"There are other ways to keep these horny goats calmed down," Peggy instructed, leaving out the gory details. It was an accepted fact of life that young people in small towns started having sex very early, perhaps out of boredom or peer pressure. It had happened to Peggy. Charlie had impregnated Peggy before she had graduated from high school.

Thankfully, blessedly, Aggie had apparently obeyed the parental constriction and had concentrated on the dream inculcated by her mother. As evidence of the possibility, aside from the miraculous rise of Donna Reed, Peggy had rattled off the biographical facts of numerous female stars who had grown up in small towns and came from humble beginnings. She would always cite Frances Gumm, who became Judy Garland, and everyone knew that Donnabelle Mullenger had become Donna Reed. By the time Aggie was fifteen,

Peggy had amassed a notebook full of possible stage names. Both favored Melody Francis as a perfect choice, a lot more interesting and mainstream than Agatha Pachowski.

Aggie's brother Ben, two years her senior, had no such grandiose ambitions and was content to work in a paint store on Main Street. Charlie worked at his brother's used-car lot at the edge of town and the Pachowskis were able, with the help of Peggy's Wal-Mart job, to squeak by financially, although it was a stretch to provide Aggie with all the expert instruction she needed to prepare for a show-business career.

It was inevitable that after high school, Aggie would head to New York to hone her acting, singing, and dancing skills and, as it was ordained, she would appear in various stage plays and follow the usual path of discovery and stardom. Both mother and daughter were not naïve enough to believe that such a discovery would happen instantly. There were dues to pay as evidenced by the biographies of stars that Peggy had read. Kirk Douglas and Sylvester Stallone both worked behind delicatessen counters, and everyone brought up on Golden Age of Hollywood lore knew that Lana Turner was discovered in a drugstore.

Peggy had also learned a great deal from watching Barbara Walters on television and was an avid reader of *People* magazine and other celebrity-featured publications that she read off the Wal-Mart magazine racks. She prided herself too on having viewed every movie on tape and DVD that was offered in the Denison public library.

Every year watching the Oscars, a very serious mother-daughter ritual, Peggy would remark: Someday, Aggie, that will be you walking up the red carpet.

It had been three years since Aggie had gone off to New York. At first, she had been a dutiful daughter calling every week reporting on her various courses and adventures, bubbling with excitement and enthusiasm, working odd jobs to pay her share of the rental of an apartment in Manhattan.

That first year she came home for Christmas. Her mother threw her a big party and invited all her relatives, co-workers from Wal-

Mart, and friends from high school, many of them now married with kids. As always, Aggie was the center of attraction, ever the local star, on her way to celebrity status in the Big Apple. She sang the *Annie* song "Tomorrow" and got a roaring round of applause.

"It will happen, you'll see," Peggy told everyone. "One day she will be walking that red carpet on Oscar night."

Aggie called less frequently from New York and on occasion Peggy called her, but, after a mild admonishment by Aggie that her calls on her cell sometimes came at inopportune moments, Peggy, out of respect and considering that her daughter was doing important work for her career, desisted.

Although the calls from New York became more and more sporadic as time went on, Aggie was always optimistic and chatty although increasingly non-specific in answering Peggy's questions about her career progress. No, Aggie had not yet gotten an agent, but she was auditioning and getting "callbacks." Peggy, from careful listening, had learned the lingo, and tried her best not to show any anxiety or disappointment when Aggie did not get chosen, although her insides raged with anger and disappointment. Most people don't know great talent when they see it, she told Charlie numerous times.

All budding actors went through the terrible disappointment of rejection she had learned from reading the biographies of stars. Undeterred, Peggy continued her cheerleading since, in her mind, it was impossible for Aggie to remain undiscovered.

"Maybe she should try something else," Charlie had suggested one day with obvious timidity, revealing that he had not entirely bought into Peggy's dream for her daughter. Peggy's reaction was thunderous and demolishing, revealing all her pent-up disappointment and frustration. It was as if she had backslid from what she had learned in her anger management course.

"Why? Because you are a loser, Charlie? Because you never had a dream or the guts to pursue anything worthwhile? All your brains and your ambition are in your balls, Charlie. Eating, beer with your buddies, sports, and fucking is all you care about. Marrying you was the worst decision of my life. I dropped my drawers for a dumb bastard and here I am paying the piper. And now you're suggesting that your daughter follow in your footsteps. That kind of negativity is what destroys people and ruins people's lives. It sure has ruined mine. No way, Charlie. I will continue to believe that Aggie will be a star as long as I have breath in my body."

"All I said…" Charlie began but words failed and, as always, he quickly acknowledged defeat. In fact, Peggy knew, that was his destiny, to reaffirm his own defeat by his clumsy submission. Worse, he had brought her down with him. Indeed, Marlon Brando's quote from *On the Waterfront* had always resonated in her mind. "I could have been a contender," was the line. Not that she had ever had an ambition for herself, a real ambition not a fantasy, to be a real contender for anything. But she was an obsessed and determined contender for her daughter and that was the focus of her life.

Peggy was well aware that she had intimidated Charlie enough to keep such negativity at bay. Then, out of the blue, Aggie had informed them that she had finally gotten a part in a play. Peggy was ecstatic.

"You see? It's happening," she enthused to Charlie and anyone else that she encountered. After all, most of their friends and relatives had begun to avoid the subject of Aggie's march to stardom. Charlie welcomed this respite from intimidation, visibly remorseful that he had dared to suggest that Aggie try something else.

The trip to New York would be a surprise. To keep to a strict budget since the trip was a financial stretch, they took a bus from Denison, a twenty-hour grind, and made reservations at the cheapest Manhattan hotel they could find. Thankfully, the bus had arrived on time and they would be able to freshen up and make curtain time at a theater somewhere in a place strangely called NoHo.

Aggie had been cautious when she announced that she had gotten a part in this new play, and Peggy had interpreted this calm as a kind of superstition that if she were too enthusiastic it would jinx her performance.

"You're on your way, baby," her mother had exclaimed. "You'll see. It will happen just as I said it would."

Aggie had told her, after much prodding, that the name of the play was *The Shape of the World*, which sounded grandiose and important. She was able to get the address of the theater from an ad in the *New York Times* theater section she found in the library, although she was somewhat disappointed her daughter's name was not mentioned. Only the "directed by" credit was given. Someone by the name of Lance Goodwin.

Peggy could not contain her excitement and it was a given that she and Charlie would, by hook or by crook, show up for the opening night and hang the expense. This was, indeed, the beginning of the dream, and Peggy felt dead certain that once people saw Aggie onstage the major career hurdle would be breached and Aggie would be on her way.

Neither Peggy nor Charlie had ever been to New York and it took a bit of research to be able to fit the trip into a tight budget. They figured that they would attend opening night, then leave the next day for the grueling trip back to Iowa. This meant that Peggy would lose only two days at work. Charlie's brother gladly gave him the time off to see his niece's debut.

It was planned as a surprise and Peggy pictured Aggie's face when she would see her parents enter her dressing room after the show. It would be, Peggy was certain, one of the great events in both their lives. She fantasized about the size of the dressing room, picturing the folding screen and the bouquets sent by admirers just as she had seen in the movies.

For the occasion Peggy had bought a new dress at Wal-Mart, getting her employee's discount, and Charlie had borrowed a sport coat from his brother. They checked into the hotel, a dingy place, where they got the cheapest room on the first floor with iron grating over the windows. Peggy worried that if she had complained they would either throw them out or move them to a more expensive room. Besides, what was a little discomfort when one was about to see their daughter's first step to stardom?

It took them longer than expected to negotiate their way to the theater in Noho, which, to Peggy's surprise and disappointment was in a gloomy area of narrow streets and dark buildings. There was no marquee, and the theater itself was entered through a battered doorway and a tiny cluttered lobby with one young woman in jeans and a spiky haircut selling tickets and giving out a paper program.

They were shown seats in the rear of the little theater, which were actually five rows of mismatched chairs in front of a tiny stage. Peggy stared straight ahead, wondering if somehow she had gotten the address wrong. Then she scanned the program and noted on the bottom of the cast credits the name of Agatha Pachowski. Not even the stage name they had both favored, Melody Francis.

Then the play began and Peggy sat stiff and unblinking, her concentration far from the action on the little stage. How was it possible? She tried desperately to confront her disappointment with a rationale that stipulated that this was merely a showcase prior to going to Broadway, an audience test of what worked and what did not. She did not turn toward her husband, fearing a confrontation with his confusion at this searing spectacle of failed expectations.

Even when she forced herself to concentrate on the action on the stage, she could not understand nor care about what was going on. It was as if she had suddenly found herself in the middle of a bad, confusing dream. What rankled more was the fact that Aggie did not appear until the last moment before intermission. The sum total of her part was to serve drinks to other members of the cast in a scene in a restaurant. She was on and off without a single line of dialogue.

A wave of anger and devastation gripped Peggy as she sat stiff and depressed throughout the intermission while Charlie went off to the bathroom. She fervently hoped that Aggie had not seen her parents from the stage. She felt torn between the desire to see her daughter or escape quickly to avoid further exposure to her humiliation.

Before she could make up her mind, the play began again and she sat through yet another bland and incomprehensible talkathon, during which Aggie as maid served tea. But this time, there was a tiny moment of hesitation, a mini-second of peripheral double take of recognition and Peggy was certain that she was seen and could no longer avoid meeting her daughter.

She spent the rest of the play contemplating her reaction. Above all, she needed to restrain and hide her disappointment. She had no illusions about what Aggie's reaction would be. Most likely resentment. They had borne witness to her abject failure. Not one spoken line. Nothing more than a walk-on. So this was the fruit of years of effort, hours of money spent on instruction back home in Denison and an eternity of hope and certainty? Peggy felt her heart pounding in her chest and her breath was coming in short gasps. She wanted to get up and run away.

"You okay?" Charlie whispered.

She nodded, but did not look at him, fearing his expression of disillusion. But then he was used to failure, conditioned to it. By the time the play was over, anger and frustration had replaced disappointment and she steeled herself to the reality of the situation.

"I can't believe this," Aggie said when they met in the cramped backstage where the actors changed immodestly and scrubbed away their makeup before a large battered mirror and a cracked porcelain sink. Obviously shocked, Aggie did not, thankfully, exhibit the feared resentment of Peggy's expectation.

"We just missed you honey," Charlie said as he embraced his daughter.

"I wish you had let me know, Mama," Aggie said looking at her watch. "I'm due at my job at eleven. I'm a cocktail waitress at one of the clubs nearby."

Peggy found it hard to absorb. Was this the beginning or the end? At that moment, a tall man approached them. He was obviously older, with long graying hair and a pepper-speckled beard. He placed an arm around Aggie and kissed her on the lips. Peggy felt a gnawing anger in her gut.

"These are my parents, Lance," Aggie said. "He's the director. He makes the magic happen, don't you, darling?"

Lance acknowledged the compliment with a smile and pulled Aggie closer, a gesture welcomed by her daughter. Peggy's anger bubbled and, and like a hot poker in her gut, she remembered Daisy's comment, which had precipitated her anger management therapy.

"So you make the magic happen, do you?" Peggy said, feeling herself on the fiery edge of rage.

"He's the man," Aggie said caressing Lance's cheek with a gesture of adoration.

"Did you enjoy the show, folks?" Lance said, hugging Aggie closer.

"You really want to know?"

"Easy, Peggy," Charlie whispered, but it was too late.

"I'd love to hear your reaction," Lance pressed, caressing Aggie's shoulder.

"Alright then." Peggy sucked in a deep breath that served to fuel her anger. "I thought it was a boring piece of shit. Aggie here has more talent in her little finger than all the stupid actors you put in this stupid play. Magic? Maybe if you put Aggie in the lead you might make something really good out of this crap."

Lance frowned and rubbed his beard, obviously shocked by this sudden onslaught.

"Mother!" Aggie cried. She turned to the director. "I'm so sorry, Lance. So sorry."

"Sorry. Why be sorry?" Peggy continued, all restraint abandoned. "He didn't give you one fucking line. Not one." She turned to Aggie. "You're being used by this middle-aged asshole, Aggie. You've got real talent, baby. Real talent. You're better than Donna Reed." She raised a finger and waved it at the director. "Not one line. You didn't give this beautiful, talented girl one line." She turned again to Aggie. "What do you have to do to get one line, Aggie?" She felt her insides quiver, her chest gasping, her face flushing.

"We better go, Peggy," Charlie said, grabbing Peggy by the arm.

"I'm so sorry, Lance," Aggie cried. "Take her away, Daddy. Please. She doesn't understand."

"Oh yes I do little girl, I sure do understand."

"No you don't, Mama."

"Oh yeah," Peggy screeched. "What the fuck do you think this horny old goat wants from you, Aggie?"

"Enough, Peggy, please," Charlie begged, grabbing his wife by the arm and pulling her away.

"Call us back home," Charlie said to his daughter, who nodded, her face ashen.

Charlie continued to tug on Peggy's arm and finally led her out of the theater into the street.

"Believe me, Charlie, I know what she's doing with that man."

"Leave it alone, Peggy. Let's go back to the hotel."

"Fuck," Peggy cried. "She was better than Donna."

"Damn it, Peggy," Charlie shouted. "Stop this."

Peggy moved, obedient to Charlie's pressure.

It took them more than an hour to find their way back to the hotel. Peggy was silent, thinking back on all those years of dreams and hope.

During the night, she awoke suddenly, screaming.

"Not one line. Not one line."

Charley embraced her and soothed her back to sleep.

ORAL HISTORY

"Why are you people so mean to Grampa?" Allison Zucker asked her parents after they said goodbye to Sam Gottlieb after their ritual Sunday brunch at the Madison Restaurant on First Avenue.

"Mean?" Allison's mother, Betty, said, responding to her daughter's assertion. "That's ridiculous."

"You don't really talk to him. I mean really. It's always like routine. 'How are you?' 'How was your week?' 'Are you feeling okay?' Stuff like that."

"Does that constitute meanness, Allison?" her father, Michael, asked.

She was fifteen, still living at home, going to the Dalton School, a fancy private school in Manhattan, and still subject to the family rituals, like Sunday brunch with Grampa. Her two brothers were off at college.

"Fact is darling, ever since Gramma died, he has crawled into a shell. He really doesn't want to have much to do with us. Besides, he's in his eighties and probably getting senile."

"Getting," Michael snickered. "He's arrived. Won't be long before he needs a caretaker or we've got to send him to a home."

"Fat chance," Betty said. "He's too stubborn and independent."

"Chronology will take care of that," Michael said. "Decline is inevitable. What does he do with himself all day, rattling around in that big apartment?"

"I don't know," Betty sighed. "He's a very difficult man."

"And gotten worse since your mother died."

"He's not exactly a bowl of cherries to be with, but he's still my father."

"He was always a pain in the ass."

"I hate hearing you talk like that," Allison said. "It's cruel."

"We're not being cruel, honey," Michael said. "Realistic."

Allison held back any rebuttal. In fact, she had many disagreements with her parents but had chosen the path of least resistance, taking refuge in her own secret life. She prided herself on her own self-awareness and believed she had the insight to realize that she was not part of the mainstream teenage culture of her class, obsessed with shopping, attitude, and sex.

She was a loner, and because she kept her distance from the power crowd at school, she knew that her peers thought of her as a bit of nerd with her nose always in a book and when not reading she was browsing through her computer. In fact, she was ahead of the pack with her knowledge of the latest technologies and, while still not certain about her career choices, she suspected that it might have something to do with the sciences.

Her father was an investment banker and her mother busy with charity work. She thought of them as a typical East Side couple, snobby, culture supporters, and very social. She thought most of their friends were boring and shallow, but she kept her opinions to herself.

"Why are you so withdrawn?" her mother would ask periodically.

What she meant was that Allison was not a typical teenager, not part of the mainstream, and she had overheard her parents on numerous occasions voice their concerns about her lack of social skills and their worries over the absence of friends. She did have one or two friends, but they were also nerdy loners like her, and their social intercourse was limited.

She knew she wasn't attractive in the traditional sense with her pale complexion, kinky hair, and squinty eyes. So far, she had never kissed a boy, although she had fantasized about having sex and she did indulge in solitary pleasures.

For years she had hardly paid much attention to her grandparents. They came and went in her life, showed the usual affection, but seemed more interested in her brothers than in her. Not that it mattered, since she paid little attention to them. But in the years since her grandmother had died, she began to wonder about her grandfather and the kind of man he had been and is. Each Sunday, he would meet them punctually at the Madison Restaurant and invariably order pancakes, say little, and then after the goodbyes on the street, he would walk away to his apartment on York Avenue near Sutton Place.

Apparently he had been retired for a number of years. He had been some sort of salesman and had made a good living. Beyond that, she knew very little about him, where he was born, who his parents and grandparents were, what his life had been like. Nor did she care.

Actually it was in history class at school where she got the idea. They were studying the presidents, and the teacher was telling them about the oral history of President Kennedy, and how people who knew him would record their memories about him.

It sort of grew in her mind that it would be cool to do an oral history of her grandfather, the only one in her family from that generation who was still living.

"Why do you want to do this?" Sam asked her when she arrived at his apartment with a small tape recorder.

"It's a school project," she lied.

"What is it you want to know?"

"All about Grampa," she teased.

"I'm not very interesting," he said.

"You are to me."

She had rarely been in his apartment, which was large and shabby but fairly neat since he had a cleaning woman come in two or three times a week. Although she hadn't paid much attention before, she was more observant now, noting the many framed family pictures scattered around the apartment. There were photographs of her mother and her sister, who lived on the west coast, and pictures of both their families. There were also many pictures of her grandfather and grandmother in various stages of their lives.

She set up her little tape recorder on a table next to his well-worn easy chair. He was a dignified man, the kind usually characterized as a gentleman. He was bald with a round belly and wore his pants high up.

"So where do I begin," he said as she started the tape recorder.

"At the beginning," she said. "Like where were you born."

"I was born in the Jewish Hospital on Eastern Parkway. My mother once told me she was in labor for twelve hours and I weighed more than eight pounds."

"Your mother," Allison reminded herself. She wanted to know about the generations before he was born. "Where was she from?"

"Both my mother and father came from Poland when they were under five years old."

"Where in Poland?"

He pondered the question, then shook his head.

"Tell you the truth, I'm not sure. It was somewhere near Minsk."

"Near Minsk? That it?"

"I didn't have a school project to find out," he laughed.

"Okay then, tell me about your parents."

He paused and grew reflective, quite obviously searching his memory.

"I think about them a lot," he told her. For a moment his eyes seemed to glaze over as if he were looking inward. After a long pause, he spoke again. "Funny. They were born in the last years of the nineteenth century. Dead now. Let's see, nearly thirty years. They are enormously vivid in my mind." He looked at Allison. "They say long-term memory is the last to go."

"Okay then, Grampa. Tell me all about them."

"The things you remember," he sighed. "We had no money." He smiled. "But who knew that. My father was a union guy, a cutter. That was when the garment district was big in New York."

"A cutter?"

"A cutter was someone who cut the patterns for dresses and suits. It was a skill and he was proud of it."

"And your mother. What was she?"

"A mother. In those days a woman who was working meant that a man was incapable of supporting his family. It was considered shameful."

"Really?"

He exchanged glances with her as if to illustrate the gap between the generations. She decided that she would not interpolate, but listen only. After all, this was his oral history, not hers.

Without interruption, he talked for an hour about his early life growing up in Brooklyn. When his father was laid off since cutting was seasonal work, they would be unable to pay their rent and would have to pile into their grandparents' little house in East New York that had been bought by his mother's brothers. Allison was, of course, tempted to ask questions, and it took enormous discipline on her part to remain silent when he spoke to the running tape recorder.

As his life unfolded, her interest grew more intense. She wanted to know more and more, and when they paused for lunch, she would chatter on like a question box about his life.

"And you went to the movies every Saturday?"

"Without fail. There was a double feature, a comedy, serial." He explained what a serial was. "I must have seen every picture made in the thirties, when the talkies started. When I see a black-and-white film I can tell you every actor and actress of that era, even the supporting players."

"What did it cost for admission?"

She was surprised that she asked such a question. Money was of no real interest to her, but she was suddenly curious about the comparison.

"Ten cents, and on weeknights when I went with my mother they gave you a dish. You could furnish a whole table with plates."

He told her that suits came with two pair of pants and cost as little as $29.95. He had been a traveling salesman carrying a full line of men's suits at the beginning of his career, then he had formed his own company and still went on the road to sell menswear. Then he told her whatever costs he remembered, from cigarettes to bananas to shoes and socks, to the cost of the subways, which was a nickel, to baseball tickets.

"Bleacher seats were fifty-five cents."

"What are bleachers?"

He patiently explained everything she asked, and she could tell he was enjoying himself immensely.

"Nobody ever cared to ask me these questions," he told Allison.

She came back day after day to her grandfather's apartment. He would look forward to her coming and would be sure to give her a glass of milk and cookies, which became a part of their regular routine. She did not tell her parents what she was doing and categorized this project as part of her secret life. Not that they would have objected, but she wanted this for herself and her grandfather alone.

When they met for the family brunch on Sundays, her grandfather would wink at her as if to say, "keep this between us," and she would nod her head in agreement. Neither her mother nor father ever noticed.

Since she was far more technically adept than him, she persuaded him to purchase a computer and taught him the bare rudiments so that he could order things online using his credit card. Having discovered his memories of black-and-white movies, she taught him how to order DVDs online and often they would share viewings of old black-and-white movies. He loved the movies of Fred Astaire and Ginger Rogers, the *Thin Man* movies, and soon she was conversant with all the old black-and-white stars of the golden age of Hollywood.

When he told her about the Brooklyn Dodgers, she searched the Internet and found old DVDs and audios of Dodger games. She loved being with him when he recalled these old baseball stories. For months she visited him almost daily, listening to and recording the oral history of his life and pressing him to tell her about all the events that were happening during his lifetime. She even went so far to encourage him to get a microfiche apparatus so that he could recycle all the *New York Times* of the thirties, forties, and fifties.

Her parents, Allison suspected, wondered where she went after school every day. Although they inquired, they were very circumspect on how they questioned her.

"I hope that wherever you go after school you are being careful," her mother warned, meaning if she had sex she should take every precaution.

"Don't worry, Mom."

"It's very dangerous today. You know what I mean."

"Of course, I do. I'm very careful." It was laughable. She was still a virgin.

"Do you have a boyfriend?"

Her mother seemed addicted to that question.

"No, Mother. I don't."

"Better to postpone that part of life, Allison."

"Yes, Mother."

"And stay away from drugs."

"I do, Mother."

She knew that she was definitely out of the mainstream of the teenage life of the privileged kids who attended her school. She knew it might reinforce their opinion about her nerdiness. She didn't care and she honestly felt she was learning far more about life from her grandfather than she learned at school.

Meanwhile, the tapes proliferated and the relationship with her grandfather grew closer. It was as if she had opened a door into his world and she had jumped right through it. Because they read the microfiche copies of the *New York Times* together, she knew a great deal about such diverse events as the Spanish Civil War, the four Franklin Roosevelt campaigns, and the names of the cars and other products of the era, especially cigarette brands, which were heavily advertised. She learned the titles of movies and the actors of that period, the stocks that went up and down, Hitler and Mussolini, the rise of the Nazis, the battles of World War II, the baseball rivalries, and especially the fate of the Brooklyn Dodgers.

"When they left Brooklyn, I left baseball," her grandfather told the tape recorder. She learned pretty much everything about his history when he talked into the recorder, including how he had met Gramma at the Freddie Fitzsimmons bowling alley on Empire Boulevard.

"Freddie Fitzsimmons was a pitcher for the Dodgers. He would wind up with his back to the batter, turn and pitch. Never saw another pitcher do that."

He told the tape recorder that he was in World War II, which he called "WW2," and was in the infantry and won a purple heart. He still had shrapnel in his tush, he told her, laughing after the session. "Only I won't show it."

It surprised her that he had never talked about that part of his life. He told too about all the cars he had owned, including his first, a Hudson, which he bought after the war and which looked like a tank. He showed her a picture of it advertised in the *New York Times*.

"Ugly, right?"

Not only did she spend her after-school hours with her grandfather, she would arrive Saturday morning and stay until nightfall. Usually they would watch a double feature of DVDs of old black-and-white movies, sometimes an extra one for good measure. After months of so-called moviegoing as they called it, she could also name many of the actors and actresses of that era. She thought Tyrone Power, Gary Cooper, and Clark Gable were the handsomest and no woman was more beautiful than Hedy Lamarr and Greta Garbo.

Then, after a year, it ended abruptly and tragically. Her grandfather had a massive coronary and was rushed to the intensive care unit of Mt. Sinai Hospital. The prognosis was not good. Allison was devastated.

Allison's mother, as befitted her daughterly obligation, spent all day in the waiting room. Allison sat beside her, unable to hold back her tears.

"No need for you to cut school," her mother said, when Allison refused to attend classes. She did not know anything about her daughter's special relationship with her father and appeared genuinely baffled by her grief.

"Life goes on," Allison's mother commented philosophically more than once as they sat together in the waiting room. "He had a long life and he was lonely after my mother died."

Allison knew better. For the past year he was not lonely. Allison's visits filled his life with interest and joy, hers as well. It had been a special year, a fabulous journey through her grandfather's memories, which were now part of her own. Still, it remained their secret, Allison and her grandfather's secret life.

On the second night of her grandfather's hospital stay, his doctor called them into his room. Her mother and father were there as well as her aunt and uncle, who had flown in from the west coast.

"He won't last the night," his doctor told them.

They stood around the bedside, watching him slowly expire. He was still conscious, his breathing difficult, his eyes barely open. Suddenly he moved his hand and beckoned with his finger, but when his daughters moved forward, he moved his head negatively and with finger signals beckoned Allison forward. She moved close to him and he made her understand that she was to lower her head against his lips.

Allison heard his thin wispy whisper, which went on for a few minutes. Then she put her lips close to his ear and said something. A minute or so later, his eyes closed, and a stethoscope check determined that he had died.

"What did he say to you?" her mother asked when they were going back to their apartment in a taxi. Her voice betrayed a slight irritation.

"What was that all about, Allison?" her father asked, when she didn't reply to her mother.

"He had something to tell me," Allison said.

"What?" her mother asked. "After all, it was his last words on earth."

"You really want to know?" Allison asked.

"Of course," her father said. "What was so important that he had to tell you, only for your ears?"

She mused over the request, then smiled. What could it possibly mean to them?

"What he said was Camilli on first, Coscaret on second, Pee Wee Reese at short, Lavagetto on third, Phelps behind the plate, Dixie Walker at left, Ducky Medwick at center and Pete Reiser at right."

. "Does that have any meaning?" her mother asked. "It sounds weird."

"Yes, it does," Allison said.

"This is not the time to play games," her father admonished.

"You asked what he said. I told you."

"Sounds like baseball," her father told her mother.

"You can't be serious, Allison," her mother said. She turned to her husband. "I can't believe this. Baseball? Ridiculous."

"And what did you tell him when you whispered in his ear?" her father asked, wary with a sarcastic edge in his tone.

"I told him that even though Durocher was manager he shared shortstop with Pee Wee Reese."

"This is not a time for jokes," her mother said. "My father has just died."

"What the hell are you talking about?" her father rebuked.

"He told me the lineup of the 1941 Brooklyn Dodgers Championship Team."

"Have you lost your mind, Allison?" her mother said.

"The Dodgers won the pennant that year but lost the series to the Yankees," Allison said.

Her mother and father looked at her, exchanged glances, and shrugged.

"I don't believe this, Allison," her mother said. "I just don't understand."

And they never would, Allison thought, chuckling.

A LOVE STORY

That spring James Pappas, nee Papanopolis, had come home to New York after, as he told himself and others, forty years of wandering in the desert. Like Moses and the Israelites. He would chuckle at the reference. Others would shrug and look at him, perplexed.

His life, so far, had been like a pinball, bouncing in a zigzag pattern from one accountant job to another. He had spent ten years in Washington State, fifteen in L.A., ten in Vegas, and the last five in Phoenix, baking bronze in what was called semi-retirement since he did a little stock speculation on the side and might kill a half day on the lush green carpet of a Sunbelt golf course.

With Sally gone, his world in Phoenix had considerably narrowed. She had been the social arranger. Without her activism in that regard he slipped into a kind of nether world of isolation. She was a good wife and he missed her.

He began to brood. Time was running out. More and more, he began to think about his life in New York City five decades before. Nostalgia became longing. He grew increasingly homesick. It was time to return.

Sally would have balked at what to her was the worm-infested big bad rotten Big Apple. She wouldn't go there and insisted that the children visit her in Phoenix. She was from Iowa, a salt-of-the-earth Midwest girl. After having put up with their many venue changes, she was happy to wind up in Phoenix. She was among her kind of people. That's why he buried her there.

Even when the illness came, Sally told him Phoenix was a good place to die. It was ridiculous to argue the point. However, in his heart, he knew that New York City had to be a better place to die and not because of the proximity to their children. With its high energy, endless activity, noise and movement, it had the feel of something worth losing, not like Phoenix, a sun-drenched waiting room for people who were half dead already.

He was the son of Greek immigrants, brought up above the family luncheonette in Manhattan's East Nineties. As a kid, he had hated the luncheonette where his father and mother slaved away their days and nights, and where all his time away from school was spent as the son-helper in the time-honored immigrant tradition.

His nostrils still twitched in memory of sizzling bacon fat and the ubiquitous effluvia of olive oil that drenched every molecule of space in their tiny upstairs flat. Once he had referred to it as a "stink." These days the stink had become perfume.

In Manhattan, he had found himself a one-bedroom rental apartment on the bustling West Side, two blocks from Central Park. He was home, a city boy in his bones, and he quickly adjusted to the environment and established a routine.

Weekdays, he read the *Times* on a bench in Central Park, then walked down to the Schwab office on Broadway to spend an hour or two watching the ticker. Later, he might poke around the books at Barnes & Noble, meander through the American Museum of Natural History, view the exhibits at the New York Historical Society, and take long walks down past Times Square, sometimes as far as Greenwich Village. Mostly, he ate in coffee shops.

Weekends he would visit the kids, an obligatory hegira into irrelevancy. Jan one week, Paul the other, a ritual of kissy-poo with the grandchildren, disinterested conversation with offspring and spouse, discovering how distance can, in the end, inhibit intimacy. He blamed no one for this, annoyed at himself for being so bored and disconnected on these bland and uninteresting weekends. After awhile, he dismissed his guilt, acknowledging his parental failure, but taking some comfort in the fact that he had been a devoted, caring father when the kids were, well, still kids.

Manhattan's diversions helped James cope with his grief, which went on longer than he had been told to expect. Nearly fifty years of marriage had considerably reduced his sense of singularity. It was tough enough in Manhattan. It would have been devastating in Phoenix.

He forced himself to consider his homecoming as a process of reconnection. As part of the process, he followed the adventures of the New York home teams: the Knicks, the Mets, the Rangers, and the Yankees, icons of his youth, although his enthusiasm had waned over the years. Unfortunately, try as he did, he had difficulty reclaiming the old rooting energy.

To fill further gaps in his time, there were movies and shows and lectures at the 92nd Street Y and, although he was in no mood to socialize, he did not feel totally isolated and was only mildly depressed. There were occasional lunches or obligatory dinners with people coming in from Phoenix, who had quickly faded out of his orbit.

As he emerged from the deep-freeze of his mourning, he began to note in himself an obsessive interest in observing the faces, mostly older faces, of those who entered his field of vision. He did not realize it at first, but it soon dawned on him that these observations were more investigative than casual. More than once he felt the sting of rebuke by the irritated gaze of those he had stared at longer than might be considered polite.

Some of these faces struck him as half-familiar, perhaps people he had known or seen years ago when he lived in Manhattan. They might be people he had gone to school with, old friends with whom he had lost contact in the decades of his "exile," old girlfriends, sweethearts, who had once stirred his romantic interest.

He was well aware that fifty years had wrought dramatic changes in these aging faces. He tried, in his mind's eye, to strip away the years and bring the faces back to some earlier focus. More than once, he was tempted to stop a passerby or someone sitting at another restaurant table to solicit their history based on a vague familiarity. Did they go to the same elementary or high school, or to the Annunciation Greek Orthodox Church on 91st Street, or come into his father's luncheonette?

So far he had been hesitant in accosting them, not wanting to seem like a fool. His mind would wander frequently as he pushed

WARREN ADLER

himself in memory back to those times of his youth when his life outside the ubiquitous luncheonette was taken up with friends, sports, school, and, indelibly, girls.

Concentration and focus brought names back. Jerry O'Haire, Tommy Stephopolus, Icarus Cotheo, Chuck Gunther, Bobby Klein, boys in his classes, boys who played pickup games of basketball in the schoolyard or softball in Central Park. Their voices, sounds, even smells, rolled back in nostalgic flashbacks as that lost world, dormant for years, resurfaced in his memory.

And the girls. Ginny Demes, Vera Vasis, Florence Delaney. Those names and the images pictured in his mind seemed especially vivid. After all, they had shared his sexual awakening and gave him his first glimpse of fleshly pleasures. He chuckled when he recalled his clumsy first efforts at his novice lovemaking, cringing more with joy than embarrassment when he remembered his inability to unfasten a girl's brassiere or fathom the mysteries of female genitalia.

With Vera Vasis, whose parents owned a grocery store not far from the luncheonette, there had been more than a hint of permanence. How old were they, fifteen, sixteen? Had they exchanged cheap silver rings? He remembered giving her a slave bracelet and they had made what passed for lovemaking on the darkened landing leading to her parents' third floor walk-up.

In those days they called it heavy petting since it would be dangerously unthinkable for a nice Greek girl of good family to "go all the way." In memory, he still saw their actions on the steps as profoundly passionate, more passionate than if they had "gone all the way." Indeed, in the mindset of those years, to force himself on her would have been an act of profound disrespect.

For a girl in that time, a virgin who came to the marriage bed was a most valuable and expected asset, a gift of great importance, a solemn pledge of purity. How long had his relationship with Vera lasted? A few months at most. Yet the echo of its memory persisted, growing stronger with his return to the city.

He wondered where Vera was today. And the others. Surely they had married, had children and grandchildren, moved elsewhere, eons away in time and geography.

It soon became apparent to James that most of his thoughts these days were turned to that lost era of his life, and the more nostalgia that insinuated itself into his memory, the more he searched the faces of the people who seemed half familiar.

He supposed he could have mounted an intensive search for his old school chums. Then what? If they had stayed all their lives in New York, he would seem to them like an outsider, dredging up memories that would not have the importance to them as it did for him. After all, they hadn't lost their world.

Mustering his courage, he did visit the old luncheonette. He sat at the Formica counter which might have been the same one, ordered a cup of coffee and a tuna sandwich, and watched the skilled Hispanic short-order cook deftly do his job. Faster than I was, he thought, although the food quality seemed to have deteriorated. The tuna looked watered down with far too much mayonnaise, and the bread seemed thinner.

Behind the counter, the battery of new-fangled machines had replaced the old ones, and various owners had added a bank of pinkish, plastic-covered booths to the seating area. The old oily smell remained, prevailed in fact, a powerful, emotionally charged jog to memory.

The visit triggered a mild hysteria complete with tears. Without finishing his sandwich and coffee, he overpaid the check and quickly retreated to the street. His early hatred of the place seemed inexplicable now to his older self. Veneration ruled his memory as he discovered how profoundly he missed that old life with his loving, hardworking, and sacrificing parents.

Such evocative recall had a rejuvenating effect on him. Investigating his past gave him a sense of purpose, a mission.

He began to intensely observe the people who passed him on the street. At times, there was a flash of recognition, an expression, a voice, some remembered characteristic that awakened his memory, then quickly retreated into doubt. The aging process, he decided, was too efficient at recasting once-familiar images. His face, too, had certainly changed in forty-odd years. A casual glance was hardly sufficient to register a positive identification. Time and study was needed for such confirmation.

One warm day in late June, he was confronted suddenly with a powerful twinge of recognition. He had been walking uptown on Broadway, having just exited the Barnes & Noble bookstore on 66th Street. The woman's face he had spotted in a brief peripheral glance did not register until a minute or so after he had passed her by.

Could it be? There was something so compelling in the recognition that he could not allow himself to ignore it.

He quickly retraced his steps to the exact spot where he had encountered the woman. His heart had begun to pound like a bass drum. Sweat rolled down the sides of his chest. Was she the Vera Vasis of his youth?

The delay in his reaction left him at a loss as to which way she had gone. Her face, confirmed by the quick memory snapshot, had been narrow with high cheekbones, her lips full, teeth uncommonly white, eyes dark, hair long, black, shiny, curled. Was there a shallow cleft in her chin? But there was more than just the visual aspect. He could, he imagined, smell her scent. Wasn't there, after all, an olfactory element to memory?

He couldn't be dead certain, but he had the sense that she had briefly glanced his way, offered a puzzled look, then passed on. Was it a look of recognition or the indifferent glance of disinterested engagement?

He stayed for a moment at the exact spot of their "encounter," moving swiftly through the crowds ahead of him. Then he doubled back, looked in every store along the way and searched the diners at two sidewalk restaurants, which lined the path of her probable movement.

For at least an hour he went up and down the street where he had imagined seeing her. That had been in the late afternoon. The streets had darkened. Still he looked in the faces of the people who passed by, again searching those in the nearby restaurants and in the stores. Anyone observing him might think he had lost his mind.

In fact, he was beginning to lose faith in his observation. Perhaps it was a mirage, that faux image that comes from a wish, not a reality.

He was concentrating too much on his past. How was it possible to recognize someone who was little more than a child a half century ago?

Yet, forcing it out of his mind proved impossible. Back at his apartment, James could not stop thinking about this vague encounter. Was that brief glance of apparent disinterest actually a flash of recognition on her part, a face recognized by the eye, without the mind knowing it or visa versa?

Nevertheless, he was in thrall to the idea, and the next day he planted himself at a sidewalk restaurant table that gave him a clear view of that spot on the street where he encountered her. He tipped the waiter with a twenty-dollar bill to let him sit there and nurse a cup of coffee for most of the afternoon and early evening.

In the end, he felt foolish, although he spent much of his time conjuring up opening gambits, but rejected most of them. What could transpire between them after he asked the basic question: "Are you Vera Vasis?"

Would he have to endure a long tale of the ups and downs of a banal life and a catalogue of her children and grandchildren and their imagined uniqueness complete with photographs? On the other hand, could he expect a rush of regrets for not seizing the moment and continuing their relationship into eventual wedded bliss? And what of him? Aside from some modest financial security, had he made a life that inspired pride? The reason for their breakup was always on the edge of his memory, although it defied recall.

He continued at his observation post for the next few days, slightly embarrassed by this sudden obsession. Then he saw her, the woman he had seen a few days ago. He contemplated her for a moment. Was she or wasn't she? Her identity was too vague for certainty. She moved swiftly through the oncoming crowds walking uptown from the direction of Columbus Circle.

Watching her coming in his direction, he saw enough old markers to spark his interest. Or was it his imagination playing memory tricks? The shiny, black, curly hair showed now as gray and the alabaster skin had lost its porcelain sheen. The narrow face had widened and softened. She wore a longish dark skirt and a beige shirtwaist and her heels were medium on plain black shoes. Yet her profile had the outline of familiarity.

When she moved within a few feet of him, he felt his pulse quicken and beads of sweat roll down his sides. He got up from the table and moved behind her, keeping an appropriate distance, still unsure and unwilling to approach her directly.

He continued to follow her. She moved uptown for a few blocks, then crossed 79th Street, moving toward West End Avenue. She continued in the direction of the river where she entered a large apartment house on Riverside Drive. After a brief interval, he entered the lobby. The building, long past its glory days, had a doorman and a desk in the lobby. There appeared to be no posted list of tenants.

"May I help you?" the man behind the desk asked.

James hesitated, then blundered the only name that surfaced in his mind.

"Vasis."

The man behind the desk looked at him, perplexed.

"Nobody here by that name. You must have the wrong place."

He feigned confusion, nodded apologetically, then moved out of the building. He felt foolish. Vasis would be her maiden name. Surely, she would have married.

It was somewhat of a victory, he decided. He did, after all, find out where she lived. Wasn't that progress? To what end, he wasn't sure, although he did harbor a quaint idea that she might be a widow herself with a yen to explore the memories of her youth. Perhaps, like him, she, too, could be looking for a point of reference to revisit her past.

Excited by the idea, he went back to his apartment in a state of euphoria, impatient to return to his investigation first thing in the morning. He had accomplished enough for one day. The idea that he was close to connecting with this piece of his early history sparked his mind to dig deeper into his past. Then the memories, like a Polaroid, slowly began to emerge and the old feelings returned. He loved her. They were inseparable. Then why had they broken up?

He was up early in the morning and headed immediately to her apartment house on Riverside Drive, posting himself on a bench that lined the strip now known as Riverside Park. It afforded a good view of the entrance to her apartment house. Expecting a long stay, he brought with him a danish, coffee, and a copy of the *New York Times*. There was, after all, a minimum comfort level to his investigation.

Interrupting his reading sporadically, he would glance upward to be certain he did not miss any activity in front of the apartment house. He felt no sense of impatience or anxiety in the process, relishing the mission, hopeful that he had guessed correctly, although he hadn't yet come to any conclusions about the icebreaking introduction.

About two hours into his surveillance he spotted her. She moved with her usual alacrity eastward, away from the river and into the more crowded areas of Columbus Avenue. Again, he followed her at a safe distance as she crossed Columbus Avenue, moved to Broadway, turned south, and headed in the direction of Columbus Circle.

By then, James had determined that her carriage and gait were indeed similar to his memory of Vera Vasis, but he couldn't make it to certainty. Keeping up with her at a distance, he followed her into the Hearst Building on Seventh Avenue where, gathering courage, he followed her into the elevator. Naturally, he avoided all eye contact, but standing closely near her in the elevator, he was able to observe her with greater detail, although from the rear.

Her hair, although gray, seemed to have the same texture and curl of her memory image. She was thin as the young Vera had been, with narrow shoulders, but an erect posture that emphasized her height. The elevator moved slowly, stopping frequently to discharge passengers. When the door opened on the 18th floor she got out with three other people. In a split second decision, he intruded his hand on the closing door and it opened again.

She was just turning the corner of the floor when he followed, noting that she had gone into a door marked "Production." Well now, he thought, he now knew where she worked. He was proud of his progress. He proceeded down the elevator and headed to the sidewalk café where he had spent long hours searching the crowd for a glimpse of her.

He could assume her weekday schedule now. She would pass the café where he had posted himself about four in the afternoon, the implication being that she worked from ten to three, then headed back to her apartment. Pleased by these perceived revelations he allowed himself more questions about her life. Was she living with her husband in the Riverside Drive apartment? Did she have children?

His mind seemed to slip back and forth between memory and contemporary deduction. There was a sense that what his memory dredged up about their encounter years ago was a kind of foreshadowing of what destiny had in store for him in later life. Was she, despite the happy years with Sally, the true love of his life? James dwelled on that idea, surprised at the romantic notions that surfaced in his mind.

This concentration on recalling the time when he loved Vera Vasis began to expand exponentially in his mind. Apparently it had exercised a powerful hold on his emotions. He remembered, above all, being jealous, not just mildly jealous, but painfully, obsessively, perhaps insanely jealous. The recall was palpable, bringing with it the familiar sensation of hurt. Was it a trick of memory? Had he been tortured by the idea that Vera might be attracted to other boys? And, if so, was it possible to feel such anxiety after five decades?

The sense of blind, raging jealousy returned to haunt him. Then, as his memory recorded it in retrospect, it had become so powerful that it soon dominated their relationship. Had they argued, he accusing, she protesting? Was it all coming back now, the fierce possessiveness of his love for her, the craziness of his jealousy? Had arguments always ended in profusions of apologies and pronouncements of eternal love? Had he written her passionate notes pledging himself to her forever?

"I cannot live without you," seemed a mantra in his memory. "You are my whole world."

Perhaps the reason for their adolescent breakup had been his smothering attention. Words returned. He imagined... or did he really remember long, tearful confrontations as they sat on the darkened stairs of her parents' apartment building.

"I can't live like this anymore. I can't. You're making me crazy," her teenage voice hurtled through the mists of time.

"I love you. I can't help myself."

"And I love you, too. But your jealousy is killing me."

He might have cajoled. She must have pleaded, but again and again he apparently could not control himself and finally, in a monumental scene that seemed to go on until dawn, she told him she did not want to be his girlfriend anymore.

The rejection most certainly must have been a challenge to his pride and his manhood. It cut deep, a Greek thing. Nor did it end there. He must have spied on her, followed her doggedly, like now.

Anger and jealousy consumed him, he supposed. Surely, he'd been too worked up to sleep, had become listless and depressed. Did he become morose and unfocused as well? There had to be a denouement to all this angst and pain, and that was the part that came back to him with fury, like a dam breaking.

One night he had followed her. She was with her new boyfriend. He saw them enter her parents' apartment building. Pacing the street, inflamed with jealousy, consumed with anger, he tried, unsuccessfully, to repress his rage.

Soundlessly, he slipped into the entrance and padded up to the landing that had been their old trysting place. He had no idea what he intended. Then he saw them. He remembered with horror how his gut had congealed at the sight. He had blinked his eyes, hoping the image would disappear. It didn't. Vera Vasis was pinioned against the wall of the landing, spread eagled, as her new boyfriend pumped away inside of her.

They were too absorbed in what they were doing and didn't see him approach until it was too late. He lashed out with his fists, striking the boy in the back of his neck. The boy crumpled to the floor and James kicked him in the ribs with all the strength he could muster. Vera looked at him in horror. Their eyes locked. She did not scream, said nothing, and dropped to the floor beside the boy who writhed in pain. He too did not cry out, perhaps fearing discovery.

For a moment, he watched them, felt no remorse, not then. Had he felt victorious? Manly? He would never know. Both the boy and Vera stayed out of school for a week or so, and when they returned not a word was spoken between them ever again. It was as if the incident had never happened.

So he had tucked this away in memory all those years, isolating it, fencing it off, never recalling it until this moment. After a brief flurry of remembered fury, he calmed. Then it was gone. High school ended and he went on to other entanglements, but never with the angst and passion of his experience with Vera Vasis.

He began to follow the woman with some regularity, starting early, routinely placing himself on the bench on Riverside Drive. She was always punctual and would move swiftly along the streets until reaching her destination at the Hearst Building. As he followed her, he studied her gait, her posture, her bearing, but always postponing the confrontation, telling himself that he required one more review, one more look, one more assurance.

He speculated, given that the Greek immigrant milieu of his youth was centered on ethnicity, that she might have married a Greek boy. To this end, he perused a cross-indexed directory found in the New York Public Library. At the address of the apartment building, he found only one Greek name, Nevius. Back in his apartment, after an agonizing debate with himself, he called the number. A woman's voice responded, but he had not found the courage to engage her. Had the voice sounded like Vera Vasis? He could not be certain. Even voices aged, he supposed.

But when he called the production house the next day asking for Mrs. Nevius, they had no knowledge of her. Thinking quickly he asked for Ms. Vasis. Women often used their maiden name in the workplace. Neither name rang a bell to the receptionist who answered.

Day after day, he followed the woman, always on the verge of confrontation but never quite finding the courage to accost her. He wasn't certain what he feared more, disappointment or positive identification. His life took on a routine. He watched, waited and followed, never losing patience. It had become an occupation.

On weekends, he sat on the bench in Riverside Park, across from her apartment. When she emerged, he followed. After a month had passed, James's life became totally dominated by this search for the truth of her identity. It took on a mythical aspect. Was he waiting for some sign? He no longer took long walks, except to follow the woman, and he eschewed lectures, movies, or those other amusements that had taken up his time when he had first come back to New York. Nor did he visit his children and grandchildren on the weekends. Usually he called, making some excuse or other, discovering in their tone that they seemed relieved.

He told himself that he needed to overcome his reluctance and eliminate his nagging fear of either a negative or unwelcoming reaction. His waking thoughts had become a mental search for a precise recall of the events of his relationship with Vera Vasis more than a half century ago.

When he was not in conscious recall mode, he dreamed these events, the reality of it so compelling, that even in that state, he felt he was "there." Every sense was tuned in. He had gone back in time. There was something miraculous in it. Perhaps, he realized, he did not confront her because he did not want the curtain to go down in what had become the movie in his mind.

One morning, he was sitting at his usual post on what had become "his" park bench in Riverside Park. When he saw her emerge from her building, he rose as usual and prepared to follow. Suddenly, two men rushed out of a car, grabbed him under each arm, and roughly pushed him back to the bench.

"Where are you going, buddy?" one of the men said flashing a badge. He was beefy and bald, his voice rough.

"Going?" James replied, baffled by the question.

"Yeah where?" the other man said. He was younger, his hair slicked back. He took something out of his pocket and began to read. "You have the right..." it began, droning on. But James wasn't listening.

"I don't understand," James said.

"We're taking you in," the beefy man croaked, lifting him roughly from the bench and beginning to drag him forward in the direction of a waiting car.

"Where?" James asked.

"You'll see," the other man said.

"Are you arresting me?" James said, dumbfounded. He had never been arrested in his life.

"What does it look like, buddy?"

The man muttered something into his walkie-talkie and maneuvered James into the car. A small group of people had gathered, watching the spectacle.

"But why?" James protested as he sank into the back seat of the car.

"Come on, man. Don't bullshit us. You know why."

James was confounded. He had begun to perspire through his clothes.

"There must be some mistake."

"No mistake. We've had an eye on you for a long time."

"A long time?"

He lapsed into silence, certain now that they had made a mistake. The car moved up the street then slowed briefly. He noted that the woman had stopped.

"We got him," the bald man said. The woman nodded.

"I don't understand," James pleaded.

"Stalking, mister. It's a serious offense."

"Stalking?"

The word seemed foreign, out of context.

"I can explain," he said.

"You'll have to," the bald cop said.

In the police station, he felt humiliated by the process of being arrested, offering to explain at every step. Finally, he was given the opportunity. He was brought into a room and introduced to a detective who sat opposite him at a table. A stenographer sat nearby taking notes on a machine.

"You realize you can have counsel," the detective said. He was a man with a dark complexion who showed little emotion.

"For what?" James asked, still certain that this was simply a misunderstanding.

"Well then," the detective said. "We're listening."

Trying to appear ingratiating, he told his story as best he could under the circumstances. Unfortunately the threatening nature of the atmosphere inhibited his intentions. He felt inept and embarrassed, and his narrative seemed disjointed. The detective listened impassively.

"I wanted to be sure it was her," he concluded. "I wanted to be sure."

The detective shrugged, lowered his eyes, and looked at his notes.

"Mrs. Martin was panicked. We had to respond."

Martin! This was the first time he had heard her name. How wrong his assumptions were. He felt ridiculous.

"Believe me," James said, his tone pleading. "I've never been in this position. It was totally innocent, really. I'm so sorry. I had no idea that the woman knew she was being followed." He corrected himself. "Not followed exactly. Observed. I wanted to be sure. I was just being overly cautious I guess. It was a long time ago. People change after fifty years."

"No shit," detective said, cracking a thin smile. Was it a sign he should feel more at ease?

"So you see I'm not what you would call a stalker," James said, believing he was making his position clearer now. "I had no bad intentions."

"How could she have known that? Older people get scared."

"I understand. I guess you might say I was foolish."

"Very. We've talked to every one along the line, the waiter at the restaurant, the messenger, the doorman, others who witnessed your conduct. You were, clearly, stalking this woman."

"I told you," he protested, unable to comprehend the thoroughness of their surveillance. He wanted to berate them for wasting time and money on such trivia, but he held his tongue. "My God. I thought she was someone I had known when I was a kid. That's the long and short of it."

"No matter. You stalked her."

"I admit it. I followed her. I told you why. But I did not stalk."

The detective left him alone in the room. It was an awful time for him. Despite the absurdity of the situation, and the knowledge of his innocence, the accusation was very real and menacing.

The time passed slowly. He tried the door to the room. It was locked. This is truly crazy, he thought. Surely, this could easily be untangled.

He admitted to himself that his obsession had gone beyond reason. He had gotten caught up in a fantasy of his past, perhaps a by-product of grief and the silly idea that he was searching to recapture his youth. He saw his actions more clearly now. Of course, this woman was not Vera Vasis. He had invented her out of the strands of an old fantasy. From the woman's perspective he supposed he could be defined as a stalker.

The outcome did not look promising and he contemplated getting a lawyer to extract him from this mess.

After about an hour, the door opened and the detectives who had brought him in appeared with the woman he was accused of stalking. She appeared wary at first, her glance washing over him in a penetrating stare. Their eyes locked.

He had not, until then, confronted her eyes. It could be her, he told himself, but he was too frightened to acknowledge the suspicion. Better to keep his mouth shut.

"Do you know him?" the detective asked the woman. "His name is Charles. James Charles." It seemed clear that they had briefed her about his story.

"I'm really James...James Papanopolis," he whispered, "I changed it. Easier to pronounce." His voice sounded nervous and reedy. As he spoke, he remained locked into her stare sensing a vague sense of familiarity. Could it be her? Maybe? The passage of time distorted recognition.

She shook her head.

"I never saw him in my life."

"I was James Papanopolis," he said, feeling foolish, clearing his throat.

"Sorry," the woman said.

"I'm not a stalker," James said, finding his voice's strength again.

"If not, it was a good imitation," the detective said.

"He stalked me. Day after day. It was awful."

"Please forgive me. It was wrong. I'm so sorry if I caused you any concern."

"You scared the hell out of her," the detective said.

"I'm sorry."

"Well then," the detective asked, turning to the woman. "Do you wish to press charges?"

The woman, still unsmiling, grew thoughtful for a moment. She stared at him again, but offered no emotional signals.

"Absolutely," she said at last, turning, proceeding toward the door.

"It was an innocent thing," James pleaded. "I meant no harm."

Without turning, the woman left the room and the detective held him back.

"Sorry, buddy."

The next few weeks were a nightmare of anxiety. He had to post bail, hire a lawyer, explain his motives. The lawyer warned him that he could serve time in prison, which shocked him.

"For this?"

"A possibility," the lawyer told him. "Depends on the woman. She is very angry. Stalking is pretty scary."

"I thought I knew her."

"Let's leave that alone. Makes it worse."

"I'm guess I'm an innocent victim of my own fantasies."

The lawyer nodded his agreement with that assessment.

"We could always cop a plea, plead guilty, invoke the age thing. Make a deal.

"The age thing?"

"Age does something to the memory."

"Like this was because I'm senile. Is that the idea?"

"It's a good ploy," the lawyer shrugged. "Might get you off with a suspended and community service."

"Plead guilty? For what? It's out of the question."

"Your call."

He tried to explain the events to his children, but they seemed perplexed, and he could tell from their reaction that they really thought he was going senile.

How could this happen? Never in his life had he been in trouble with the police. Never! It was a bad dream and darkly colored the renewal of his New York experience. He contemplated going back to Phoenix after this was over.

Events dragged on. Court dates were made and postponed. He lived his life in a kind of limbo. No longer did he search the faces of people for signs of his past friendships. No longer did he take advantage of any of New York's amusements. He stopped talking to people, stopped reading the *New York Times,* stopped visiting his children. Instead, he brooded and stayed in his apartment all day. He missed Sally. There was no one to talk with, no one who understood, no one who would regard him sympathetically. He felt alone.

Then one day, his lawyer called to tell him that a meeting had been arranged between the parties at the office of the assistant district attorney who was handling the case. When he asked for an explanation, the lawyer told him that they might want to plea bargain. He wasn't sure what that meant, but it did sound hopeful, although he was determined not to plead guilty to a lie.

When he met the assistant district attorney in his office with his lawyer present, he was surprised to see the woman.

"Mrs. Martin has requested that she meet with Mr. Charles privately."

"Is she withdrawing her charges?"

"The charges remain," the assistant district attorney said. "The issue is whether she will testify."

"And without that there is no case," his lawyer said, turning to Mrs. Martin. "Am I correct?"

Mrs. Martin said nothing, not responding by gesture or expression. Suddenly the assistant district attorney stood up.

"We will give you ten minutes, Mrs. Martin. Defense counsel and I will be in the next room."

The woman nodded. The men left the room. James was puzzled by this turn of events. They sat in chairs a few feet from each other.

When the lawyers had left, the woman turned to him and began to speak.

"What you did was terrible, disgusting."

The woman's expression became a snarl. Her anger was palpable. In her eyes, James saw unmistakable contempt.

"I'm very sorry," James said, stunned by the energy of her outburst. "I meant no harm. It has been a terrible ordeal."

"Good," the woman said. "I hope it has been painful."

"Yes, it has," he said with a sigh. In his mind the punishment somehow did not fit his alleged crime. What had he done?

"I thought of this many times," she said.

James remained silent. He was totally confused by her bellicose attitude.

"I am her," she whispered through tightly pursed lips.

"Vera Vasis?"

She nodded.

"You were the hate of my life," she said, sucking in a deep breath. "I could never get it out of my system."

He started to speak, but she held up her hand to stop him. He had many questions to ask.

"Please. No explanations. No apologies. No words. We were trapped into silence. I spent a lifetime fantasizing revenge."

"I was a stupid jealous teenage boy..." he began.

"I don't want to hear your story and I won't tell you mine."

"People forgive..." he began again.

"Not me," she said.

He studied her face, looking for signs of the young girl he once loved. He knew now why he could never be certain. A lifetime of anger had distorted her aspect.

"I wish I could have gone further than this," she hissed. "It will have to do for the moment."

"For the moment?" he muttered.

"I will take this to the grave," she said, turning her head, as if to remove him from her sight.

They waited in silence until the lawyers returned.

THE SEED THAT GREW

Late spring, cerulean blue sky, sun-dappled terrace of this pleasant Greenwich Village café and here he was, Harry Waldman, thinking strange thoughts about Milton Horowitz. He hadn't thought about Milton Horowitz for easily forty-five years. He wasn't even in his radar range. In fact, he thought he had forgotten him entirely, wiped his mind of all memory of this man who had for a brief time touched his life, profoundly. For how long? Two, maybe four years.

Then, out of blue, he had gotten this e-mail. And then he knew the man had touched him for a lifetime.

"My name is Shirley Tannenbaum. I am the granddaughter of Milton Horowitz. He died twenty years ago when I was three. He was a writer and I am trying to find out more about him and his writings. You were one of the writers in an anthology of short stories published years ago that I discovered on a used book site on the Internet. I am taking my masters in creative writing at New York University and would be happy to hear from you to discuss my grandfather. Thank you, Shirley."

His first thought, once Milton had been retrieved from the mud of memory, was astonishment that Milton had died. His second thought was surprise that instead of the warm nostalgia the name suggested, an odd anger had assailed him. It wasn't at all like the kind of anger inspired by ugly disagreement, insult, or personal abuse and betrayal. Milton had always been kind, interested, respectful, and mentoring.

Harry had met people before who seemed to be born to the cloth, surefire success stories. They were the stars of high school and college, the chosen ones, who lived in the glow of promise, as if they were anointed by destiny. He used to be in awe of these people. It was certainly jealousy. That didn't explain the anger toward Milton.

What afflicted him was another kind of anger, an anger generated by Milton's failure to find his destiny, to realize the full flowering of his talent, to lose his way. It was like suddenly coming upon a tattered college yearbook and finding under Milton's picture that most prophetic and dangerous line, "most likely to succeed." How dare him not to have lived up to that promise.

Since that e-mail from Milton's granddaughter, he had become obsessed by thoughts of Milton Horowitz. Why hadn't Milton Horowitz realized his full potential? Milton was the best of all of those wannabe writers of his youth, the very best.

He had met Milton when they were both taking creative writing courses at the New School in Manhattan. It was after the war, the big one, and the thirty-odd students were a grab bag of types of all ages, a number of them veterans, a couple of gray heads, about a third women and one black. He remembered the one black because he had a name that sounded Irish.

Milton was the class hero, the golden boy of promise. He had already published a couple of short stories and poems in small literary magazines and was clearly marked, by everyone including the kind wonderful inspiring and encouraging Professor Fox, who taught the course, as someone with greatness engraved on his forehead.

Creative writing courses in fiction were a kind of aberration, since about all that could ever be taught was craft. Talent was innate, a mysterious gift, perhaps a genetic hand-down from some unknown ancestor. No one knew. But craft, of course, could not be ignored and so everyone listened carefully to Professor Fox as he analyzed the offerings of his students and filled them with red-inked chicken marks of delight when he came across an image, a sentence, or a passage that conveyed some special way of presenting a work of the imagination.

Everyone in the class shared the same dreams of fame and fortune. Why were they there? They lusted for the fame of Hemingway, Fitzgerald, and Faulkner. Of John O'Hara and Thomas

THE SEED THAT GREW

Wolfe, the heroes of the day. Some, of course, were merely experimenting with hopes and dreams. To some of the others, like him, they knew in their bones they were pursuing a calling, a compulsion for which there was no cure and would obsess them for the rest of their lives.

At twenty he knew it was true and at seventy, his age now, he knew it was true. Nothing had intervened in those years, no traumas, failures, rejections, no slings and arrows pointed in his direction, drawing blood and breaking skin, had ever turned him away from that bedrock truth. Milton knew, not only that it was true for him, but he had an uncanny instinct for spotting others with the same affliction.

Among this group of obsessed kinsman, Milton was clearly the cream of the crop. His writing was praised, lauded actually, when he stood up to read his material. The fact was that he was an awesome reader, which gave his work added heft and impressed the hell out of all those wannabes. His future success was undeniable. He had the look, the demeanor, and attitude of a winner.

And, of course, there was the talent, recognizable, natural, inherent. It seemed a consensus, and listening to him reading his work, one could not fail to join in the mutual appraisal. It was the prevailing view.

The class met weekly, but Milton formed an inner circle of those he had chosen, anointed actually, to what he called a "true writers" group. He had recognized instinctively who possessed this fierce need to do it, to pursue it to the death. Any true artist would understand. For them writing works of the imagination was everything, the world, the only activity worth living for. Rarely was it articulated. Every one of the half dozen in Milton's group, two women and four men, knew it in their gut.

There were six of them. About a decade separated the youngest from the oldest. Harry was the youngest and, to be honest, thought he was outclassed and outgunned by the talent of the others. The group would meet on a different day weekly at the home of one of the six to showcase their efforts to each other.

It was strictly a coffee-and-cookie event since everyone was pretty close to the edge financially. But to be chosen by Milton to join that charmed circle was, indeed, a feather in one's cap. Admittedly, by being chosen, Harry Waldman thought he had arrived in nirvana, a first step on the road to literary recognition. Milton had laid his hand on him. He had been anointed.

Of the various offerings read by members of the group, Harry's memory had become collective. They were, he was certain, great, vivid, wonderful, inspiring, more than promising, the best of the best. By some strange chemistry of mutual admiration, there seemed to be no competitive back biting, only praise and astonishment, as if they were all rooting for each other. Milton, as always, was the principal cheerleader.

The school did arrange for the work of most of the class to be collected and published in a hardcover anthology, *Which Grain Will Grow*, the title taken from a couple of lines from *Macbeth*: "If you can look into the seeds of time and say which grain will grow and which will not, speak then to me." Milton's story, naturally, was the first story in the book. Harry's was somewhere in the middle.

There was a big celebration when the book came out. It seemed then that this was the opening gun in the race toward fame and fortune and, perhaps, as everyone silently believed in their heart, immortality.

As predicted, Milton was the first of the group to receive a publishing contract for a novel. It was, of course, predictable. Indeed, it was a necessary validation that he was marked for greatness. Milton, as usual, was gracious in accepting his success and encouraging to the others, as if to say, I'll point the way and you will all follow. Everyone was sure it would come true.

How long did their little group stay together? At most a couple of years. Life intervened, he supposed. Love, marriage, children, the necessities of earning a living, the usual. He knew, of course, that none of them would ever let go of their dream. It was destined to be their blood-sucking leech, forever feeding on their blood for nourishment as it had for the rest of his life and still would as long as he his heart beat. Imagine, Harry thought, all this had occurred in a mere blip of time. Nearly fifty years ago.

But as he waited there for Milton's granddaughter on this pleasant spring day under a cerulean sky, nursing his Bloody Mary, protected from the sun by the umbrella over the outdoor table, he still could not shake his anger. How come he had heard nothing, nothing about Milton Horowitz for forty-five years or more?

"I recognized you from the picture on your book jackets," a voice said. He looked up at her face, blocked by the sun. "I'm Shirley Tannenbaum," she said, sitting down, smiling, open-faced and eager, her hair glossy with youth, her teeth sparkled by the sun. He noted that she was carefully groomed, wearing a crisp white blouse and jeans, with a bright yellow scarf artfully wrapped around her neck.

He studied her face for any trace of what he remembered about Milton. The eyes, he decided, but he couldn't be sure. Had he ever looked that deeply into Milton's eyes?

"I'm so happy you could see me, Mr. Waldman. I've read all your books."

"Really?"

How could he not be flattered, especially by her generational applause? He had done well, he supposed. At least in retrospect. What she did not know or could not know was that this affliction that plagued the real writer could not be cured by worldly success. She would think such an observation was ingenious and he merely thanked her. He thanked her politely. Readers were always welcome.

They ordered brunch and he craftily got her to tell her own story. On the surface it seemed fairly routine. Her father was a lawyer, her mother, Milton's daughter, was a doctor, obviously super achievers, comfortable, upper-middle class, liberal, savvy, supporters of the arts, traditional. No rebellion here, no sixties angst. She was the daughter of baby boomers. Milton was an Air Force veteran, stateside through most of the war, he remembered. He had been too young to serve. Shirley had majored in English, at Harvard, and was now getting a masters in creative writing at NYU.

It was, he thought, wonderful to listen to her, full of hope and ambition, self-effacing, modest. I could love her, he thought, if I was forty years younger. He had been married twice, been in love six or seven times, had a rocky history with women in general and was now content to be alone with his muse, although it had been years since his muse had provided worldly success. There had been moments, of course. A movie made from one of this books, a number of foreign sales. He was financially comfortable, drifting forward on the stream of life heading toward the open sea. He liked that metaphor.

Expertly, writers of the imagination were adept at such biographical mining; he drew from her the bare facts of her life. No, she was not involved in a relationship. Relationship was the operative word of her generation. What he was doing, he realized, was deliberately postponing the reason for their meeting. The fact was that he had not yet formed a proper response. What he really wanted to know from her was why, why in the name of God, had Milton not made it as a published writer. Not one book published. He felt his rage return and he ordered another Bloody Mary. Finally the subject became unavoidable.

"So, tell me about my grandfather." she asked.

"Why do you want to know?"

She seemed startled by the comment, perhaps it seemed belligerent.

"What I mean is," he corrected. "I think I know why."

"Obviously," she said. He realized that he had touched a nerve. "He was a writer. I mean I was only three when he died, but my mother told me that he had always wanted to be writer, that he had published some short stories and a few poems and had once written a novel that was never published." She paused. "By some strange genetic chemistry. I don't understand it myself. You see, I want to be a writer. That's all I ever wanted to be. Nothing else interests me. I have two brothers who are both in med school. My parents wanted me to go to law school and my mother just hates the idea that I want to be a writer."

"Why?" he asked. He knew he was being cagey, but it was at the very heart of this interview.

"She thinks that it had nearly ruined their lives. Her father's ambition. She says it drove him into depression. He was, how did she put it, beyond joy. Oh, he was a fair provider. He was a candy salesman. Not a great living. But she and my uncle, her brother, had it okay. Good education. They lived for years in a rental apartment in Rego Park. My Uncle Ben is a businessman. My grandma lived about nineteen years after my grandfather died. Apparently she had never been happy and never did marry again." For a moment she had drifted off the subject, then she came back again. "I read his short stories and his poems. I think the novel is missing. Apparently, he stopped writing. I don't know when. He was only fifty when he died. Grandma said he couldn't make a living as a writer. No way. She had a conniption when I told her what I wanted to be. She said in the end, it killed him."

"From what?" he asked. Why was it suddenly important to ask?

"Heart attack, I think." She paused and their eyes met. He was sure now she knew, that she was one of the afflicted. "Broken heart, probably."

"But why? He had other novels in him. Why stop? Nobody knows for sure about the worth of anything in this game."

He felt his rage begin again. He had the talent. Why didn't he have the courage to go on? The staying power? The decision makers fade quickly into the dustbin of history and others take their place. Rejection was an occupational hazard in his world. He had been rejected by battalions, long dead and gone, along with their choices. He had a test. Name five of the Nobel Prize Winners for Literature. Name a half dozen who won a Pulitzer. Inevitably most failed the test. He decided against making his point.

"That's why I'm here, Mr. Waldman."

He nodded, drained his Bloody Mary. He knew he was about to play a duet with his mind. His words would not match his thoughts. In his thoughts, he was enraged by Milton's cowardice, his retreat, his surrender. He was a fucking coward. A real writer goes on the attack, never retreats, wages war to be heard, to be read, to be discovered. His voice must be heard. There is no other choice for a real writer. Why didn't this stupid son-of-a-bitch know that? Was he so inundated with praise and the surety of success that he could not arm himself against the motley crowd of pigmies who would bar his way? Damned, fucking cowardly fool.

This was your life, you stupid schmuck. Nothing had to stand in your way, certainly not the stupid bleats of the untalented, the unannointed, the pretenders, the fools that barred the door. If you can't find one door open, find another, then another, then kick down the next fucking door you come to, you goddamned idiot. Life is war. Your talent is your armor. Let the arrows come. They will not dent your armor. He felt the blood rise in his head. He was conscious of her watching him, perhaps wondering why it was taking him so long to respond. Had his lips or his eyes mimed this diatribe of rebuke?

"If you have half the talent of your grandfather for writing works of the imagination, you will win the game handily. There was no one I knew that was a better writer than your grandfather, including yours truly. Without his being there, just being there at a certain time of my life, I might never have realized even my far more modest potential. We were part of his hand-picked group of real writers, the true committed, who met every week and read our material to each other. It was, believe it not, the truly greatest, most defining moment of my life. You know what I think?"

He felt a sob coming from deep inside him and knew that tears were starting. He reached from a napkin and blew his nose, then coughed away the sob.

"Damned pepper," he said.

"What do you think?" she asked.

"I think…" He paused. "I think that, by some miracle, your grandfather's spirit has reached out to you and handed you a relay stick."

Really, he thought. Where did that come from? He sounded like some preacher in the Southern sticks. Nor had he ever believed in such things.

"But you've never read any of my work," she said.

Nor will I ever, he told himself, hoping she would not ask.

"Let's say I am psychic about the power of DNA," he said, rebuking himself for what was little more than clumsy, cheerleading stupidity.

She laughed, perhaps seeing a joke in it. He hoped so. The irony of it was that he believed implicitly in his judgment despite the silliness of the sound of it coming from his mouth.

"I am so happy to hear that," she said. "It makes it all worthwhile."

He searched her expression to see if it reflected either ridicule or sarcasm.

"This was important for me, Mr. Waldman. Really. I couldn't find anyone else who knew him at that time. You are apparently the only seed that grew."

"Really?" he said, feeling the sob begin again. This time he let a few tears drop before he wiped them away with his napkin. "I'm sorry to hear that."

They sat for a while longer and he told her other stories about her grandfather's generosity and kindness, his mentoring and his fondness for other writers. Real writers, but he did not allude to that. If she were a real writer she would know.

When she left, he watched her pass out of his life.

Later he discovered that he was no longer angry.

MY FATHER, THE PAINTER

"Cynthia Barish?" the voice said, cracked, clipped, harsh.

Normally cautious and skeptical, unafraid to show her irritation with unsolicited calls, she answered "yes." Then it was too late.

"Your father's dead," the voice said.

"So?"

She hadn't seen or heard from him in twenty-five years, not since she was five. Her meager memory of his presence, occasionally reinforced by her mother's remarks, had become less sporadic as time passed.

"Who is this?"

"Feschetti, Mario. Actually I was his landlord. I wouldn't say he was my friend, but I kind of traded out on some of the rent. He did odd jobs. You know, took out the garbage, cleaned the halls, washed the front."

"Where did you get my name? I haven't seen him in twenty-five years. Am I supposed to cry?"

He ignored her question.

"He had this heart attack. Died a few days later in Bellevue. His wallet gave you as next of kin."

"You're kidding," she said, expelling air through her teeth.

"The thing is he left instructions to be cremated, which he was. What I got here is this, his ashes, and a basement full of paintings, which has to be removed. I mean, I don't really have a choice in this. I don't know, maybe hundreds of paintings, stashed away. What am I supposed to do?"

"I haven't got a clue."

"I suppose I could dump them somewhere, burn them. I don't

know. So I called. He had you as next of kin with an address in Scarsdale. So I took a chance."

She was baffled by the explanation. Contrary to some practices, she hadn't used her maiden name since her marriage to Todd. How could he possibly know she lived in Scarsdale?

"And what am I supposed to do, Mister... What was the name?"

"Feschetti. I guess all this stuff is yours. It's why I called. Somebody has got to move it out. And I got the ashes."

"What the hell am I going to do with the stuff? As for the ashes, I just don't know."

"It's your stuff, lady. Not mine. You're the next of kin. You think he left a will?" He snickered. "Look. Here's my number." He gave her his number. "Think it over. Call me. I'll let you into the place. You decide. I really don't know what to do with all the stuff. You tell me. Call me later, okay?"

"I'll give it some thought," she said, finally reacting to the weirdness of it. "By the way," she asked before he could hang up. "Where did he live?"

"The Village," the man said. "Little Italy, actually. It's no palace. Got eight apartments but I'm sort of holding it for, you know. Developers buying it up now. 'Gentrification,' they call it."

"I don't believe this," she said.

"Listen, the man is dead. You're the next of kin. He was your father. Lou Harris, right? I have his ashes, for Christ's sakes."

"I don't mean that," she said. "I thought maybe he was far away. Gone, maybe the west coast. But Little Italy. We go there for Italian food."

"The best in the city." He gave her his number again and the address of the apartment. "Call me when you decide. I mean tomorrow at the latest. I got to clean out this stuff. Man painted day and night. Paintings all over the place."

"That's what my mother told me. Never sold one when she knew him."

"Looks like he never sold any since. Not that I know about art. Not my cup of tea. Day and night he painted. That I could tell you. As far as I know he never sold anything. I think he was on welfare or something. He paid part of the rent and worked off the other part."

"I'll call you, Mr...."

"Feschetti. Mario Feschetti."

It was mid-afternoon, April, a bit overcast, but that was to be expected in April. The baby was sleeping and Todd would be home in a couple of hours. Oddly, or coincidentally, she was a commercial artist working at home, designing logos, book covers, advertising layouts. Somewhere in back of her mind, she did acknowledge the genetic thing. Her mother embellished the connection by recalling that all he wanted to do is paint and never sold a damned thing. No tickee, no shirtie, she told him, in ultimatum after ultimatum until one day he upped and disappeared.

She got a divorce on desertion grounds, married Jack Nolan, had two other kids, and moved to Texas, where her stepfather had a Toyota franchise. But the picture she painted, the image another irony, was of a man consumed, obsessed with plying his art, unable to make a buck, forcing her to be the breadwinner as a secretary where she had three jobs to do, take care of baby Cynthia, do the housework, cook the meals, the usual cliché.

Okay, her mother admitted in those early days. She loved him, in the beginning at least. But, she averred time and time again, he was a wastrel, didn't lift a finger. Painted from morning until night. No dealer bit. The paintings were probably shit. This was the story Cynthia was weaned on, which got increasingly bitter as her mother struggled to raise her only child who was five at the time.

Cynthia's memory was vague, although the turpentine aura that hovered around him was something that stuck in her mind. She supposed the memory of odor was quite powerful since she could barely remember what he sounded like. Sometimes it took her a moment to remember his name. Lou. Her mother destroyed all the old snaps, although, for some reason, she retained the one showing the young couple at City Hall, where they were married. The man, her father, had black hair, a long thin face, like her. He was smiling and wore no tie. She had no idea what happened to that picture.

Her mother's attitude toward her missing husband was contemptuous. Her anger about him accelerated as time passed, and

Cynthia's early life echoed with one long harangue about her missing father, the ungrateful, unfeeling bastard, who left wife and daughter in the lurch. Not that he was missed as a breadwinner. Finally it became good riddance to bad rubbish and that tolled the end of any possible fond memories for his daughter. The man had turned his back on her and not once, not a single time, in the twenty-five years had he ever attempted to contact her. There were no letters, not even a postcard, no phone calls, nothing. The man had faded into oblivion. Is this someone she should cry over? Is this someone for whom she must disrupt her life? Was she supposed to care about his ashes and his paintings? "He's your father," the man Feschetti said. Really?

After a few years, especially when she met Jack Nolan, her mother stopped talking about Cynthia's father and he became a kind of legendary ne'er-do-well who disappeared, abandoning his wife and only child, the son of a bitch. Cynthia supposed he had reasons, since her mother was something of a shrew, but now that she had her own baby girl, she could not imagine her being abandoned, certainly not by Todd, who was a most loving Dad, who was steady and smart and climbing the ladder of financial success at Morgan Stanley.

After she hung up from Mr. Feschetti, she called her mother and told her the story.

"What can I say," her mother said. "He lived so close and didn't have the decency to visit his only daughter."

"He wants to know what I should do with his paintings. I guess I'm the heiress."

"Burn the shit. He never could sell them."

"The man said he would do it, if I didn't come up with some solution."

"Your call, darling. To me, he doesn't exist any more. As for his demise, I really don't give a tinker's damn. I spent six years with the man in some ancient history time warp. He gave me nothing but trouble and misery."

"And me," she said. She felt a sudden sensation of loss, which disturbed her.

"Do whatever you want, darling. As you say, you're the heiress. From what you tell me he was nothing more than a janitor. The man was off the wall. Do whatever you want. Oh yes, there're the ashes. Might make good fertilizer."

The idea was ghoulish and, while she had never thought about her father affectionately, she was insulted by the remark. *No matter what, he's still my father.* Todd was on that same page.

"He's your blood."

"Fruit of his loins," she said, being sarcastic.

"There's something to say for the genes," Todd said. His father was a professor of mathematics at Columbia, and Todd was a whiz at math and working on derivatives for the company. He often expressed the idea that such talents are handed down in the DNA.

"I think you should go down there and see what it's all about," Todd said. She knew he would give her that advice. He was a family man to the teeth, a beloved son, grandson, brother, and husband. Being taken in by Todd's family had been a blessing for Cynthia, who had felt like a third wheel when her mother married Jack Nolan.

"You're such a family-values person. Don't forget my father abandoned me when I was five years old. He was a real shit, never getting in touch with me."

"Apparently he had your name in his wallet."

"How the hell did he sniff that out?" she exclaimed, intrigued now.

"Clinches it. It's a mystery. You've got to go."

"And what will I do with the damned paintings. Apparently no one was ever interested in buying them. Feschetti said there are hundreds of them."

"We'll cross that bridge when we come to it," Todd said. He was logical, sensible, and practical. He always did know the math. Got that from his dad, she thought, thinking of her own artistic bent. One day, too, she secretly yearned to be a successful painter. But then, what commercial artist didn't aspire to that.

Leaving the baby with a sitter, she drove into the city and met Feschetti in front of the building on Mulberry Street. Feschetti was accurate. The building was a dump, a four-story walk-up with eight apartments, waiting for gentrification. Feschetti was a heavyset bald man, probably in his fifties, which was about the age of her father.

She'd have to check his exact age on her birth certificate. But then, why would even that detail matter to her.

The apartment was a mess. It reeked with paint and the stink of turpentine, which set off strange memories in her mind. The man lived as if he was homeless, sleeping on a crippled cot, with a paint-stained mattress. In fact everything about the place looked like a Jackson Pollock painting.

"Okay," Feschetti said. "He was a slob. Wore paint-stained overalls. The place is like a cyclone went through it. But you gotta understand, he cleaned the place's halls real nice, kept the front clean, took out the garbage."

"How long did he live here?"

"Jesus, twenty years at least, maybe twenty-five. Who knew? My mother made this deal with him. And when she died and I took over, I kept it going. Hell, it paid for itself. No mortgage."

"What kind of a man was he?" Despite herself, the crummy atmosphere in the apartment made her curious. What kind of a man could live in this squalor?

"Actually, tell you the truth, he wasn't a bad guy. He did a good job with the place and all he did was paint as far as I knew."

The paintings were piled in all the rooms, and in the back where the furnace was there were more paintings. There was a shack in the back that Feschetti said had even more paintings. They were piled flat, floor to ceiling. She pulled one from the top of the pile. Not bad, she thought. Apparently he was an experimenter. Impressionist pieces, many snow scenes depicting New York sites, cityscapes in all seasons, Central Park scenes with the trees in bloom and green grass, lots of images of what appeared to be Little Italy, the bridges, river scenes, street scenes, also abstracts, even drip paintings like Pollock. Portraits in different styles of people of all ages.

"I guess he painted his life history."

"Looks like it," Feschetti said. "I got six of his paintings around the neighborhood."

"And he never sold any?" she asked, baffled.

"Can't tell by me." He looked around the apartment. "This look like he made a buck?"

She moved through the apartment to a back room filled floor-to-ceiling with paintings. There were additional paintings placed upright against the wall near the furnace. Suddenly she stiffened and she felt her stomach lurch.

It was her. Recent. She felt that she might faint. Feschetti was behind her.

"That's you," he said.

Her knees shook and she began to rifle through the other paintings. There she was again and again, painted in all ages.

"I don't believe this." She could barely get the words out. "How?"

Had he stalked her in some way? Photographed her? She rushed through the apartment, opening closets. One was filled with shoeboxes. Opening one, she found photographs of her from every age but never front-faced.

Feeling faint again, she had to sit on the broken cot, baffled and deeply disturbed.

"You okay?" Feschetti asked again. "You're white as a sheet."

She nodded, but couldn't get the words out. She opened her purse and reached for her cell, wanting to call Todd, but her fingers shook too much and she put the phone back in her pocketbook.

"Why?" she mumbled, looking up at the round face of Feschetti, who shrugged. She took a deep breath and stood up.

"He could have made himself known to me. Why?"

"You're asking the wrong guy," Freshetti said. "I got kids."

She was slowly recovering, looking now around the room, trying to imagine what was going on in his mind.

"He had this thing," Freshetti said.

"What thing?"

"Painted all the time. I saw him lugging his stuff every day. Looks like he painted everything in sight."

"Even me," Cynthia said.

"Lots of you. That's for sure. But then, you were his daughter."

"Big deal. Did he ever once come over to me, speak to me?" She felt herself turning angry now. "Crazy bastard." She raised her voice. "Why didn't he ever acknowledge me?" It wasn't a question directed to Feschetti, but he answered it anyway.

"Hey, lady. Didn't acknowledge you? He painted you over and over. Means something. Doesn't it?"

She didn't answer him, but agreed with the thought.

"I'll just have to deal with it," Cynthia said. "All these paintings."

"They gotta go, lady. Can't get away from that."

She took a deep breath and nodded, then she called Todd and explained what she had observed.

"What shall I do?" she asked.

"They're yours."

"So?"

"We'll have them appraised. Make a market. That's my business. We'll put them in storage and go from there. Maybe...just maybe this is your lucky day, baby. One thing," he said, before signing off. "He didn't forget you."

That set her off and finally big sobs heaved up from her chest and tears rolled over her cheeks. For some reason she leaned against Feschetti, who embraced her.

"Jesus," Feschetti said. "It's okay."

"Daddy," she said, when she found words. "My Daddy."

After awhile she untangled herself from his embrace, reached into her pocketbook, pulled out some tissues and wiped her eyes and cheeks.

"We'll take everything off your hands. Everything. We'll be making arrangements."

"That's good. He wasn't a bad guy. I guess he didn't want anything to interfere with his painting." He looked around the room. "This was his life. It takes all kinds."

"You have a point. He shut everything out but this."

She started to move out of the apartment, then stopped and turned to face Feschetti.

"His ashes."

"Nearly forgot." He looked under the bed and pulled out an urn. She took it from him.

"He was my father," she said.

"My father, the painter," he said, perhaps trying to get her to smile.

She did.

About the Author

Warren Adler is the author of 24 critically acclaimed novels and four short story collections. The film adaptations of two of his novels, *The War of the Roses* and *Random Hearts,* continue to enjoy great popularity throughout the world. A previous short story collection, *The Sunset Gang*, became a successful trilogy on PBS. His most recent novel, *Funny Boys,* is published by The Overlook Press.

Mr. Adler is a native New Yorker and a graduate of NYU. He studied creative writing at The New School. His wife Sonia is the former editor and owner of the *Washington Dossier.* They have three sons and four grandchildren.

NEW YORK ECHOES

Reading Group Questions and Topics for Discussion

Reading Group Questions and Topics for Discussion

A collection of short stories makes for especially interesting readers group material since it ranges over a wide landscape that can make for lively debate and commentary. Here are some suggested topics and questions that can provoke interest and inspire insightful discussion in connection with *New York Echoes* by Warren Adler.

1. Does one get the sense after reading these stories that New York City is a land unto itself, circumscribed by its own mores, habits, and attitude than the rest of the country?
2. Of all the stories in the book, which one resonated the most to you?
3. There are a number of stories that deal with parents and grandparents like "The Cherry Tree" and "Oral History" and the divide between the generations. Do you believe this divide is growing more so than in previous generations?
4. A number of these stories like "My Father, The Painter" deal with the obsessive needs of the creative artist where the pursuit of one's art trumps all human relationships. Is the artist justified in pursuing such a single-minded pursuit?
5. Some of these stories like "Good Neighbors" and "The Mean Mrs. Dickstein" deal with coping with living in close proximity to others in a bustling, frenetic, high-energy city. How do you cope with this phenomenon in your daily life?
6. As the story "The Obituary Reader" implies, guilt and shame for past actions magnifies itself as time goes on. Do you believe that time enhances or blunts such feelings?
7. The pursuit of celebrity through show business is passion that apparently brooks no hardship. In the stories "Actors" and "Better Than Donna Reed," one confronts the reality of this hardship. Is it worth the candle?
8. The story "A Dad Forever" deals with the irrelevance of a parent to a grown child. Do you believe this is an accurate portrayal?
9. Memories of young love and passion permeate a number of stories in this collection, as in "A Love Story." Do you believe

that such early experiences of love and sex are as endurable and powerful as portrayed?

10. There are a number of stories like "A Birthday Celebration" that deal with loss and loneliness. Do you believe that living in a crowded city like New York enhances such feelings?

11. Stories like "I Can Still Smell It" and "That Horrid Thing" deal with the trauma of 9/11 and how it continues to impact people's lives. Although more than six years have passed since that traumatic event, does the anxiety and fear engendered by it still generate the same amount of anxiety and worry as it did immediately after the event?

12. In the story "Epiphany" latent and hidden cultural anti-Semitism rears its ugly head in a divorce dispute. Do you think it will ever be possible to erase this hateful strain that afflicts the human psyche?

13. In the "Dividing Line" and "Oral History" fading generational memory is explored. How much does historical memory really matter?

14. Because the author is a father, it is natural that a number of the stories deal with fatherhood and its consequences. Do you think this has been a neglected topic in recent fiction?

15. The short story, once a staple of reading formats, has experienced a decline in recent decades because of its elimination from magazine content. The Internet is now responsible for an upsurge in interest in short imaginative fiction. Do you believe the short story format is now on the upswing?

16. Would you like to see another volume of short stories dealing with life in New York City?

Enjoy the first chapter of
Warren Adler's new novel

FUNNY BOYS

Published by The Overlook Press

The adventures of a budding young comedian in a Catskill
Mountain, "Borscht Belt" resort where, circa 1937, the era's
gangsters, dubbed Murder Inc., stash their wives, children, and
girlfriends for the summer. Grim, sexy, violent, authentic, and
hilarious, this story of love and danger stirs tears of nostalgia for a
lost era and immerses the reader in a pulse-quickening, unforgettable
narrative.

FUNNY
BOYS

WARREN
ADLER

Bestselling author of THE WAR OF THE ROSES

CHAPTER ONE

The woman opened the door to Gorlick's suite and two men emerged. The shorter one grabbed the woman's buttocks and squeezed.

"Is that a tush, Pep, or what?"

"World class," the taller man said.

Mickey Fine, who had been waiting in the corridor puzzled over the men. The shorter one wore a brown pin-stripe double-breasted suit with a red rose in its lapel and a beige fedora. His glance washed over Mickey like a spotlight in a prison movie, freezing him in its glare like a pinned insect.

The other was taller, handsomer, dressed to the nines in a blue serge suit and matching satiny blue tie on a white-on-white shirt. He wore a pearl gray fedora and his black shoes were spit-shined, in contrast to his shorter companion's scuffed browns. He was also handsome in a hard way and his lips wore a thin smile that was anything but warm.

Mickey watched them both swagger toward the elevators. It was the tall one who looked back at Mickey, studying him briefly, as if trying to recall him from some previous occasion. Mickey had the same sensation.

"Mr. Gawlick will see ya now," the woman said, dissolving his effort at remembering. She was tall, with a voluptuous figure and a low-cut dress that showed much fleshy cleavage. He followed her as she pranced into the suite on swivel hips that swung at an exaggerated wide angle. A tush like the Pied Piper, he thought, confirming the earlier comment. Follow it anywhere. Does it come with that swing? he wanted to say, then thought better of it. But the idea did boost his energy level and chase away the edginess that the appearance of the two men had brought on. He came into the suite with a theatrical bounce and a face-aching smile.

Clouds of smoke layered the air in Sol Gorlick's suite. He was a short corpulent man with squinty eyes and thick lips. As Mickey entered, he was just lighting a long expensive-looking cigar. The jacket of his double-breasted suit was open, showing sweat puddles on his blue shirt. His pants were high-belted over a balloon-like stomach and his bald head appeared lacquered, reflecting the slanting rays of late afternoon sunlight.

His complexion was waxy and although his face was round and fat, his skin did not hang in jowls. Greeting Mickey with a nod, he pointed with his cigar to a chair beside the coffee table.

"Sit," he grunted.

Mickey sat in an upholstered chair beside the coffee table, on which were a number of used highball glasses, a half emptied bottle of seltzer and nearly empty bottle of Johnny Walker. Salted peanuts were strewn around the table. There was also a silver pistol cigarette lighter and an ashtray filled with smashed cigarette and cigar butts.

The woman who had shown him in sat opposite Mickey on a matching chair, crossing her legs, showing an expanse of pink flesh on either side of her black stocking suspenders.

"This is Mickey Fine, Mr. Gawlick," the woman said. Gorlick's big behind sank deeply into the soft cushions of the couch. He sat upright, his back stiff, his belly resting on his thighs. Mickey noted that he had star sapphire rings on the pinkies of both hands.

"Here I'm Fine," Mickey said. "But finer in Caroliner." Keep the one-liners coming, he urged himself. He prayed that his nervousness wouldn't erase his memory.

Gorlick smiled thinly, nodded and picked up a paper from the coffee table. Mickey watched him as he puffed on his cigar, blowing thick smoke rings as he read. Mickey could see it was the letter he had sent outlining his experience. Not earthshaking. He had been a waiter and substitute tumler at Blumenkranz' in Lock Sheldrake for two summers. For three summers before that he had been a bus boy at Grossingers and been in some of the weeknight shows.

Off-season he played small club dates, mostly Jewish veterans
and women's groups. Days he helped in his father's ladies underwear
store on Sutter Avenue in Brownsville. Nights he went to CCNY.

"It's short," Mickey said. "I ran out of lies."

"You're twenty-two?" Gorlick said, inspecting him.

"All year," Mickey replied.

"He looks like a Jewish Tom Mix. Don't he, Gloria?" Gorlick
said, tossing his head toward the woman.

"And here I thought I was passing for a goy. I know. You saw
my horse, Tony." Mickey turned toward the woman. "He's
circumcised. How can you hide it?"

Gloria made a sound like a Bronx cheer.

"Sometimes I forget and say 'Oy Oy Gold' instead of 'Hi-Yo
Silver.'"

"That's the Lone Ranger," Gloria snickered.

"You think he's not Jewish? Why do you think he travels with
his tanta?"

Gorlick, not reacting, puffed a smoke ring into the air, then
picked up a stray peanut from the cocktail table and popped it into
the smoke cloud belching from his mouth.

"Such a tumler," Gloria said winking. "He's a real cutie pie.
The girls would get a kick out of him."

Mickey felt her inspection, distracted by the swell of the upper
part of her full breasts. But when he forced himself to shift his
glance, he found himself watching that stretch of pink bare thigh.

"What kind of a store your father got?" Mr. Gorlick asked,
looking over the paper again.

"Foundation garments," Mickey said, not with a slight twinge
of embarrassment. People always reacted with a snicker and Gorlick
and Gloria were no exceptions.

There was humor in it, he knew, but mostly to others; less to
Mickey or his mother or father or sister. To them the store meant
survival and they lived above it. To the Fines foundation garments
were serious business, although Mickey had developed a repertoire
of jokes about it.

"Corsets, girdles, things like that?" Gorlick asked, smiling.

"We fix flats, too," Mickey said, looking pointedly at Gloria, who needed none of his father's wares. As if to emphasize the obvious, Gloria straightened in her chair and flung out her chest.

"Bet you seen plenty," Gorlick chuckled.

"Plenty is the word for it. It's turned me into a vegetarian."

Gorlick grunted another chuckle, then turned his eyes back to the paper.

"What kind of courses you taking?"

"General," Mickey said. "If things don't work out, maybe, as a last resort, I'll become a shyster." Despite the joke it was a bone of contention between him and his parents. To them becoming a tumler was not a proper career path, although they often laughed at his jokes. "I get a kick out of making people laugh," he told them. You can still be a lawyer and make people laugh, they would say. It was a never ending complaint.

"A shyster." Gorlick nodded. "At Gorlick's a shyster would have a field day." He turned and winked at Gloria, who smiled thinly.

"That's if show business doesn't pan out," Mickey said, reluctant to reveal his secret yearnings for comedy stardom.

"A putz business," Gorlick said.

"Maybe he wants to be a movie star," Gloria interjected. "The Jewish Tom Mix and his faithful horse, Moishey." She laughed heartily, her big tits shaking.

He felt a sudden twinge of resentment, wondering if they were taking his ambition seriously. That part was not a joke.

"What we are seeking here," Gorlick said, "is a special kind of tumler for 'Gorlick's Greenhouse'—a classy boy, a diplomat, an organizer, a social director with "tum," ya know whatimean?"

"Also funny, Solly," Gloria said. "Goes without saying. Sure funny. It also helps if you can sing a little."

Mickey nodded. He had a fair voice.

"And a good dancer. A refined talker. Ya know whatimean, a smart classy funny boy who can keep the guests happy."

"They liked me at Blumenkranz," Mickey said. He was at somewhat of a disadvantage over that. He had been set for the season at Blumenkranz, another Catskill hotel, then Mrs. Blumenkranz hired her brother's son for the job. With ten days until Decoration Day, when the Catskill hotels traditionally opened, he was in no bargaining position. It was Blumenkranz who had recommended him to Gorlick, who had apparently had some disagreement with the tumler he had hired then fired.

"Blumenkranz," Gorlick sneered, "A pigsty cockeninyam operation. We're not like the other hotels. We're special. We got a special clientele." He took a deep drag on his cigar and looked at Gloria. "Small but eleganty. One-fifty guests max on weekends. A showplace. Great coozeen. Kosher but gourmet. We don't even have to advertise. All woid of mouth. In the middle of the week we got the wives, the kids, the girlfriends. Weekends when the boys come up we expect you to put on a show, sometimes we hire a specialty act, and we got a three-piece band all week. I say sometimes, because mostly the boys want action."

"Action?"

"Big time action. Poker. Crap tables. Slots."

"Is that legal?" Mickey asked, instantly regretting his hasty response. Blumenkranz and Grossingers had been straight places. But Sullivan County, which covered the Catskills, was considered wide open for gambling in some of the hotels. He had played slot machines at hotels near Lock Sheldrake.

"Legal shmegal. Not my business."

Mickey shrugged, watching Gorlick use his big cigar as if it were a baton.

". . . it's the weekdays I worry about, especially when it rains. When the boys come, ya know, they inject a happier prospect, if you get my meaning. But on the weekdays the girls get bored with the machines and not all are not into cards. You gotta tumel them, keep them happy. They get bored, moody, start to complain about the coozeen. On the weekends they tell the boys and we got tsouris." Gorlick raised his eyes to the ceiling, as if he needed validation from a higher source.

"Tell him about last year's, Solly," Gloria piped. She extracted a compact from her bag and began to fix her makeup.

"A schmuck. Not bad on a stage. A good dancer. A schmoozer.

He could tell a lotta jokes. A genius at Simon Sez. But on the floor, he was not a diplomat. Worse, he was a schmuck with a schmuck, if you get my drift." He looked toward Gloria, who peeked out from behind her compact and giggled.

"I love it, Solly."

"In the right place, at the right time, a young schmuck with a schmuck is a valuable asset. At the wrong place at the wrong time it's tsouris. This schmuck's schmuck gave me tsouris."

"One thing I know is my place, Mr. Gorlick," Mickey said seriously, calculating that the matter was a serious issue with Gorlick.

"It's your schmuck that's got to know its place," Gorlick said, looking down at the paper on the coffee table, "Mickey."

"No question," Mickey said. He was remembering Blumen- kranz. On weeknights the women were barracudas. To some, he hadn't been averse, but he knew it was tricky business. "I know how to draw a 'Fine' line." The pun sailed right over Gorlick's head.

"Last year's social director is still in the hospital," Gloria said from behind her compact. "It's a miracle they let him live."

"I won't even tell you what they did to him," Gorlick said. "But you can imagine."

"Jesus," Mickey said, feeling a sudden chill as he envisioned what they might have done.

"We gotta cure, tumler," Gloria said, winking. "Only it costs."

Gorlick looked at Gloria and shook his head.

"Hey, Solly. What about our two minute special?" Gloria giggled.

"Now funny. Show me funny," Gorlick said, flicking an ash into the ashtray on the coffee table.

But the stab of fear had dampened Mickey's enthusiasm. He was also confused. He thought he had been funny, showing them his funny attitude and his ability to integrate funny patter into the conversation.

"Tumler shtick," Gorlick prodded.

"I've got a terrific file. One liners and routines. Lots of blackouts." Mickey said. But when they didn't react, he cleared his throat and stood up.

"Now take my boss. He's the biggest man in who owes who. If he can't take it with him—he'll send his creditors. He gives me plenty of exercise. When he gives me a check I have to race him to the bank."

Gloria giggled.

"Boss jokes are okay," Gorlick said.

"Except for Garlic. He hates to be called Garlic," Gloria interjected. Gorlick nodded.

"That would be in bad taste," Mickey said, searching Gorlick's eyes for a glint of acknowledgement. He found none.

"Jokes on wives are okay. Shvartzers. Pollack jokes. But be careful on smut. There are kids around."

"Stinky little brats," Gloria piped. "Course they think they're all Little Lord Fauntleroys and Shirley Temples."

"And that's the way you treat them. Make nice, nice, nice," Gorlick said. "And be careful with the ladies. They like dirty but not in front of the men. The boys get edgy, think you're try to . . . you know . . . heat up the frying pan. With the men everything goes. They love smut, smuttier the better. But the biggest no-no of all. Hear my woids." Gorlick put a fat finger in front of Mickey's nose. "Absolutely no wop jokes. You put that one in your tuchas." Gorlick tapped his temple. "Get in the habit, just in case."

"You have wops in a kosher hotel?" Mickey asked innocently.

Gorlick bent forward and glared at him. His cigary breath was not pleasant.

"Nobody tells a wop joke in front Albert Anastasia."

"Albert who?"

"Mr. Anastasia is a very important man," Gorlick said. He scratched his head.

"I get it. A celebrity. What is he? A bandleader? An actor? A ballplayer?"

Gorlick's eyes narrowed and his thick lips seemed to grow narrower with pressure. He looked toward Gloria, who shrugged.

"Goomba goes crazy when anyone makes fun of wops. Even Mussolini. In a kosher hotel, a tumler says the word guinea or wop or makes Italian jokes, Anastasia has a shit conniption." Gloria explained.

"And who gets the blame?" Gorlick shrugged and pressed a thumb to his chest. "Yours truly."

"They get real mad, they play with matches, " Gloria said, lowering her voice.

"Burn me down, like they did to Shechters."

"With the Jewish boys, it's different," Gloria said. "They like the bad-boy rep cause people think Jews are, you know mollycoddles, mama's boys, fraidy cats. Like they been kicked around because they didn't fight back."

Gorlick glanced toward Gloria and raised his eyes to the ceiling.

"You're from Brownsville and I suppose you never heard of Kid Twist or Pittsburgh Phil?" Gorlick asked.

"An old vaudeville act, right?"

"It's no act, Mickey," Gorlick said ominously. "You just seen em come outa here."

"Those ones," Mickey said. "Bad actors both of them."

"Jesus," Gorlick said. "You never heard of Abie "Kid Twist" Reles and Pittburgh Phil Strauss? The guy they call Pep. Where you been? In China? They got reps a mile wide."

"Reles? Strauss? Kid Twist? Pep?"

His memory kicked in and he felt his stomach turn to a block of ice.

"You okay, boychick?" Gorlick said.

"He's like a white sheet," Gloria said.

Reles and Strauss! Kid Twist and Pep. Those two he had just seen come out of here. He wiped a film of icy sweat from his forehead. It took him a moment to recover.

The image of his father's battered face surfaced in his mind. They had come into his father's store one night. Mickey had been upstairs. Luckily his mother was playing cards at a friend's house.

It had all happened so quickly. Mickey had heard muffled sounds and ran downstairs to the store. His father lay on the floor writhing in pain, his face bloody and bruised. Reles, the short one, was standing over his father with what looked like a piece of pipe wrapped in newspaper. The other man, Strauss, started to move to intercept Mickey who was heading for Reles.

"No, please," his father had shouted. "Mickey, please. Leave us alone."

"Leave you alone?" Mickey said dumbfounded, stopped in his tracks. "They're trying to kill you."

"Kill him? Whatayou crazy?" Reles said, shooting Mickey a glance with feverish agate eyes and a twisted grin. "Shmeckel knows da score." He looked at his father on the floor.

"Dis is business, kid," Strauss said.

"I owe them money," Mickey's father croaked.

"Nothin poisonal boychick," Reles said. "Ya borrow money from Roth's bank, ya pay on time." He looked down at Mickey's father, then swung the newspaper-coated pipe, hitting him on the shoulder. His father screeched in pain.

"I promise," his father whimpered. "Please go way now."

"Hey, looka dis," Strauss said suddenly, holding up a pair of women's pink satin panties. "Dis is real pretty." He stuffed it in a side pocket. Then he picked up the box from which it had come. "I'll take em all. Ya want some faw yaw hooers, Abie?"

Reles looked up and laughed.

"I got no hooers, Pep. Youse da guy wid da hooers. I got my Helen."

"I fawgot, Abie," Pep sneered. "Lucky you."

"Put em on my tab," Pep said to the older man.

"You can't take that," Mickey cried. "That's salable merchandise."

"Mickey, please," his father cried. He was trying to shimmy up one of the display counters to stand upright. Mickey ran over to help.

"Dese are not fun times faw us, Fine," Reles said. "Pay up and save yourself da tsouris."

"I promise."

"Not nice, Fine. Passing bum checks. A shanda."

"I thought it was covered," his father said.

His father had finally managed to stand upright, although

unsteadily. Blood was gushing from his nose. His shirt was heavily sprinkled with it.

Reles pointed the end of the pipe to his father's chest. Then he nodded toward Strauss.

Mickey felt himself grabbed in a hammerlock from behind. He struggled but to little avail; Strauss pressed a hard bony knee into his spine, doubling him over.

"Ya got any scratch to pay off Daddy's markers, schmuck?"

"Please. Don't hurt Mickey please. He had nothing to do with this," his father pleaded. Then he heard a cry of pain. Lifting his head, he saw his father sprawled on the floor again. He started to crawl on his belly toward Mickey. Reles stepped on his fingers and his father screamed in pain.

"I asked ya nice," Pep said to the helpless Mickey. "I don like to repeat."

"It's not his fault," his father pleaded weakly.

"Whose talkin to you, putz?" Reles said, kicking his father in the ribs. Then he turned to Mickey. "Pep asked you nice. Even a down payment shows good fate."

"I give him da toilet, right, Abie?" Strauss said.

"Got a can?" Reles asked Mickey's father, who lay on the floor watching Mickey. Blood and tears were running down his cheeks. Reles walked behind a counter to the one dressing room. Beside it was a door. He opened it.

"Fat ladies take a pea heah," Reles said, as Mickey was manhandled and forced to his knees on the floor in front of the toilet.

"Now we goin to play submarine, kid."

"How much?" Mickey gasped.

"Whats da number?" Pep asked.

"I feget, Pep," Reles said. He dipped into a side pocket and brought out a notebook he opened, searching for a name with spatulate fingers.

"We need tree hunert," Reles said. "But we take a down payment. Say fifty."

"I'll go to the bank tomorrow," Mickey said. Actually he had three hundred fifty saved in his account just in case he needed it for law school in the fall. Or to go to Hollywood.

"Ya got nuthin in the house?" Pep asked.

"Please. Leave my boy alone," Mickey's father shouted. He had managed to lift himself off the floor once more and was standing looking into the cubicle using the walls for support.

"Again he don answer, Abie," Strauss said. Mickey felt Strauss grab him by the hair and begin to force his head down.

Mickey's father made an attempt to step forward into the cubicle, but Reles pulled him out by the back of his belt and hit him solidly on the underside of his knees. The man screamed and fell to the floor, writhing in pain.

"Bastards," Mickey screamed. But he could barely get the word out as Strauss forced his head into the toilet and pulled the overhead chain. Water and noise swirled around him as Strauss emersed his entire head in the toilet bowl. Mickey struggled but Strauss held him fast. He felt as if his lungs would burst.

Then, suddenly, Strauss pulled his head out and Mickey, approaching hysteria, took deep gasps of breath. Mickey's father, writhing on the floor, began to sob hysterically.

"I got about forty in the house," Mickey blurted through his gasps.

"See what a nice boy ya got, Fine," Reles laughed. "Fine pays a fine."

"And tomorrow I'll see you get everything."

"Evyting?" Pep asked.

"Whatever my father owes."

"Dis is one fine kid, Fine. Ya oughta be proud."

"I like dis, Fine," Strauss chuckled. "Knows da score."

"Whats ya name, kid?" Reles asked.

"Mickey."

"Mickey. Hey, dats fine," Reles roared.

"Like Mickey Finn," Strauss said giggling. For a moment he relaxed his grip on Mickey's hair. "You tink he needs one more reminda? I kinda like dis shit."

"Maybe one maw fa good luck," Reles said.

"Down da hatch, kid," Mickey heard Strauss say. Then came the pounding water and soon he was gasping for breath. Strauss pulled him up again.

"You get da drift? " Reles said.

Mickey nodded. Pep still held him in a viselike grip.

"Next time we keep ya down dere," Pep said.

Mickey nodded. There was no point in resisting. He saw his father reaching out an arm in his direction. Strauss pulled Mickey to his feet.

"Fawty now, right?" Reles said.

Mickey nodded. Strauss walked him upstairs, to the little chest next to the cot where he slept. Opening a drawer, Mickey took four tens from under his underwear and gave it to Strauss.

"You're lucky, kid. I'm da easy one. That Abie's an animal."

They came downstairs into the store. His father was slumped on a wooden chair, his eyes glazed, his face bloody.

"And tomorra da whole marker, right?" Reles said.

"Ya don play round wid Abie," Strauss said.

"I swear," Mickey said. "I swear. Only go now."

"We tank you faw da hospitality," Reles said.

"And I tank you for the panties." Pep held up the box.

"Dey gonna be more awf dan on," Reles said laughing.

Later that night, after his father's wounds had been attended to, he had confessed what he had done. He had borrowed money from "the bank" in the candy store on Saratoga and Livonia under the El. A man, the son of the owner, got approval for $300 for ten weeks with a payback of $60 a week.

"I gave them post-dated checks. They're "shylocks." I knew it. What could I do? I can't get goods, we can't sell anything."

"Papa, that's double interest."

"I needed it. What bank would give it to me?"

His father started to cry. "You should have told me, Papa."

As promised, Mickey paid off the loan the next day. Odd, he thought, how he couldn't remember the men right away—as if he had blanked out the whole experience.

"Sure," Mickey told Gorlick soberly. "I think I know who you mean."

"You think?" Gorlick said. "They enforce things. But don't ask."

"Like shylocking?"

"Like everything," Gorlick shrugged. "I told you, don't ask. Never. It's not your business. Not mine neither. I run a hotel."

"It bothers you?" Gloria asked Mickey.

Mickey thought about that for a moment.

"Not me," he said, almost choking on the thought. He needed this job. "Live and let live."

Gorlick tapped his temple again.

"So use your tuchas." Gorlick, having made his point, stuck his cigar in his mouth and nodded. "Remember the rules. We got here a very special clientele.

"Explain about the combination, Solly."

Mickey must have looked puzzled.

"You never heard of the combination?" Gorlick asked.

Mickey shrugged and looked helplessly toward Gloria, who shook her head in a kind of flouncy disgust. He knew all he wanted to know about these men.

"Brownsville and Ocean Hill," Gorlick explained. "The sheenies and the wops. These are the boys that run the show."

A hotel for gangsters and their families, Mickey realized at last. A cold chill ran up his spine.

"Combination. Get it. We got Jewish customers and Italian visitors. They come to Gorlicks to meet. So no wop jokes. Never eva."

"Jew jokes are mostly okay," Gloria said. "Jews like to laugh at themselves."

"I got lots of those," Mickey said. "Like 'Don't give up. Moses was also a basket case.'"

"Yeah," Gorlick chuckled.

"How about 'We got a sign over the urinal. Says the future of the Jewish people is in your hands.'"

Gloria giggled.

"Save that for weekdays. The girls love shmeckel jokes."

"But talk only, Fine. Talk only."

"Got it. We swat flies at Gorlicks. We don't unbutton them."

"No fly jokes, Fine. We got horseflies in August." Gorlick turned to Gloria.

"You think he understands the emmis."

Gloria looked him over as if he were a prized race horse.

"Believe me, I got it," Mickey said. "Their business is their business and my business is funny."

"It's inspiring, right, Solly? The combination." Gloria said.

"Yeah," Gorlick said through a smoke cloud. "An American success story, the way these boys do business and love each other. Catolic and Jew. They come to Gorlicks for the relaxation and the action and this is where the Jew boys put their families for the summer. The wops have their own places, but they come here to meet. The wops like the kosher coozeen."

"So no wop jokes," Mickey reiterated, groping to get back into a tumler mood. After all, his father had healed, the money had been paid back. Even his father had agreed, despite the brutal methods used, that this was business. "I went in with open eyes," he told Mickey. "So who is the real criminal? Them or me?"

"It's a respectable Jewish place, strictly kosher. We gotta lot of goyem help." Gorlick went on. "We got shiksa waitresses and maids. You'll hear things, Fine. You know what I mean. Bad Jew stuff."

"Don't listen," Gloria said. "It's expected."

"Mostly they know better," Gorlick said. "If not . . . if the boys hear. . . ." He made a slashing motion across his neck.

Mickey nodded, his stomach fluttering.

"And no gangster jokes," Gloria said. "Especially not in fronta the girls. They are very sensitive about this subject."

"Gangsters consider themselves businessmen and wish to be referred to as such," Gorlick said. "And they must always be called Mister."

"Like Mr. Kid Twist and Mr. Pittsburgh Phil?" Mickey asked. When Gorlick and Gloria didn't laugh, he said, "Just a joke."

"Monickers are for them and the news boys. Not for you," Mr. Gorlick said. "We had an incident with Mr. Buchalter. One of the waiters called him Mr. Lepke."

"Even though he used Mister," Mickey said.

"These are very sensitive men, Mickey," Gorlick said.

"What happened to the waiter?"

"Don't ask," Gorlick muttered.

"They can be very demanding," Gloria said. "Right, Solly?" Gorlick nodded. "And they are very possessive of their women," he said. "Hence my earlier reference to shtupping."

Gorlick puffed his cigar and watched him.

"Discretion is the better part of value," Mickey said, the pun chasing the pall of gloom.

"Yeah. Yeah," Gorlick said. "Something like that." He turned to Gloria, who had closed her compact and was smoothing her skirt. "So whattaya think, Gloria?" He glanced back at Mickey. "Gloria is a specialist in entertainment." Gorlick winked. "Right, Gloria?"

"Bettah believe. Teddy Katz would have been a mistake to hire," Gloria said. Apparently this was the man they had fired before the season.

"She thought he was too pretty."

"All we needed was a tumler who looked like Clark Gable. In my opinion we saved him from a not-too-good fate. These boys don't play games about things like that."

"This ones so so," Gorlick said.

"At least he's no Gable," Gloria said. "He doesn't look like a chaser."

Mickey faced her and showed his good white teeth. He was picturing her spread-eagled under Gorlick's corpulent body, her smooth white thighs hugging his whale-like middle. In his mind, he saw the porch swing of her hips in double time.

"Not a world beater," Gloria said. He noted that she had lipstick on her teeth. "And his jokes stink."

"I didn't show you everything. I got the whole Jessel routine with the mother down pat." He put one fist to his ear and one to his mouth. "Hey Mother, this is your son Mickey, the one with the checks..."

"I'll say this," Gorlick interrupted. "He's a real tumler. He gives me a headache."

"I do imitations, too," Mickey persisted, summoning up his Edward G. Robinson. "Ya ya, you boysh get your gats and come wish me to the Soush Side."

"How many guesses?" Gorlick said.

"Want to see my Eddie Cantor?"

"Not today," Gorlick said.

"Who's this?" Mickey said, summoning up his Joe Penner. "Wanna buy a duck?"

"You're shpritzing me." Gorlick said.

Gloria's continued contemplation was an elaborate routine. She lit a cigarette with the pistol lighter that had been lying on the cocktail table then got up from the chair, brushed down her dress, looked behind her to straighten the seams of her stockings, then walked across the room, hips swinging, her cute ass bobbing.

At the other end of the room, she stopped, took a squinty drag on the cigarette, picked a morsel of tobacco from her tongue, then, throwing out her ample chest, she posed against a doorpost, eyeing Mickey up and down.

"Great audition, kid," Mickey said, imitating Cagney. "You got the job."

Gorlick moved his head from side to side.

"Not bad," he said, barely cracking a smile.

"You a fagele?" Gloria asked suddenly.

"Oh my God," Mickey said mincingly, waving a limp wrist. "You do know."

"A fagele they wouldn't like," Gloria said. "They like a real tease."

Mickey hid his embarrassment. He did not like being judged like horseflesh.

"Considering the others we seen," Gloria said, "and since we need someone in ten days, maybe you should give him a try."

Gorlick turned to Mickey. "I personally am not overly impressed."

"I swear, Mr. Gorlick," Mickey said, raising his right hand. "If I let them down may I drop dead."

"Believe me, boychick, that's no joke."

"They kill people that aren't funny?" Mickey asked with elaborate innocence.

"For less than that," Gloria said as she came back to the chair and sat down.

Again Mickey caught a peek at pink flesh beside her stocking suspenders. The sight, with its resultant twitch of lust, somehow mitigated the sense of the ominous. Their warnings seemed unreal, make-believe, a kind of initiation ritual for a tumler rookie.

"The important thing," Gorlick said, shifting his body on the couch and lowering his voice. "No matter what you see, what you hear, you gotta always make like them three monkeys."

"See no evil, hear no evil, speak no evil," Mickey said acting out the words, walking around the room like a gorilla.

"Enough already," Gorlick said. "You got it."

"You mean BO or the job?" Mickey asked, sniffing under his arms.

Gorlick looked at Gloria.

"There's a fine line between a tumler and a nudnick." Gorlick said.

"Finally you're getting the message, Mr. Gorlick. A 'Fine' line. That's me. That's what I feed them. Fine's line."

Gorlick took another puff on his cigar and shrugged.

"Step outa line, boychick. It's your funeral," Gorlick said, pausing, as he relit his cigar, which had gone out. "And my hotel."

"You won't be sorry, Mr. Gorlick."

"It's twenty a week with free meals and a room. From Decoration through Labor Day."

"I was hoping for thirty," Mickey said. He knew he was being lowballed because of his weak bargaining position.

"First thing we argue about money," Gorlick said. "For this opportunity, you discuss money. You be a good boychick, you'll get tips—you'll double what I pay you." He took a deep puff on his cigar and displayed a scowl.

"All I'm asking is a fair deal," Mickey said.

"Talk to President Roosevelt then. Gorlick pays twenty. By

right, you should pay me for the privilege."

"Twenty-five then."

"Right away with the money. There's a depression, Mickey. Haven't you heard?"

"Blumenkranz mentioned thirty," Mickey said.

"Sure, it's not his money," Gorlick said. "Twenty or nothing."

"All right then, Mr. Gorlick," Mickey said. "This is my last offer. Twenty a week with room and board. I warn you. Not a penny more."

"This Mickey is a mensch," Gorlick said, stuffing the cigar in his mouth and putting out his fat stubby hand.

Mickey Fine took it in his. He wasn't sure whose hand was sweating more, his or Gorlick's.

Then he moved to the door, stopped and turned.

"I leave you with one thought, people."

"Please," Gorlick said. "Enough."

"Anytime someone orders a pastrami sandwich on white bread from a delicatessen, a Jew dies."

"Getoutahere tumler," Gorlick said.

Mickey did a skip and jump movement, saluted, opened the door and left.